ELI

LOST AND BOUND

MISMATCHED MATES SERIES

Copyright © 2021 by Eliot Grayson

No parts of this publication may be reproduced, stored in a retrieval system, or transmitted in any form or by any means, electronic, mechanical, photocopying, recording, or otherwise, without the prior written permission of the copyright owner.

This book is sold subject to the condition that it shall not, by way of trade or otherwise, be lent, resold, hired out, or otherwise circulated without the publisher's prior consent in any form of binding or cover other than that in which it is published and without a similar condition including this condition being imposed on the subsequent purchaser. Under no circumstances may any part of this book be photocopied for resale.

Cover design by Fiona Jayde

Published by Smoking Teacup Books
Los Angeles, California

ISBN: 9798470217288

Chapter 1
Together

When they didn't take me out of my cell for a few weeks, I knew my time was up.

Or maybe it was a couple of months. I'd long since stopped bothering to scratch marks into the walls of my cell—or into my own flesh, since I healed too quickly and the entertainment value of hurting myself paled after a while.

There'd been that time a while back…sometime, in the past…when I hadn't healed. When I'd clawed my own arm and then watched, glazed and still too sedated to care, as the blood didn't stop welling up. That had been after one of the trips to the lab.

And that had lasted for a few weeks. Maybe.

And now *this* had lasted for a few weeks, maybe, the guard only opening the door once a day to slide in some food and maybe a sliver of soap or a roll of toilet paper, and then slamming it again without saying a word to me.

My cell had concrete walls and a concrete floor, a mattress in one corner and a toilet and sink in the opposite one. The concrete had a hairline crack to the left of the door. It split into a Y-shape near the end.

It was by far the most interesting thing in the cell, and I'd examined it in detail, day after day, staring until the light from the slits along the top of the other wall faded away, and I had to imagine the crack there, tracing it in my mind over and over.

Some days, I'd thought about getting a tattoo of the shape of that crack if I ever got out.

I knew I wouldn't be getting out.

Either they needed me for something—the endless vials of blood, the occasional injections that left me itchy or screaming or unable to heal, or once, shifting back and forth from wolf to man over and over again within minutes, uncontrollably, until I didn't know my own skin and could only scream in both my voices until I lost consciousness—and they wouldn't let me go, or…they didn't need me anymore.

Footsteps echoed distantly from the hallway.

I looked up from my lap, where I'd been idly contemplating the shape of my knuckles. Gloomy gray light filtered in, so it was still barely daytime. Whatever that meant. Not food time, though. That had already come and gone.

My heartbeat started to lift out of its usual slow tempo, skittering into an unsteady reel. I'd thought the prospect of death didn't matter to me anymore, but apparently my body disagreed.

The footsteps stopped; the door opened. Two guards stood partially framed in the doorway, the blond one who usually didn't hit me and the bald one who usually did. No matter what I'd tried, I'd never been able to get either of them, or their several equally laconic colleagues, to give me a name.

"Get up," the blond said.

I got up. Slowly, though, or as slowly as I dared, anyway. There was a fine line between pissing them off and not rushing to get my throat slit. My heart pounded away, double-time.

"Sometime this fucking year," Baldy grunted.

My feet felt numb, but I got on them and crossed the cell to the door. The blond took me by the elbow and tugged me out and along the hallway, the concrete out here rougher against my bare soles than in the floor of my cell. Maybe from all the jackbooted assholes marching around out here and scuffing it up.

The hallway lacked windows, but dim fluorescents hung at intervals along the ceiling. One of them kept flickering. I resisted the urge to fight, to struggle, to try for a few more minutes of living. It wouldn't matter, and I'd end up beaten or tased into unconsciousness. I'd never even see how they were going to end me. Somehow that seemed worse than at least knowing how I was going to die, for the few seconds between finding out and actually, you know, dying.

Blondie led me to the left, and I stumbled, my legs trying to carry me the other way. The labs were to the right, along the hallway and up the stairs. I'd been heading that way on autopilot, even though every time I'd been there I'd been some combination of bored, hurt, and terrified.

But we went left, and the bald guard fell in behind us.

The urge to fight hit me again. A couple of years—I thought? But I couldn't be sure—of living in that cell, alternately experimented on and ignored, had left me thinner and weaker than I'd been. But werewolves were resilient, and I'd started off tall, muscular, and able to fight.

I could still fight.

Except that every time I'd fought, I'd lost. They had weapons, and these guards might not smell like much except the sharp, acrid tingle of magic that obscured their natural scents, but they weren't human. They were stronger than me, and armed. I'd lose again.

I walked down the hallway, the blond's grip on my arm firm but short of punishing. He knew I wouldn't run. He knew I wouldn't fight.

Somehow, paradoxically, that drained the last of the impulse to fight right out of me. I didn't used to be like that. I used to be a contrary bastard.

We reached the end of the hall, and Baldy pushed past me to put his hand against a panel set into the wall by a metal door that stank of magic. The panel glowed faintly purple for a moment, and a heavy thunk and click echoed from inside the door.

The blond pulled it open. The room beyond lay in murky shadows, and I could only see a glint of something metallic. He shoved me through, and I stumbled and tripped a few steps inside.

"Brought you something to play with," the bald guard said, his voice thick with something foul and anticipatory, making my heart skip a beat and the hair stand up on the back of my neck.

And then the door slammed shut behind me.

The scent hit me first. It wasn't a bad scent, exactly, although no smells in this place had ever been mouthwatering.

It was a terrifying scent. Hot iron and bone-freezing chill, like fresh blood spilled on glacier ice, with a vein of uncontrollable wildness running beneath.

I blinked and stumbled back again, my shoulder blades hitting the door hard. I pressed my palms against it, clammy flesh on unyielding cool metal. A faint chink of metal sounded in front of me, and I blinked again, adjusting to the lack of light. After a moment, dim slits of twilight gray resolved out of the darkness, tiny windows like those in my own cell, high up in the wall across from me. I focused on them, hard. If I looked at those, I didn't need to see anything else. Whatever was in this cell with me, I didn't want to know. The scent had intensified, richer and sharper both, becoming mesmerizing.

And the sense of menace that came with it had grown too. I *really* didn't want to know.

Finally I had to know. Night had almost come, and in a few moments there'd be no light at all to see what lurked in the cell with me, no matter how much my werewolf senses compensated for the dark.

I looked down, away from the window slits.

Something sat against the wall on a pallet similar to my worn mattress. Something big. Three faint gleams: a metallic reflection, and twin pale stars, the glow of alpha eyes. Not golden, like the alpha werewolves I'd always known before, but bluish silver.

It didn't move.

I didn't move.

Whatever it was took deep, even breaths, slow and calm, and it didn't move a muscle.

My legs started to shake, protesting their rigid tension after weeks of sitting on the mattress twenty-three hours a day without even the exercise of walking to the labs.

I'd long since given up on exercising in my cell.

I slid down the door until my ass hit the concrete, drawing my knees up to my chest.

Darkness fell. I could still see a little, the faint starlight filtering in through the wall slits giving me enough to make out shapes, at least.

My heart still pounded in my throat at first, but after some indeterminate time of nothing fucking happening, it settled down. I got cold and stiff, but at least calm again.

And nothing happened.

Something to play with.

Either I wasn't a tempting toy, or the...whatever it was across from me wasn't in the mood to play.

The air between us hung thick with nauseating uncertainty.

I couldn't take it anymore. I'd almost forgotten this aspect of my own personality, the inability to keep my stupid mouth shut. It'd been so long since I'd had anyone to talk to. My lips and tongue practically ached with the need to move, even though my throat felt so dry I didn't know if words would emerge.

"Who are you?" It came out a hoarse whisper.

The shape across from me moved slightly. I had the impression of size again, of something massive shifting in the depths of the ocean, or of a predator moving in the darkness of a forest. All my hackles would've gone up, except that they'd hit peak *up* the moment the guards opened the door.

"Does it matter?" I twitched, adrenaline jolting through me. That voice, oh fucking gods, that *voice*. Deep and raw, and not human. Not remotely fucking human, not even in the way shifter voices were human.

I swallowed hard, peering into the darkness at those faintly glowing eyes.

"Since we're stuck in here together, it matters to me?" My voice came out high-pitched and weak. "I'm Jared."

His laugh scraped along every one of my nerves, a rusty knife dragging over concrete.

And it was definitely *his*. No way did that voice, that laugh, belong to anyone not male. What kind of male creature, though...that I couldn't even guess at. His scent was like nothing I'd ever encountered.

"I don't give a fuck what your name is," he said. "It

doesn't matter to me. I doubt it matters to you, either. Not in here."

Something about the note of utter indifference, bordering on despair, hit a nerve I'd thought long numbed into the same kind of deadness.

No, dammit. *No.* It mattered. My heart beat faster. *I* mattered. I still mattered. Jared Armitage was still alive, still here. Even if *here* meant buried alive in a concrete prison, waiting to die.

"My name is Jared," I gritted out. "I'm a werewolf. I'm—" I stopped, struggling for anything else I could say about myself. I hadn't exactly been the most interesting, charming guy before all of this. In fact, I'd been kind of an asshole. My lips quirked, into the first attempt at a smile I'd managed in so long I almost didn't recognize the feeling of my muscles moving that way. "I like jazz concerts, long walks on the beach, and having fun."

He made that sound again, that horrible not-laugh. "You're never going to hear music again, Jared the werewolf," he said, very low. "Or walk on a beach. Or have *fun*." He spat that last word like it tasted foul. "You're going to die here. And soon. Now shut the fuck up."

The two points of glow winked out.

He'd closed his eyes. He wasn't even bothering to look at me anymore.

And the implication that I'd die a lot sooner if I kept talking definitely wasn't lost on me.

Anger surged up, warring with terror and despair, and oddly tinged with embarrassment. What had I expected, that my pathetic attempt at humor would've mellowed him out and given us a moment of jocular camaraderie?

And why hadn't he done anything? Was he restrained in

some way? That little glint of metal, and the clinking...chains?

I shuddered, and my fingers dug into the concrete floor, my fingertips aching.

This place was impossible to escape from. Judging by the window slits, the walls were two feet thick. The doors weren't that thick, but they didn't need to be. Given the number of bones I'd broken trying to hammer at the one in my cell early on in my captivity, they were made from some kind of alloy that was harder than steel. And the whole place was steeped in magic. That would've held me, and presumably my new cellmate, even without the physical barriers.

And yet they had him chained, and his door was even stronger than mine.

Gods, I was going to die here.

The night passed slowly—and silently, except for our breathing. His was still slow and even, mine faster and rougher. I didn't sleep, really, although I dozed off a few times, my head tipped back against the door, jolting upright in a panic after a few minutes each time. I didn't dare to move, even to stretch out my legs. If he was chained, then presumably his chain didn't reach to the door, ensuring the safety of the guards when they opened it. I didn't know the exact length of the chain, though. Pressed against the door with my feet tucked up so he couldn't lunge and grab my ankle was the only place I could be relatively sure of being out of his reach.

I started and blinked for the fifth or sixth time, and then blinked again. The sun had come up, somewhere out there where there was sky and breeze and warmth and...I shifted my stiff, chilled limbs and rubbed the crud out of my eyes.

My cellmate came into focus.

He sat on his pallet, with his back to the wall, long legs stretched out before him. Pale blond hair, all matted and hanging down to his shoulders…and those shoulders wouldn't have been out of place on an ox. He was big. Very, very big, probably six foot six, and though he'd clearly been borderline starved like I had, he still had the build to match, his bones heavy and his limbs lean but powerful. I could clearly see his ribs through his skin, though—because he wore only a pair of the same kind of cheap prison-issue-style gray pants I did, with no shirt.

But he had one accessory I lacked. A heavy, dark chain attached to the wall in the corner of the room to my right, leading to an even heavier collar around his neck.

I looked up from the collar. His face was as pale as the rest of him, with thick blond stubble on his cheeks and jaw, matching the hair on his chest and arms. Strong features, with high cheekbones and a beaky nose.

And then his eyes opened, and I couldn't see anything else.

They pinned me in place. Pale, pale blue-gray, with the silvery glow of his alpha power shining through.

And he seemed to be looking right into me, seeing past my skin to the veins and arteries and muscles and bones beneath, cataloguing each jagged beat of my heart.

He stared, long and hard, and I gazed back at him, eyes wide and lips parted, like a fucking frozen prey animal instead of the predator I was myself.

His lips twitched, stretching into the parody of a smile, showing too-sharp teeth.

I pressed back against the door so hard my spine ached.

Without a word, he rose fluidly from his pallet, the chain rattling and hanging down his back. My breath returned, and I panted for every bit of air, suddenly released from that intense, unbearable gaze, like an actual weight had been taken off of me.

He stretched his back with his arms over his head, and his hands nearly reached the ceiling. I craned my neck, looking up and up and *up*. Christ, he had to be *more* than six foot six. I was six feet even, with a build to match, and I felt tiny, huddled there on the floor.

He turned his back to me and went to the side of the cell, lifting the lid of the toilet and taking a piss.

And that was when it sank in: both the toilet, and more importantly, the small sink—otherwise known as the only source of water in the cell—were within the limits of his chain. I'd die of dehydration if I didn't move away from the door.

I hadn't had anything to drink since…hours before the guards took me out of my cell. I swallowed, my throat clicking.

He finished his business and washed his hands, splashing water on his face. I could imagine it, moisture on my dry skin and in my parched mouth. Cool and soothing.

All I could think about was water.

And I needed a piss, too. Badly enough that my bladder ached.

He strolled back to the pallet, the chain rattling, and resettled himself against the wall, crossing his ankles and leaning back like he didn't have a care in the world. He closed his eyes, blinking slowly, and then opened them slightly, a gleam of silver under blond eyelashes.

He didn't seem eager to try to reach me. He hardly seemed to give a fuck about my presence in his cell one way or the other. Had the guards been trying to fuck with me? Maybe he wouldn't do anything to me at all, if I moved into range.

"What did he mean?" I rasped. "Something to play with."

He sat still and silent long enough that I started to wonder if he'd ever speak again. I shifted around, trying to relieve the ache in my belly, in my back, in my cramping legs.

"I can smell your blood," he said at last, his voice as low and rusty as before. But he spoke softly, conversationally, like he'd made a remark on the weather. Goosebumps rose on my skin. "I can almost taste it on the air."

And then it clicked. The scent of him that I hadn't been able to identify…it wasn't completely foreign, but I hadn't been able to parse it, because of the conflicting information it was giving me.

Vampire. At least partly vampire, mixed in with the rich scent of a powerful alpha shifter, and tinged with raw, wild magic that I still couldn't pin down. My blood, hot and rich and aromatic…I could feel every pulse of it through my veins, too quick, fluttering.

"I can smell how afraid you are, too," he went on. "Terrified. And weak."

"I'm not weak!" I cried, sounding…thin and reedy. Pathetic.

He chuckled and shook his head slightly, and I closed my eyes tightly, biting my lip raw.

I couldn't possibly have said anything more calculated to reveal my weakness than that defensive, pitiful denial.

"We'll see how you feel after another day without water."

I opened my eyes.

They met his, that glow undiminished. Steady. Mesmerizing.

"You don't want to kill me," I whispered, my fists clenching. "Why would you? I'm a prisoner. Like you. I've never hurt you. We're in this together."

"Together?" His lips twisted in a sneer. "No. You've never hurt me. But I'm going to hurt you."

It wasn't a threat. Just a statement of fact.

Gods, we could find a compromise, couldn't we? My mind spun in circles, faster and faster, panic starting to build.

"Feeding doesn't have to hurt," I said desperately through numb lips. "Vampires can make it..." *Feel good*, I didn't say. But it was true, I'd heard. Being fed on could be ecstatic. I'd never tried it to find out for myself. Werewolves didn't go around offering themselves up to vampires, and I didn't submit to anyone, anyway. "It doesn't have to hurt."

The chain rattled as he shrugged slightly. "I'm not a vampire."

I blinked at him. "I don't understand."

He bared his teeth at me. "You've spent some time upstairs, I'm guessing."

"Yeah."

"I'm not a vampire. I don't know what I am," he said roughly, and then stopped abruptly, as if he'd said more than he'd meant to. "Anyway, whatever vampires do to make their prey enjoy it, I can't do it even if I gave enough of a fuck about you to want to." Those massive shoulders moved a little as he shrugged again. "I'll feed on you. And it'll hurt."

All right, okay, it'd hurt. I could take pain. I'd taken a lot of pain over the last couple of years, and here I was, still kicking.

Well, twitching, at least. Alive.

And fuck, but I really, really wanted to stay that way. What the hell was up with survival instincts? I ought to want to die. Part of me, a large part, the conscious part, *did* want to die rather than live in this cell as this...creature's...victim.

But that part of me couldn't overrule the pounding, insistent drive to keep my heart beating for as long as possible, no matter the cost.

"Hurt doesn't mean kill," I said. "Let me...get some water,

okay? Use the john. You can take what you need. I don't care if it hurts, as long as you leave me alive, after. We can—coexist."

He stared at me. "Coexist."

I ignored the heavy overtone of skepticism. "Yeah, why not?"

"Because rabbits don't coexist with wolves."

"I'm—fuck you, I'm the wolf in this cell!"

"Maybe literally, but not in the analogy. And can you even shift?"

I flinched, stung and pissed and patronized and without a good response. No, I couldn't shift, not after whatever they'd done to me. The forced shifting episode had…burned it out of me, I guessed, and I hadn't been able to escape my human form since.

It ached, and it burned in me, and he'd figuratively poured acid into the open wound of it.

"I may not be a wolf right now," I gritted out, "but I'm no fucking rabbit."

"Might as well be." And he closed his eyes and tipped his head back against the wall.

Dismissing me.

Like he would've dismissed an actual, twitchy-nosed, cotton-tailed rabbit.

Fuck. That.

I was a werewolf, and maybe I wasn't an alpha but I was close enough, damn it, and I needed to piss and take a drink of water, and he wasn't going to stop me by just…*sitting* there.

I pushed myself to my feet, ignoring the pins and needles and the stiffness by sheer force of will, and steadied myself against the door.

I crossed the room to the sink, my steps firm and my head held high.

Chapter 2

Something to Play With

With my back straight and my stance wide and confident, I took a piss and flipped the lid shut, even though my neck itched and I was almost in agony from the need to turn, to run, to escape the presence I could feel behind me.

I washed my hands. I cupped them, taking a long, deep drink, the relief instant and overwhelming. The cool of the water rushed down my esophagus, soothing everything all the way down.

He hadn't moved. I'd have felt the motion in the room's air currents, heard the rattle of that chain.

Like a belled cat lurking right behind a mouse.

No, I wasn't a mouse any more than I was a rabbit, dammit.

I rubbed water on my face, my confidence growing for real, instead of being just something I was putting on for show.

Maybe he didn't want to try to take me on. I wasn't that much smaller than he was, right? A few inches shorter. Okay, half a foot or so. And narrower, but not like I was willowy. I was a werewolf, a fighter, a predator. People mistook me for an alpha all the time.

Sometimes, anyway, and mostly humans.

But it happened, because I had the strength of four or five humans and the resilience gifted by all the magic flowing through my blood.

I turned.

He hadn't moved.

I took a step back toward the door.

The rattle of chains gave me warning, but it didn't matter. Arms like iron bands wrapped around me, and he dragged me back, my feet brushing over the floor as he lifted me right off the ground.

We landed on the pallet, with me sitting in his lap, my back to his chest.

Thrashing in his lap, more like, kicking and trying to slam him with my elbows, knocking my head back in an attempt to break his nose.

Until he got one arm around my torso, pinning my arms, and pressed the other forearm across my throat, hard.

I sucked in air, but black spots swam in my vision and my airway compressed, one tense of his muscles away from being crushed. The arm around my waist pressed down too, trapping me in the cradle of his thighs. He wrapped his legs over mine.

And that was that. I couldn't move so much as an inch, and I couldn't breathe, I squirmed frantically, trying to communicate that I was done, I wouldn't fight any more, he didn't need to kill me…the door, the cell walls, flickered and blurred as my eyes watered and my vision failed.

The arm across my throat eased up a little, and I gave in. Completely. I went limp, my head leaning back against his shoulder.

A thick, long, and very hard object pressed into my ass.

I squeezed my eyes shut.

Something to play with.

I lay in his arms, panting for breath, not quite sobbing. Well, that hadn't taken long.

What was left of my life probably wouldn't, either.

He bent his head, inhaling deeply. His hot breath brushed over my ear.

"You want to survive this?" he asked softly.

I let out a whimper.

He chuckled, very low, and I felt it all through me, vibrating my chilled, sweaty skin. His cock against my ass felt like sitting on a metal rod. "I'll take that as a yes. Tilt your head to the side and hold still."

What was the point of disobeying? I'd taken my shot. I'd failed.

I tilted my head to the side.

He bent down further, his nose brushing my ear, until his stubble scraped me and his hot mouth pressed against the curve of my neck. I expected something else, a few words, an adjustment in his position or his hold on me. Some kind of preliminary.

So I wasn't ready when he opened his mouth and tore into my flesh.

It hurt. Not more than anything I'd ever felt, but a lot. I screamed, and only his grip on me held me still after all. His throat worked against my shoulder as he swallowed, and swallowed, and swallowed, gouts of my blood pulsing into him.

I writhed, rubbing my ass over his cock and accomplishing exactly nothing else.

The blood flowed, my blood, leaving me weaker and weaker as he gorged himself on my life.

Just as my eyes started to slide shut, the world going dimmer and dimmer around me and my extremities losing sensation, he stopped. His open mouth stayed on the torn wound in my neck, his tongue lapping at me, but he wasn't drinking anymore and his teeth had withdrawn.

Would I heal, I wondered distantly? Maybe. I blinked slowly, since it was taking extreme effort to lift my eyelids. Probably. That not-healing thing hadn't lasted long. If he'd taken too much blood, though, I could still die from that. Possibly. I didn't know. I'd never lost enough to test it.

Would he rape me now? No idea. His cock still pressed insistently between the cheeks of my ass. Did I care?

I blinked again, and what felt like a tear leaked out. Yeah, I cared.

But I couldn't do anything about it, anyway.

The wound in my neck burned and itched, starting to close over. Well, there was one question answered.

My front felt icy cold, from the chill of the air and blood loss, but my back was toasty warm, the huge, solid body behind and under me radiating heat. His arms felt good, bands of warmth around me. I could feel his heartbeat, hammering hard but starting to slow.

I could smell his arousal, his lust, his satisfaction. He nuzzled into my throat, lazily rasping his tongue over the closing wound. It stung a little, but it also felt like my skin regenerated faster as he licked me.

At last his grip loosened, and he rolled me off his lap and onto the pallet beside him. I thumped down like a sack of potatoes, flopped on my side with my legs still tangled with his. He extricated himself and rose with a clinking of chain, and then I was alone, cold and numb. I heard him moving around, his rasping breaths, and then the quick slap of skin on skin. I tried to turn my head enough to see, and then thought better of it, letting my face rest against the rough fabric beneath me and allowing my eyes to slide closed again.

He was almost certainly jerking off, and I didn't want to see that.

Part of me did. The part of me that hadn't had any human contact except for the rough handling of the guards, pulling me from my cell, beating me when I fought—and the warlocks who'd taken my blood and injected me and performed rituals in between, as I lay numb and half-conscious on their examining table.

The guards had never forced me, used my body. Maybe they weren't allowed, or maybe they simply had no interest. That was a mercy.

And the...man, or whatever he was, who'd just nearly torn out my throat...well, it should feel like a mercy that he was taking care of his own needs without forcing himself on me. It *was* a mercy, and the relief nearly overwhelmed me.

But part of me still wanted to watch. To see another person's pleasure. To have a glimpse of some kind of sexuality outside of my own nearly nonexistent libido. Outside of my own fucked-up mind.

He let out a low, raspy groan, and the scent of semen wafted over me.

It smelled like he smelled, sharp and cold and hot and rich, only more so.

I inhaled deeply, hating myself for it. I hated myself even more when my cock gave a feeble stir, the first sign of life it'd displayed in months.

The tap squeaked, and water splashed in the sink. My mouth felt like I'd swallowed a sand dune.

He loomed over me, and his fingers nudged my chin. "Open up."

I cracked my eyes open. He had his cupped hands held up

to my mouth, full of water, which dripped down onto the pallet next to my face.

Too dazed and thirsty to really feel the humiliation of it, I opened my mouth and slurped the water from his hands as he tipped them, some of it running over my chin and trickling down my neck. I licked the last few drops from his palm, his skin hot and rough under my tongue.

And then I fell back down and passed the hell out.

***

When my eyes opened, slowly and grittily, it was still daylight. Half a peanut butter sandwich sat on the edge of the pallet a few inches from my face. My stomach growled at the sight and smell of it, even though I'd have cut off an arm for something hot to eat—but that would've required bowls and utensils and crap the guards would've needed to deal with later. Sandwiches were easier for them than even shitty prison slop would've been.

I levered myself up, painfully pushing up on my arms until I could turn and lean back against the wall.

He sat beside me in the same position. We were shoulder to shoulder—or at least, shoulder to bulging bicep. I picked up the sandwich a little warily, even though I wanted it more than I'd ever wanted anything in my life.

"You saved me food." I couldn't quite bring myself to turn my head and look at him.

He grunted. "Eat it before I change my mind."

I stuffed half of it in my mouth, and the rest disappeared within seconds. It tasted fucking amazing, even though it was crappy peanut butter on stale bread. Fuckers. You'd think that with all the other shit we had to endure in here, they could at least spring for the nutty peanut butter and a jar of jelly, for fuck's sake.

And that half sandwich was about a tenth what I needed to keep up with my body's caloric requirements. I didn't know how *he* was surviving on what passed for full rations here, let alone half. No wonder his ribs stuck out.

No wonder I didn't have any fight left in me after all.

The meaning of the half sandwich finally filtered into my sluggish brain, and I froze.

"They only gave us one sandwich," I said, sounding like a fucking moron.

"That's right."

"They're expecting you to kill me. Maybe they thought I was already dead, lying there."

I felt his slight shrug against my shoulder. "They didn't bother to check either way."

If I hadn't already felt chilled down to my bones, that would've done the trick.

But it also made my mind start turning, trying to work everything I'd learned over the past twenty-four hours into some kind of coherent whole, adding it to what I already knew and guessed.

My first probably-a-year in this place, I'd been dragged out of my cell frequently, if not exactly regularly, subjected to a variety of horrors. Jonathan Hawthorne had been there most of the time.

I closed my eyes, forcing down a wave of nausea. Hawthorne. That motherfucker. My former lover's father, and the architect of every fucking thing that'd gone wrong in my life.

Well, no. I'd made a lot of bad choices, no matter how much I wished I could blame Hawthorne. But some of those choices had been influenced by magic. He'd all but admitted, once when he had me laid out drugged and helpless and surrounded by bits of foul-smelling herbs and candles, that he'd done something to my mind, nudged me into thinking of him as an ally. Someone who could help me get what I thought of as rightfully mine: leadership of my family's pack.

No one could possibly have been more unsuitable as the leader of the Armitage pack than me, but that revelation had come slowly, painfully, and miserably over the course of the first year spent alternately alone in my cell, battering at the walls or lying in a ball of pain and despair, or subjected to Hawthorne and company's not-so-tender mercies.

And my willingness to work with someone like Hawthorne really underlined that. I'd spied on Nate Hawthorne for his father, and more than that, worse than that, I'd slept with him to keep him focused on me, rather than making other friends, other connections. I hadn't exactly spied on my pack for Hawthorne, because they were my family and I had *some* fucking morals, but I'd definitely let slip a lot more than I should have when Hawthorne plied me with expensive bourbon and nodded sympathetically, listening to my mostly imaginary woes.

And then, Hawthorne had faked his own death. I'd known it was bullshit. He'd kept in contact with me, laying a piece of strong magic on me to keep my mouth shut.

A little less than a year later, he'd summoned me to a meeting, furious that I'd let his son break up with me. I got out of my car and walked to the meeting point, and then it was lights out. I'd woken up in my cell, and I'd been here ever since.

But I hadn't seen Hawthorne here for a long time. Maybe even as much as a year. Had he finally gotten himself killed for real? I hoped it'd been agonizing. But with a fucker like that, you couldn't count on it. He could just be busy. Working on some other horrifying, nightmarish project in some other godforsaken place.

Anyway, he had a couple of colleagues who'd taken up the slack.

For a while, at least. My trips to the lab had slowed, with much longer gaps in between, and then finally stopped.

And it had been weeks since the last. Thinking harder, I was inclined to believe it had been more like a month.

All right. That had been my situation before yesterday.

What did I know now, that I hadn't before?

Well, I knew my captors didn't have any further use for me. I knew they'd tossed me in here expecting my cellmate to kill me. I knew they were so confident in that expectation that they weren't bothering to feed me.

I didn't know, but I could guess, that my cellmate's tolerance for sharing what little food they gave him would run out sooner rather than later, and he'd finish me off.

And the guards hadn't bothered to look to see if I was dead…

There was something there, I just hadn't quite managed to figure it out yet.

I got up, wobbly and lightheaded but feeling like I wouldn't die quite yet. My werewolf physiology had been busy while I slept, replenishing my body's blood supply in double-time.

I drank, I pissed, I washed my face, and I wished they'd let me bring my worn-out toothbrush from my cell. I eyed the equally decrepit toothbrush lying on the back of the sink. Did I dare use my cellmate's, and did I want to?

A glance over my shoulder showed him sitting quietly, completely still. Only the faintest gleam from under his lashes let me know he wasn't asleep, but watching me. I reached for the toothbrush, and then jerked my hand back.

"Go ahead," he said.

I didn't wait to be told twice. No toothpaste, of course, but scrubbing my teeth with water was better than nothing. Had he brushed his teeth after he drank half of my blood?

Another handful of water chased down the nausea that thought brought up, and then I had nothing to do but sit down again. I hesitated. Would he allow me to share his pallet, now that I'd gotten up? Apparently so, because when I dropped down next to him again, this time leaving a few inches between us, he didn't react at all.

Did *I* want to be sharing the pallet with *him*, was a better question. No, but the bare concrete didn't leave me a lot of palatable options.

We sat in silence for a while, as I stared at the wall. His bulk beside me grew more menacing rather than less as time went on and the faint light through the window slits began to fade into gray nothingness. I was conscious of his every breath, of the heat of him, of his bare chest, of the sizable bulge in his thin pants. Of his hand resting on the pallet a couple of inches from mine. Of the aura of coiled power emanating from him, almost palpable.

I looked around a little, trying to distract myself from his presence.

My eye caught on something tucked under the edge of the pallet on his other side—some kind of plastic?

"What's that?" My voice echoed in the stillness. I hadn't heard anything from the hallway since I woke up, either, I realized. Not even the footsteps of a passing guard. "Under the mattress."

"Lube," he said casually.

My heart stopped for a second. "What?"

"The blond asshole dropped it off with the food. I think he likes you," he said, his tone so sardonic it could've dried out an entire ocean.

I didn't know what to say to that. If the guard was showing his soft spot for me by bringing lube so the psychotic bastard he'd thrown me in a cell with could use it to tear me up a little less when he raped and killed me…who needed enemies, with friends like that? And if I was going to die, and Blondie knew it…well, who needed lube?

My eyes stung. I thought I'd been beyond anything resembling tears, that they'd dried up permanently after the first few months here.

"I'm not going to use it," he said abruptly.

"There's more than one way to take that," I muttered.

That drew out another of those deep, blood-freezing laughs. "Always the optimist, aren't you? I'm not going to fuck you. So I'm not going to use it."

"Why not?" The words popped out of my mouth before I could think. I could almost see them hanging in the air in front of me, taunting me with their stupidity. I froze.

It was a reasonable thing to wonder; I didn't know how long he'd been here, but he clearly had a sex drive—he'd jerked off after biting me. And here I was, totally at his mercy and available. He'd drunk my blood and didn't seem much concerned with the fact that he'd kill me, now or later. I didn't think compassion or morals had much to do with his forbearance.

But there were a lot of ways this conversation could go wrong. My cellmate didn't laugh at me, though, or say, 'You know what? You're right, why don't I?' like I half expected.

Instead, he shrugged again, and said dismissively, "Not interested."

Not interested.

Not fucking *interested*?

Okay, that was a good thing. A very fucking good thing, that even though this bastard was literally going to be the death of me, he was one of that percentage of men who apparently...what, stayed a through-and-through heterosexual even after being deprived for the gods only knew how long?

But this still represented a new goddamn low. He'd been alone for probably years, if he'd been here long enough to be experimented on to the point that he was...whatever he was. He had lube. No one would stop him. He'd had a hard-on and the will to do something about it before, so presumably he could get it up again. Maybe I wasn't the handsomest guy in the world, with my reddish-brown hair and dark blue eyes and average features.

But still.

Not interested.

Yep, new low. Ninety-five percent of me felt nothing but relief. But that other little chunk of me withered away and died a bit, at the insult and the dismissal and the knowledge that even this insane fellow-prisoner thought of me as nothing more than a bag of blood.

Fuck this. I couldn't deal with consciousness anymore. "Can I sleep here? Instead of on the floor?"

"Don't care," he grunted.

I lay down again, curling up in a similar position to the one I'd occupied before.

I thought I'd be awake for a long time, but I fell asleep between one breath and the next.

Chapter 3
They're Not Paying Attention

I woke to the sound of the door opening. Reflex, born of long experience with what happened when I didn't respond quickly enough to a guard, had me almost popping up off the mattress.

But I forced myself to be still, with my eyes closed.

Because I'd started to get a theory, before, and I wanted to test it.

There was a soft thump as some kind of food, probably another sandwich, hit the floor.

"Is he dead? Has he even moved?" Baldy's voice, mostly unconcerned, but with a slight undertone of annoyance. He'd probably hoped I'd die on someone else's shift so he wouldn't need to deal with the corpse.

"Not yet," my cellmate said, equally unconcerned, not specifying which of the questions he was answering.

"Huh," Baldy grunted, and the door shut with a thud.

I sat up as soon as his footsteps had faded.

"They didn't know I'd been up and around since the last time they were in here," I said breathlessly.

He pushed himself up and went for the sandwich,

dropping back down beside me and ripping it in half without comment, handing me the smaller side. More peanut butter. Joy. And with the dust of the filthy floor all over it.

I tore into it, and he did the same with his half. It took about thirty seconds for it to be gone.

"What's your point?"

I turned my head, daring a look at him, and found him doing the same. Our eyes met, and I was transfixed again, the way I had been when we'd first looked at each other. Up close, I could see the color of his eyes more clearly. They really were gray, nearly the same as the alpha glow—which never seemed to fade. Most alphas only displayed that when they were shifting, or in the grip of some strong emotion.

Not this one. "Why isn't your alpha glow golden?" It came out low, intimate, in the space between our faces.

"Who says I'm an alpha at all? Maybe this is just another side effect."

I scoffed at that. "You're an alpha. Whatever they did to you, that didn't change." I knew that as well as I knew my own name. Alpha shifters had a scent, a feeling, that no other shifter could miss.

"Whatever they did to me," he growled, his eyes narrowing.

He sounded angry. Angry? What the—before I could get it together, his hand shot out and caught me around the throat, shoving me down onto the pallet.

He landed on top of me, crushing me with his weight, his fingers tightening, his face hovering an inch above mine, his eyes filling my vision and freezing me in place like that rabbit he'd called me before.

"What's the test?" he snarled. "The fucking game. What is it this time? You want my 'subjective impressions of the results'? Or to see what the 'treatments' did to my libido this time?"

The quotation marks in what he'd said were clearly audible. I gaped up at him in horror and dawning comprehension. "No," I gasped. His hand tightened, and I flailed up with my own, tugging uselessly on his arm. "I'm not," I wheezed. "Please, I'm not..."

The pressure let up suddenly as he yanked his hand away, and I sucked in deep, choking breaths, coughing and sputtering.

"You're not what?" he demanded, his eyes glowing more brightly.

"I'm not working for them, or, or collaborating with them. I'm not testing you. Or if they're testing you using me, I'm not part of it. I swear to you I'm not. I'm not trying to trick you into saying something they want to know." He stayed silent, staring down at me, his expression terrifyingly neutral. Measuring. "Obviously they've asked you to tell them how their fucking *treatments*," I spat the word, "made you feel. And you've refused. And now you think this is the way they're trying to get to you."

He nodded slowly.

"I'm just here to die," I said. "That's it. So obviously they're not expecting me to report back. And—if you haven't noticed, that's what I was trying to get at before. They're not paying attention anyway, so it's not like they'll hear anything you tell me."

His hand moved again, from the mattress to my shoulder. Claws pricked into my collarbone, a clear warning. "The fuck does that mean," he said flatly.

Jesus, I'd still be floundering around trying to explain myself clearly when he lost his patience and gutted me. I drew a deep breath, closing my eyes for a precious second to gather my wits.

I opened them again. He was still staring down at me. Was it my imagination, or had his cock thickened against my thigh? Fuck.

"Look, you think I'm here to spy on you." And wasn't that ironic—the one time I truly wasn't spying on or betraying anyone. He nodded again. "Okay. I'd either have to survive long enough to tell someone what you said, or they'd need to be listening. Surveillance of some kind. Right?"

He frowned down at me, and his grip on my shoulder loosened, the claws retracting, leaving little points of pain. His eyes flicked down, and he inhaled deeply.

Little points of pain, and little welling droplets of blood. I could smell it too.

I had to keep him on track. "Listen to me!" I said desperately, and his gaze pulled away from the blood on my chest, reluctantly returning to my face. "They obviously don't care if I'm alive or dead in here. So they can't be expecting me to report on you. And he didn't know I'd been up! Remember? He didn't know! So no one was watching. I think they used to have surveillance in the cells. Magical, not electronic. But it's not there now. For whatever reason. They're not watching us anymore."

Slowly, he sat up, still straddling my legs but not crushing me anymore. And keeping his hands to himself.

"So you're not a spy, and they're not watching us," he said at last. "So fucking what?"

I stared up at him in disbelief. "So you don't need to kill me for spying on you, just for starters?"

He looked down at me, his lips quirking. Just a little. Not a smile, and if it'd turned into a smile after all, it wouldn't have been a pleasant one.

"I'm going to end up killing you anyway," he said, his tone oddly, horrifyingly gentle. "Ripping your throat out and draining you dry." He laid his hand against my neck, his fingers stroking over the pulse in the side. "This collar drains me. My magic, my strength. It's spelled. I can't shift. And the need to shift is—you know how it feels." He traced a little circle over my jugular, claws scraping my skin. Not breaking it. But close. I lay still, frozen in place. "I have a little strength right now. Enough to pop claws, but that's it. From your blood, Jared the werewolf. But I want the rest of it. And I'll take it. Even though it still won't be enough. I'll take it all."

I swallowed hard, feeling my Adam's apple bob against his palm. "You don't need to. You don't need to kill me."

He leaned down, sliding his hand off my throat, and pressed his face to my neck. I tipped my head back without being able to stop it, and my stomach clenched. No, no, I shouldn't react like this. I was—not an alpha, never an alpha. But stronger than other werewolves. More powerful. I never submitted to anyone.

Except him, and I couldn't help it. His tongue flicked out, lapping up the drops of blood on my collarbone. Tasting me. Teasing out a few more drops from the closing punctures.

"But I do," he whispered against my skin.

And then his mouth opened, lips sealing over my flesh.

And suddenly, I was fighting him like a madman, thrashing, shoving at his chest. "No! Not now, not yet, wait, please wait…"

I struck him a hard blow in the back of the neck, enough to have stunned a normal shifter, and he grunted, rising up and seizing hold of my arms, pinning them over my head with one hand.

The other hand landed in the middle of my chest, the force of it knocking the wind out of me. One of my ribs cracked with an audible pop.

"Wait," I gasped, eyes watering from the pain of it. "Wait. Please. Not now."

"There's no reason to wait," he growled, gazing down at me, his eyes glowing feverishly bright. "Why draw it out?"

Why indeed? Why should I want to live? What did it matter, after all?

But it mattered. It *had* to matter, because I'd been here for years, and my family hadn't come looking for me. I'd brought that lack of care on myself, giving my cousin Matt—the young and inexperienced pack leader, who needed my support desperately—hell for having the position I thought I ought to have. Undermining him with the pack council. Trying to turn his brother Ian, who loved and trusted both of us, against him.

Fucking Nate Hawthorne, even though I'd known for years that Ian was hung up on the guy. Working with Jonathan Hawthorne, even though I'd known what a psychopathic piece of shit he was.

I didn't matter to them, and I didn't matter to anyone here, and so I had to matter to me. Right? I had to. Or my life had meant exactly nothing, to anyone, ever. Except maybe my parents, briefly, before they fucked off and left the pack when I was nine.

"Please," I repeated, because I couldn't think of anything else, because the corners of my eyes were wet and my chest hurt, and I couldn't die like this. "Please." That came out almost a sob.

He let me go.

I lay there, unable to move, as he got off me and crossed the room, running water in the sink, drinking from his hands.

Reprieve, for now, and my heart pounded away like a kettledrum.

I pulled my legs in and curled up on my side, burying my face in my arms.

He sat down next to me again a minute later and let out a long sigh.

"Tomorrow," he said. "I'm not waiting longer than that. There's no fucking point, for either of us. And I won't be able to help it anyway," he added softly.

I didn't answer. There wasn't anything to say.

***

Sleep would've been a blessing, but it didn't come. I'd already been unconscious for as long as my brain was willing to give me.

I lay there, perfectly still, and gave in to all the thoughts I'd tried to repress. All the fears, and griefs, and regrets.

My life really hadn't meant anything.

To me. To anyone.

I had another twenty-four hours, at the outside, to *make* it mean something.

Escaping was the obvious way. Get out, redeem myself. Do something with my life. I rolled my eyes at myself, because that obviously wasn't fucking happening.

And then my eyes popped open again.

Why the fuck not? What did I—what did either of us— have to lose? The guards were sloppy, not even checking on prisoners who might or might not be dead. They weren't watching the inside of the cell, which meant anything we did to prepare for them would go unobserved.

Alone, I hadn't stood a chance. But with him? I doubted

their tasers would have any goddamn effect on him at all. And he'd overpowered me without the slightest difficulty. The guards were stronger than I was—but not stronger than him. If I could lure one into his reach, the guard would go down. I was sure of it. And if another came running, surely I could tackle him, get him into my cellmate's range too. Even if I got tased, so what? I'd recover from it pretty quickly. I always had before. One of the guards might have a key to the collar and chain.

It was worth a shot.

And it was the only chance we'd ever get.

The tiniest flare of hope, like a flicker of a candle in the darkness…more than I'd had for longer than I could think about.

I rolled over onto my back. My cellmate had taken up his usual position, sitting with his back to the wall and his legs stretched out in front of him. I pushed myself up on my elbows.

After a moment, he turned and looked at me.

"Will you tell me your name?" I asked. It wasn't what I'd meant to say, but—I needed to know. I needed at least that much of a connection.

"No."

"Why not? What's wrong with me knowing? It's not like I have anyone to tell."

"No," he repeated, in a tone of complete finality.

He regarded me steadily, unblinkingly, out of those unsettling, glowing pale eyes.

I cleared my throat. "Okay. Fine. Keep your anonymity. You should have some sunglasses and a hat." He didn't even crack a smile, and my attempt at one died on my lips. Jesus, tough crowd. Not that I'd had much of a reputation for being hilarious even before I got myself landed in this hellhole.

"Look," I started again. And then stopped. How would I ease into the idea? "We should try to escape tomorrow," I blurted out. Yep. Very smooth.

A pause. He stared at me. "No."

What the fuck did he mean, just...*no*? A proposal like that merited at least something! "Did someone steal your vocabulary when I wasn't looking?"

That earned me the faintest, most barely-there upwards tick of one corner of his mouth. "No."

Dammit. I sat up all the way, leaning in toward him in a way that was probably suicidal. "We can escape," I said urgently. "Together. I can get them into your reach, lure them, distract them somehow. You can take them down. Right? Don't try to tell me you couldn't. That's why they have you chained out of reach of the door."

He sighed, and said, in the tone of someone humoring an idiot, "Yes. And I'd still be chained out of reach of the door. And without me, you'd never get out of here alive. That plan leaves us both fucked. It's not going to happen."

"But there has to be a key to—"

"The fucking warlocks have it," he growled, his eyes flashing. Yeah, he hated them at least as much as I did.

"Are you sure?"

He glared at me. That glare, out of those glowing eyes and over that ferocious nose, could've terrified a much braver man than me. It was a testament to how desperate I was that it didn't even faze me.

"Yes. I'm sure. One of them always comes along to unlock the collar from the chain when they bring me out of here. It's opened with a key and with magic."

I dropped back on my hands, tipping my head up to stare at the ceiling. Well, fuck.

I tipped my head back again to look at him. "Have you ever tried to break the chain?" The look he gave me after that little bit of stupidity could've melted the concrete floor. "Okay," I mumbled. "Obviously you have. But what if you…" I swallowed. I had one more idea. One more stupid, fucked-up idea I shouldn't even consider, but that still sounded better than lying down again and waiting for him to lose control and kill me. He'd been starved, and whatever they'd done to him to make him what he was, he needed food and he needed blood. Lots of both, probably. And he'd had nothing. The fact that I was still alive was a testament to his self-control, but that would have a limit; he'd admitted it.

I forced myself to go on. "What if you took my blood? Most of it. Not—all of it. Enough that I'd still have a chance. You said my blood made you stronger. Maybe strong enough to break—"

"No."

"What the fuck?" I shouted, my voice echoing off the concrete box we were in, reverberating, and somehow sounding all the shriller and more desperate for the amplification. "What the *fuck*?" I repeated, not shouting this time but still rough with my fury and frustration. "Why not? Why not even consider it?"

"Because it wouldn't be enough." His voice sounded even rougher than mine, low and gravelly and raspy enough to make the hair on the back of my neck stand up. "It simply wouldn't be enough. Draining you dry wouldn't be enough. If it would, you think you'd still be alive?"

"Oh," I managed, faintly.

"I'd need a lot more than that," he said. "More than your lifeblood. I'd need your actual *life*. And to get that—" He stopped abruptly, his lips parted, giving me a glimpse of those too-sharp teeth. And then he focused on my face, the glow in his eyes intensifying. His expression went as sharp as his canines, and his face hardened. "To get that, I'd need to mate you," he said at last.

I moved faster than I'd ever moved in my life, scrabbling backward and flinging myself across the room. I smacked into the opposite wall with bruising force and huddled there, nearly choking I was breathing so hard, my heart trying to thump its way out of my chest. My cracked rib had nearly healed, but the last bit of the injury throbbed like a fucking bitch.

He stood slowly, unfolding himself to his full, ridiculous height.

And that was when I realized he hadn't been trying to catch me. He hadn't moved a muscle when I fled from him in terror.

He wasn't doing anything threatening at all, in fact—but he still felt too close, and he loomed over me, menacing and compelling and terrifying. Monstrous. An enormous silhouette against the faint light from the window slits.

Death incarnate, without doing more than standing there.

And he wanted to *mate me*.

"It wouldn't work!" I said, my voice cracking. "It wouldn't work, forced matings don't create a bond strong enough to—"

"You're the one who was willing to risk anything for a chance to escape," he snarled, his voice going from vaguely-human to completely inhuman, a bestial growl that made the instinctive part of my mind roll over and whine in mindless terror. "And I know it wouldn't work."

"I'm willing to risk everything if there's a chance—wait, what?" The rest of what he'd said caught up with me belatedly. "You know it wouldn't work?"

"Of course I know," he said, his lip curling. "Mating 101. Those fuckers upstairs know that too. You wouldn't be in here with me if it was possible for me to escape by raping and biting you. Nothing good comes of a forced bond. Not strength, not power. Nothing but disaster."

The bitterness in his voice took me aback. Had he…? I had no idea. But I did know asking would be the stupidest decision I'd ever made, in a long line of incredibly stupid decisions.

I slumped back against the wall, not quite willing to get up and move back into his reach yet, whether he planned on trying to force a mating or not.

"Okay," I said, trying to breathe evenly and get my heartrate under control. "Okay."

I dropped my head into my hands, rubbing my palms over my burning cheeks, squeezing my eyes shut. I needed to think clearly. Focus. Consider all the possibilities.

I could do nothing at all. I could hide out over here by the door. I could die of thirst, or of starvation, if I lasted that long.

And then the variation on doing nothing at all…letting the hunger and thirst wear me down until I couldn't resist going for the sink, and then he'd catch me. His instincts would overwhelm whatever faint desire he had to spare me, whatever little shreds of compassion were left to him after what he'd endured here. He'd drain me and kill me, and that would be that. Maybe I'd fight him. Maybe he'd force a mating after all, the instinct to survive taking over, even though it wouldn't work out well for him: a forced mating created a forced bond, weak and twisted and deformed. He might be able to pull some of the force of my life through it, some of the magic that set me apart from mundane humanity, but not all of it.

Not enough, if he needed every last drop.

It also wouldn't work out well for me. Obviously.

So I could die for nothing, terrified and brutalized and unmourned. No good to anyone.

Just like I'd been no good to anyone, ever, here or before. I'd be an anonymous pile of rotting bones in an unmarked grave, or tossed into an incinerator like so much garbage.

Or…or. I'd had no control at all over my life for years. No decisions to make, stupid or otherwise.

Right now, I still didn't have any control over my life.

But I did have a decision to make. And I had control over how I died, and why.

I had to be smart for once. Smart, and not ruled by my fear and my ego.

My survival instincts flared up again, but I squashed them down ruthlessly. I had to accept that death was the likely outcome here, and that I wasn't an animal, struggling in a trap—I was a sentient being, more than my instincts, more than my biology.

If he escaped, if he really did rip that collar off his neck and burst out of this cell…

When I finally lifted my face from my hands, all my panic had drained away, replaced with *purpose*. It burned, a good burn, like the useless parts of me, the frightened and pathetic parts, were withering away to ash and leaving only the undamaged core of me behind.

He hadn't sat back down again, still poised to move—which kept me wary. But I ignored that.

"Hypothetically," I said, craning my neck to look up at his impassive face, "if you got out. Out of the chain and the collar, out of this cell—"

"I won't," he growled.

"Hypothetically! Christ, bear with me a second." He frowned at me but kept his mouth shut. "*Thank* you. If you got out. What would you do?"

His instant answer made my heart leap. "Rip them to shreds," he said. "Limb from limb. All of them. Burn this fucking place to the ground."

I could picture it, so clearly. The screams, the fountains of blood, the limbs flying through the air. Flames leaping up from the lab, consuming everything in their path. The bald guard who'd tased me and beaten me and dragged me to and from the lab to be tortured over and over again, crumpled and gray on the floor in a pool of crimson.

It made me smile.

Revenge. I might not live to see it, but I could bring it about. I could die knowing I'd made it possible, that they'd all die because I'd made the right fucking decision for once in my life.

What was left of it, anyway. My last few minutes, and they'd *matter*.

I looked up. He still stood there, waiting. Watching me.

"I'll do it," I said, with only the faintest little hitch in my voice. "But I have some conditions."

His brow furrowed. "Do what?"

I drew a deep breath. "Mate with you. Let you mate me. Drain me. Use me to escape."

I thought he'd been standing still before, but he went so motionless he looked like a statue. "Why?"

Did I owe him an explanation? No, definitely not. He'd owe me, when this was done. But I might as well tell him. Maybe Ian and Matt would want to hear it.

"I haven't had a lot of choices for a long time. And when I did, I always chose wrong." My throat clicked as I swallowed. "I get one last choice. I don't want to die scared, and in fucking pain, and with no one knowing what happened to me. Most of all I don't want to die for nothing. If we mate, and you drain me, and you pull everything you can through the bond, until you're strong enough to break the collar. I might survive it, right? I could survive it, bonded to you."

I'd meant to sound confident, but it came out plaintive. Like I was begging for him to agree with me.

He didn't. A muscle ticked in the angle of his jaw. "Probably not."

I agreed with him, actually, deep down. But it didn't make any difference. My mind was made up.

"I want to do it anyway."

A look I couldn't completely interpret crossed his face, a shadow of something like grief or regret. For the barest second, his eyes flickered.

"You said you had conditions."

I blew out a long, long breath. That was tacit agreement. "Three." I stopped, considered the last two years, the way I'd felt day after day, endless hour after hour, the isolation and the blood-chilling loneliness, and the likelihood that he'd be the last person to ever touch me. Not to mention the mechanics of mating, and one very important sexual act I'd never participated in.

I said, "No, four." He nodded at me. "First. You have to go find my cousins. I mean, if I don't survive," I added, in a pointless sop to the idea that I might live through this. "Ian and Matt Armitage. Matt's the leader of our pack, or he was a couple of years ago. Near Laceyville, in northern California. Tell them I'm dead, so they don't wonder." If they even gave a shit, which I doubted at this point. But at least they'd *know*.

I couldn't go on for a second, vivid images assaulting me of my cellmate showing up at my home without me, telling Ian he'd killed me without a trace of emotion.

"What else?"

I shook my head to clear it. "Second," I said a little hoarsely, "you have to do what you said. Kill them all. No mercy."

That earned me a quick, flashing smile, a baring of his teeth that might've had me cringing back against the wall if I hadn't already been pressed to it. "That doesn't need to be a condition."

"Good. Third, I have a request about how we—do it. The mating. And fourth, you'll—look, I know you think this won't work. For me, anyway. And I can live with that." I couldn't help laughing. It came out a rusty croak. "See what I did there? Anyway, I get it. But try, okay? If you can do it without killing me, I want you to try. I want your word. Swear to me."

He licked his lips, and shifted a little on his feet. Just the slightest involuntary movement. It was the first sign of uncertainty I'd seen in him.

His brow furrowed. "No one's asked me for my word in a really, really long fucking time," he said slowly, very low. "Not without threats or coercion. I could lie to you."

I looked him in the eye, confident about this as I hadn't been about anything in so long it felt like a completely foreign emotion. "You won't."

Something in his posture changed, those massive shoulders and broad chest straightening a little. "You have my word," he said.

Chapter 4
Like I Fucking Matter

"Sit down," I told him. And a little to my surprise, he did what I said, resettling on the pallet with his back to the wall.

Now that I'd really decided to do this, my temporary calm was dissipating, turning into a sick, belly-clenching anticipation. I stepped forward, following him to the miserable excuse for a bed that was all we had. I'd committed now. No going back. Like the few, nauseating seconds between jumping off a cliff and hitting the ground.

I knelt down next to him, almost touching. Close enough to reach out and touch, if I wanted to run my hand down over the heavy muscles of his chest. To touch his cock. Brush my fingers over his lips. They weren't the kind of lips I'd usually want to kiss. Too firm, too masculine. I'd usually fucked women, or sometimes very pretty men. Like Nate, for example.

But it was all I had. He was all I had.

Could I say this? Gods, I didn't want to admit it. I mean, there was nothing wrong with always having topped, obviously—it'd used to be a point of pride for me, even, douchey as that sounded. And I'd hate every second of him fucking me, either way—but the fact was...beyond my distaste for the idea,

I was scared. And I didn't want it to hurt. That was pathetic and cowardly, and probably irrelevant, considering how much it would definitely hurt when he drained me. But I didn't want to spend possibly the last hour of my life getting hurt that way, too.

"I've never—I mean, I'm not a virgin, but—" I stopped, my lungs laboring, my throat closing. He reached out and wrapped his huge hand around my wrist. I didn't have dainty wrists at all. Muscular forearms, and heavy bones. At least compared to an average person.

But his hand more than wrapped all the way around. He could've squeezed, ground my bones together, turned them into powder, disintegrated me.

Instead, he held me, the heat of his skin seeping into my chilled body.

I stared down at his hand on me. "I've had sex. Lots of sex. But…I want you to hold back a little. Ignore your instincts. Because—because I'm, okay, definitely not a virgin, but…a virgin for this."

The hand tightened. "What."

I could feel my face burning, like all the blood in my body had rushed there. I definitely didn't have any left in my brain; I'd gone lightheaded and dizzy.

"Look, I've never gotten fucked, okay?" I looked up at him, challenging, daring him to laugh at me for my blushing embarrassment. He didn't. He just stared at me, stony-faced. "Don't just, you know, stick it in. Let me get some lube up there first, at least. Try to make it not hurt. I'm not going to enjoy it, I get that, but—*fuck*," I snapped, goaded into real anger by the humiliation that rushed up and tried to choke me. "Can you stop staring at me like that? I know this is fucking awkward, I mean, awkward doesn't even begin to cover it. But it's been years. Fucking *years*, and you may be the last person to ever touch me. I don't want it to be totally impersonal, like I'm a means to an end, just a hole you need to use for another reason."

And shit, fuck, *fuck*, now my eyes were stinging, my face tingling with that crumpling feeling of trying to hold back tears. "Make me feel like I'm a fucking *person*, okay?" I choked out. "Like it matters to you. Like I—like I fucking mat—" I stopped dead, because his expression hadn't even flickered. Gods only knew what was going on behind those unreadable silver eyes. Probably he was hoping I'd shut up soon so we could get on with it. I yanked my arm away and covered my face with both hands, resignation settling in like a heavy weight on my shoulders. "Forget it," I muttered. "Just do what you need to do. Maybe try not to rip me open if you can help it. I know you never wanted to fuck me in the first place. I know you'd rather just get it over with."

My chest heaved, and I couldn't hold it in anymore.

"Enough," he said, low and firm, and it worked to cut me off. "Enough. Come here."

I couldn't move. I couldn't pull my hands away from my face. He'd see my eyes all wet and shiny. He'd see me, big bad werewolf, a twenty-seven-year-old grown-ass man, an anal virgin and fucking crying about it. Really goddamn impressive.

Big hands found my waist, pulling me inexorably in. I was forced to shuffle forward on my knees or topple over. His hands tightened, and he picked me up. Just like that, without any apparent effort at all, lifting me into his lap so that I straddled his thighs. My breath came hoarse and quick, and his slowly, in counterpoint. He rubbed his thumbs over my hipbones. The heat of his body surrounded me.

"Look at me."

I didn't want to. But I had to, the command in his voice vibrating through me.

I lifted my head and found his face an inch from mine, eyes glowing steadily, features composed. That muscle jumped in the angle of his jaw, the only sign that he felt anything at all.

He leaned in and set his mouth over mine, and I froze from the shock of it.

A kiss? He was *kissing* me?

Not really, though, because for a moment it was only that, a touch. Skin against skin. No more than his hand around my wrist had been.

And then he tilted his head and kissed me for real. His lips moved gently, coaxing me open. Softly. Tenderly, even. My skin itched with humiliation and shame, my cheeks burning all over again. Yeah, I'd never taken it up the ass, but I didn't need to be treated like a sheltered virgin bride on her goddamn wedding night. Was he fucking *mocking* me?

I struggled, trying to pull away, to protest and tell him to take his condescending mockery and stuff it up his own fucking ass, but it was like fighting a brick wall.

He held me in place without any effort at all, and his tongue flicked out, teasing my lower lip, brushing my tongue, asking me to let him in.

I wanted to keep fighting, try to shove him away from me.

But it'd been so long since I'd kissed anyone…only I wasn't kissing him. He was kissing me, and I couldn't believe how different it felt.

I couldn't believe how it drained the resistance right out of me, like he'd cut my strings. The surety of his mouth moving on mine mesmerized me.

He carefully persuaded me into parting my lips and teasing back with my tongue, feeling the shape of his mouth and learning the way he moved.

He dipped in, withdrew, nibbled my lower lip. Always gently. Not even the threat of breaking the skin with those very-sharp teeth that'd ripped my throat to shreds the day before—that would inevitably do it again, and soon. He had to be mocking me.

He *had* to be. And yet I couldn't seem to stop him, or even muster up the will to try again.

My hands had been resting on my splayed thighs, but they moved without any conscious input from me, drifting up to press open-palmed against his chest. The hair there felt softer than I expected. I let my fingers move, exploring the firmness of his flesh. He ran warm, like all alphas, and between the heat of his mouth and my position cradled in his lap, the chill I'd felt for days—or maybe years—melted away.

I melted, going boneless and loose, but still with that core of hard tension deep within me. He slid his hands under my shirt and stroked up and down my back, around my waist, letting one hand travel as far as the waistband of my pants, fingers slipping just under to trace the swell of the top of my ass.

He'd gotten hard under me, even though he hadn't moved his lower body at all. His erection pressed against my balls, poking up in front of me, tenting his pants. Apparently he was interested enough after all—although that could simply be due to having been alone as long as I had.

He released my mouth at last, pressing kisses along my jaw and ducking his head to my neck.

I tensed automatically. The last time he'd had his mouth on my neck he'd meant to kill me, before I argued him out of it. And the time before that…I shivered. And next time…

But I still tipped my head back.

He pressed a line of soft, closed-mouthed kisses down the line of my throat. "Easy," he murmured into my skin. "No teeth. Just this. I'm going to taste you on the outside first. I won't hurt you. Not until I've given you what you asked for."

I shuddered, a little moan rushing out of me completely out of nowhere, as he kissed along my collarbones, as he started rucking up my shirt to push it over my head. What I'd asked for…was this what I'd asked for? No, I hadn't asked for this, for kisses and caresses and tenderness. I didn't want that. I'd asked for some straightforward consideration, not just the kind of brutal possession of my body that his unfettered alpha instincts, and all that rage he had simmering under the surface, would have naturally led him to carry out.

But it was sick, how much I seemed to be craving his, what, his approval? His care? His…it felt like he was making love to me, as he stroked me and cradled me in his big hands. As he pushed my shirt up and I lifted my arms, letting him pull it off and toss it away. The cold of the room brought goosebumps up on my skin, pebbled my nipples.

My belly clenched. I didn't want this. I'd never wanted this, in either direction. I'd been a predator, a tall, muscular, cocky, aggressive werewolf, pursuing his lovers without any subtlety or care. I'd wanted to fuck.

Gods, I'd always been the aggressor, and now I had this man who could've crushed me with one hand bending down, tracing his tongue around my nipple, closing his lips over it and tugging, sending bright sparks of sensation winging through me. My nerves were coming to life, like pins and needles of the soul, my body waking up from two years of hibernation.

My cock was hard, I realized. Hard, and aching, and

pressing into his belly. I'd started rocking my hips, rubbing it against him, riding the ridge of his erection beneath me in turn.

He moved to the other nipple, kissing it, flicking it with his tongue, as delicate as if I'd been made of crystal. Soft. Tender. The way no one had ever touched me, because who bothered to be careful with someone like me? His arm wrapped around my back, and he shifted his hips, tipping me back against his arm so that it was all that held me up.

I let him take my weight. What the hell was I doing, trusting him, letting him treat me like this…closing my eyes and spreading myself wantonly, legs open over his hips and my whole neck and chest and belly exposed. He bent further, kissing over my ribs, teasing my navel with his tongue. My cock brushed his stubbled chin, and I started and groaned.

"I'll get there," he said.

My head swam. He'd strongly implied he was straight, hadn't he? Or was it just me he didn't like that much? "You don't have to do that," I slurred, my voice seeming to have melted down as much as my brain and my oddly pliant body. "I'm not a fucking virgin, I told you. And I'm a sure thing. I don't need to be talked into this."

He stopped, his hot breath brushing over my chest, his whole body still. "You don't want me to."

Part of me really, really wanted him to—the part currently standing up and straining for his attention. Gods, my cock *ached* for it. I'd hardly felt any kind of sexual desire in so long, and now I suddenly wanted a blowjob like I wanted fucking oxygen.

I didn't want a pity blowjob, though, even through the haze of fear and confusion…and arousal, gods. And maybe a small voice in the back of my mind was also telling me that I didn't want those terrifying teeth wrapped around my vulnerable cock.

The vulnerable part in question pulsed, getting impossibly harder, and I whimpered, my hands clutching at his chest.

Oh.

Maybe I did.

"Up on your knees," he said, an unmistakable command. He pushed me upright again, and I rose shakily, bracing my hands against the wall over his head.

He slid down a little more so that his mouth was right at a level with my cock, and tugged my pants down around my thighs.

"Take these off."

I obediently lifted one knee and then the other, letting him work the pants off each leg and foot. The concrete of the wall felt rough against my palms, the cool air chilled my ass and legs…every little sensation pinged at me individually, more overwhelming that way, somehow. His breath heated the tip of my cock. I closed my eyes and let my head hang down, panting even though I hadn't been moving almost at all.

He kissed and licked at my cock the way he had the rest of my body, every light touch making me quiver, sending sparks arrowing into my balls and pooling heat behind them. A long lick, from the base of my cock and up the side, with a flick of his tongue at the tip. I shook and moaned. A soft kiss to the ridge of the glans, and my fingers flexed against the wall as I tried not to thrust forward. He slid even lower down the wall and lifted my balls, kissing them one at a time.

And then he went lower still, pressing his face into the space between my thighs. Mouthing over the tender flesh at the very top of one, and then the other. When he turned his head, his hair tickled me and his stubble scraped me. My legs shook. My face felt too hot, my head too light and too heavy all at once.

He nuzzled deeper between my legs. Strong hands spread over my ass cheeks, pulling them apart, pushing me so that I angled myself toward him.

His lips brushed over my hole.

The cry that came out of me didn't sound remotely human, raw and desperate and helpless.

I'd known he'd fuck me. Planned on it. But this…my cock and balls were external, meant to be touched and explored by a lover. This part of me was hidden, intimate, secret. No one had ever touched me there. I hadn't wanted anyone to touch me there.

He flicked his tongue over that soft flesh, kissed me again.

Kissed my hole, oh gods, kissing me like he'd kissed my mouth. My legs trembled and burned as I bent my knees, canted my hips, tried to open myself as much as I could for that…kiss. For his kiss. For the way he opened his mouth over my hole and *sucked*, swirling his tongue in circles the way he'd explored my mouth a few minutes before.

This wasn't…it wasn't desire. It wasn't lust. Not like I'd ever felt. My body wasn't doing what I expected it to do, what I wanted it to do. My body liked to fuck, and this wasn't fucking. I had no idea what it was. I'd never been harder, now that the ache of arousal had spread, moving deeper—not from inside me to my cock, like an orgasm, but the other way. Moving in, making parts of me I hadn't known I had beg mutely for something I couldn't define.

It went on and on, his mouth plundering my hole and his hands kneading me, until I couldn't hold myself up anymore. I collapsed. He caught me, his fingers digging into the flesh of my ass and taking my weight completely, shoving me against him, burying his face between my legs.

I wanted to touch my cock, but my arms had dropped, my hands resting on his shoulders, and I couldn't get them to move.

It didn't matter; my cock didn't need it. I felt the orgasm building, my legs splayed wide around his head as I shook and whimpered.

And then he let me down, right before I came, moving up at the same time so that I slid down and landed on his lap again. Frustration and confusion had my head spinning, and I couldn't help rutting my cock against his body—but it wasn't enough, not without his mouth doing things to me I'd never imagined wanting, needing. My head dropped down on his shoulder, my face pressed against his collarbone. I had his skin right next to my lips, that scent of him thick and rich. Icy and burning, metallic and spiced. I opened my mouth, letting my tongue flick out and taste him, all salt and alpha and magic.

A growl rumbled in his chest, and I froze.

He leaned over, taking me with him because I was plastered to his chest, and reached a hand out, rummaging around.

The lube. He was getting the lube from where it'd been tucked under the pallet, and that meant he was going to fuck me now. His cock pushed hard and insistent against the crease of my ass, still covered by the thin, scratchy fabric of his pants, but hot as a brand against my skin even with that barrier.

When he fucked me, he'd bite me. It'd be over. My life would almost certainly be over unless he could save me. And the logistics of that hadn't really occurred to me until now, when it was far too late. Ripping through the collar, tearing the door off of its magic-reinforced hinges. Me in the process of dying, if not dead already. How could he keep me alive and still get out? Healing a mate through a bond took time and concentration. Effort. Sacrifice.

Even if he wanted to, he'd fail.

And my cock still throbbed against his abdomen. Maybe I wouldn't even get off before he ripped into me. I wanted to beg him to at least jack me off, let me come before the pain and humiliation of getting fucked took away all the strange, uncomfortable need he'd stirred up in me.

I couldn't get the words out.

I pressed my face into his chest, and my own hitched with something like a sob. I shook in his arms, and he petted me, soothed me, huge rough hands stroking over my back.

"Up," he said softly. "For a second."

I lifted my hips enough for him to work his own pants off, but I couldn't make my upper body move. I clung to him, my fingers clenching against his sides, my chest and face glued to him, needing the expanse of his hot skin against mine. Feeling his heartbeat, feeling my own heartbeat thundering in tandem. How many more beats did I have left? My heart felt like it was speeding up, desperate to squeeze in as many more as it could before it stilled forever.

I might live. I might survive. I had to believe that.

A click told me he'd opened the lube. He put his other hand around my hip, guiding me back down again so that I rested on his legs. Slick fingers pushed into my crease, unerringly finding that hot, wet opening he'd already worked over so thoroughly. His fingertips rubbed over me.

And then he pressed one in. I clenched around it. Everything narrowed down to that penetration, the first time I'd ever had another man, anyone, anything, inside me. I'd never even sucked a cock. Maybe I'd nibbled on someone's fingers, at some point. But I'd never been penetrated, at all.

His finger drilled deeper, twisting inside me, calluses abrading tender flesh. I panted into his shoulder, my mouth as wet and open as I was below, my lips slick against his collarbone.

He pulled back, and then delved in again, this time with two fingers stretching me. They worked in and out, his knuckles pushing against my ass cheeks. Those two fingers felt so strange, so alien, but his whole hand lodged between my legs almost felt more so, even though most of it wasn't inside me.

I burrowed closer to him. Three fingers, now, making me shift in discomfort, trying to spread my legs as if that'd relieve the internal pressure. It didn't. My ass burned, the rim of my hole stretching to the limit. He kept moving his hand, pumping in and out, his other arm around my back and pressing me close to him.

He leaned his head down so that his mouth brushed my ear. "It's time." That raspy growl finished me off. Tears leaked out of the corners of my eyes.

I didn't resist as he lifted me a little, pulling his fingers out of me, leaving me feeling almost numb where he'd worked my body open. He took a firm grasp on my ass cheeks, pulling me apart and positioning me over his cock.

Slowly, he lowered me down. The head entered me, lodged just inside. I froze, thighs trembling, straining to keep myself still. He had a big cock. A thick, long, alpha cock, the size of an average forearm. Too big to fit in me. So big that I'd never recover from it.

I didn't want this to end, this moment, poised between life and death. Wrapped in the heat of his body, with my burning cheek resting on his broad shoulder. I wanted to get even closer, until he absorbed me into his strength and solidity. Melt into him. Let him hold me and stroke me and caress me forever.

He waited patiently, not pushing me down, not thrusting

up, until at last my legs gave out and I sank down onto his cock, taking it in a slow, unstoppable slide. My body swallowed him, adjusting inside until he filled me up. The pressure took my breath away. There simply wasn't room to breathe. He ran his hands over and around my ass, tracing the contours of my body as if they'd changed to accommodate him within me.

His hips shifted, and he thrust up. And again, shoving deeper into me. It didn't even feel like being fucked, or not like I'd imagined being fucked would feel. It wasn't an intrusion anymore. Or...it was. But an intrusion suggested he didn't have the right to be there, or that I had the right to stop him. So he couldn't intrude, because my body belonged to him.

He'd claimed those secret places in me, hidden away, and made them his. He moved in me like the wet heat of me only existed to sheathe his cock.

I let him, not like I had a choice. I lay pliant against him, breathing hard, my own cock the only part of me that hadn't gone completely limp.

It still pressed into his skin, still eager. Why did I...pressure built inside me as the thickness of him rubbed over and over a little bright spot of sensation, a nub of pleasure that tightened and grew brighter still, my muscles clenching all around.

He moved faster, thrusting up harder. But still carefully, still gently. As if I might break.

I almost laughed. This place had already broken me. He couldn't do it again.

Except that I was wrong about that.

I moved up and down with his motions, my chest and belly rubbing against his, my cock stiff between us, that heat and pressure building inside me, my eyes sliding shut.

And then the base of his cock started to swell, catching on

the rim of my hole.

His knot.

My eyes popped open. I started to lift my head, and he wrapped a hand around the back of my neck and held me in place.

It got bigger, harder, until I thought I'd tear. And then with one hard thrust up, he buried it inside me, lodging it against that place where the pleasure had been sparking in me.

That spark caught fire, blazing through me, every muscle in my body going rigid.

Feeling something good, something searingly bright, after all that darkness…I moaned, long and loud, a broken, helpless sound.

And I broke again with it. I came, shuddering, my cock spreading wetness between our bodies. I almost blacked out from it. He crushed me in his arms and let out a long, low growl, shoving his knot deeper. He spilled in me, hot pulses of come that filled me to bursting, and his hips stuttered, his arms tightening around me.

I could have drifted there for another two years.

I felt his mouth against my neck.

"No," I whispered. "Not yet." His fingers stroked through my hair.

"Yes," he said. Not cruelly, but implacably. "The mating bite first. And then I'll—"

"I know, I know what comes next, don't say it."

He sighed against my skin, pressed a heartbreakingly gentle kiss to the curve of my throat. I sobbed and buried my face in his chest, squirming against him, writhing on his knot, aftershocks of my orgasm rippling through me.

Why had I wanted this to be less violent? Why hadn't I held out until he couldn't control himself anymore, let him take me by force, brutalize me while I fought and struggled to the end? This hurt so much more.

He bit down.

I gasped and stiffened. His teeth pierced me, and our shared shifter magic swirled between us, in my blood and his, around and around the points where our bodies were one. I felt the bond form, a pull between us, threads of magic that stitched us together soul to soul. It felt like coming home, sinking into a warm bath, the embrace of someone who loved me.

And it hardly hurt at all, except that every cell in my body ached and burned, knowing I was about to lose it again. That I'd only have this for a few fleeting moments.

That all of this was a lie, anyway.

He lifted his head. "Can you feel it?" Was that a note of wonder in his voice? Something, anyway, that I couldn't quite identify.

"Yeah," I said hoarsely. "I can feel it."

It, me, him. Bound together. Wrapped in ancient blood magic, something no witch or warlock could duplicate.

He leaned down again and kissed the bite, kissing all around it, like it was something precious to worship with his mouth. One hand cradled my skull, the other rested on my waist.

Like *I* was something precious to be held close and tenderly.

I tilted my head, turning my face away from him, baring more of my neck. The air felt cold on the throbbing heat of the bite mark. His knot still stretched me to bursting, the shaft of his cock buried deep.

He leaned down and kissed my neck again. "Nothing's going to hurt after this," he said against my skin, so low I felt the vibration of it.

"What?" I opened tear-glazed eyes and stared at the concrete wall. The last thing I'd ever see.

"Nothing's going to hurt," he repeated, kissing the bite again, and his arms tightened, his fingers stroking through my hair. "One way or another. You have my word on that too."

I couldn't follow that, couldn't understand. Of course nothing would hurt after I died, but...one way or another? Why didn't he do it, get it over with, end this agonizing suspense, because every second made it harder to let go? Every touch of his hands made me want more. How had I gone my whole life without being touched like this, even when it was a mockery, a parody, a sardonic commentary on my partial virginity? And I was going to lose it, this feeling. This beautiful lie.

My head whirled.

And then he said something else, even lower and quieter. "Calder. My name. It's Calder."

"Calder," I whispered.

He shuddered, and stroked my waist, and his teeth tore into my throat, ripping me open.

I screamed, and screamed, and he bit deeper, and the gray concrete of the wall faded into blackness.

Chapter 5

Little White Seashells

Pain twisted in the darkness. My body hurt.

I had a body.

Wasn't the advantage of dying that the pain stopped?

And if this was surviving, I wasn't sure it was worth it.

More pain, more weakness, and I couldn't turn away from it. And I couldn't see, not in this impenetrable dark.

Had I been dreaming? I couldn't open my eyes. Motion. Screams, and heavy thuds, cacophonous noise. More jolting motion, more pain, silence, heavy breaths and heavier footsteps. Rattling and a roar.

And through all of it, one searing brightness in the dark, pressing into me, like a hot poker cauterizing a wound. I wanted to scream as it burrowed into me, wrapped around me, jolted me into awareness every time I tried to slip away.

And then the brightness dimmed, pulled away, and the pain rushed in to fill the space it'd occupied, and I still wanted to scream, but I couldn't find my mouth.

That lasted a long time.

Warmth, at last, and I hadn't realized I'd been bathed in icy chill until it surrounded me.

That bright thing had come back, only this time it didn't hurt.

Consciousness slipped away again.

And then it returned, only this time it wasn't a dream.

I could feel my body. Really feel it, from my scalp down to my toes. All of it felt battered and beaten.

Eyelids. I had those. I forced them open. And then blinked, unsure what I was looking at. I finally figured out it was a chest, hard with muscle and furred with blond hair.

I had arms around me. I had legs tangled with mine.

We were both naked.

And alive, fucking *alive*. I closed my eyes again for a second, dizzy with the realization.

I'd lived. He'd gotten me out of there. Somehow, he'd done it.

My neck protesting the movement—and gods, why shouldn't it, hadn't it been ripped to bloody shreds...recently? It felt like years ago—I tipped my head back.

Tipped it back on his bicep, it turned out, because I found myself staring into his hard, expressionless face, his glowing eyes meeting mine, icy silver and frozen flame.

Calder. I swallowed hard.

"Calder," I murmured.

A tremor went through him, shaking that impassivity for a second. His mouth tightened.

"You remembered."

I swallowed again, my throat horribly dry. "Hard to forget the last word you think you're ever going to hear."

He flinched, actually *flinched*, his eyes flicking away from me like he couldn't bear to look at me. My own eyes widened in shock. His arms tightened around me, as if he could get me any closer. I was tucked against him, completely wrapped in him.

Calder stared over my shoulder, jaw clenched so hard I expected to hear his teeth grinding.

"How am I alive?" I finally asked, when it looked like he was going to stay stony-silent forever. "You didn't think it would work. I didn't honestly think it would work." I stopped, horrified, as belated panic slammed into me. Oh, fucking gods, *maybe it hadn't worked*, maybe this was some kind of dream, a hallucination or a horrific afterlife made of false hope and—I struggled, shoving him away, trying to sit up. "We didn't—oh fuck, we didn't—it didn't work, it didn't—"

He let me go enough that I could wrench myself up, propped on my elbows and staring around me wildly.

It took a second for what I was seeing to penetrate the fog of terror.

No concrete walls. No cell door. No toilet and sink in the corner.

A bedroom. Pale-blue walls with dark wood trim. A dresser, with some pictures and a vase on top. A window, a real fucking window, framed in white drapes and with sun shining in. An open door, with a glimpse of a bathroom through it.

An actual bathroom. With a shower. I could see part of a blue shower curtain.

With little white seashells printed on it.

They looked so incredibly real. No hallucination or afterlife would've included that detail, would it?

The seashells blurred as my heartbeat rocketed up into the stratosphere. Everything blurred. I couldn't feel my limbs.

Calder dragged me back into his arms, cradling me against his chest. I huddled there as he ran his hands all over me, pushing heat and strength into me.

The bond. I felt the bond, and I knew that had been the bright thing in the darkness. Strong, living magic pulsed through it and suffused me until I sang with it.

That bond couldn't be anything but real. Magic didn't lie like that.

And the panic ebbed away.

I peeked out from the shelter of his arms. I couldn't see the fucking shower curtain from this angle, thank the gods, with its overwhelmingly cutesy normality, its terrifyingly pleasant mundanity...but the dresser was still there.

We still weren't in that cell anymore.

We'd escaped.

And I had lived.

We were somewhere safe, somewhere clean. He was clean, his matted hair washed out, although still a tangle of something like dreadlocks.

And *I* was clean, that gritty, sticky, all-over residue of living and sweating on a dusty floor completely gone.

He'd washed me too, and I had to swallow down bile at the thought. My limp body, flopping around as he held me under a shower spray or dunked me in a tub, scrubbing off the blood he'd drenched me with.

Washing my ass, where he'd fucked me. He hadn't even wanted to fuck me. How disgusted must he have been, dealing with the sloppy aftermath of claiming a body he'd never desired to begin with? The fact that I'd been unconscious only added to the humiliation, somehow, even though I hadn't had to see his face while he dealt with it. With me.

More bile. I swallowed again, hard.

I lifted my head. There were more important issues, and I had to get my head out of...well, my ass. My now-clean ass. Ugh, gods.

"We escaped," I rasped. "How? How did you—*how*? I didn't think you could do it. *You* didn't think you could do it. Get me out. Where are we? How did we—" I broke off in a cough, as my too-dry throat gave out on me.

Calder regarded me seriously, seeming to have gotten all his composure back when I flipped my lid and lost mine. "The bond was a lot stronger than I expected it to be."

I waited. He didn't say anything else. "Fucking talk, or I'm going to shake it out of you."

His lips quirked in that little sardonic smile of his, only this time it didn't look like he was mocking me. I'd had those lips on mine.

I'd had those lips on my ass.

My face flamed, and now he had an eyebrow quirked too. Bastard.

He scooted back until he could lean against the headboard of the bed we were in, and it finally hit me viscerally that *we were in a bed together*.

Both naked, as I'd noted but somehow ignored, with the blankets rucked up around our waists. His chest looked broader in a real bed, like normal furniture was made to a miniature scale. I glanced down at my own nudity. Werewolves got naked around each other all the time, so I wouldn't normally care. But I resisted the urge to pull the covers up over my chest like a virgin on her wedding night.

I was in bed, naked, with my mate. My *mate*.

My hand flew up to my neck. The bite mark was there, a little raised scar in otherwise unmarked flesh.

Of course the other wounds had healed, since I was alive. Werewolves healed just about anything—except wounds made with magic, sometimes.

And mating bites were part of one of the oldest, and most

fundamental, types of magic in existence.

I traced the bite with my fingertips. When I glanced up, I found Calder's eyes glued to it, wide and glowing, but darker than usual.

"What?" I snapped. Gods. He couldn't be happy about this. Would he kill me after all, to get out of the bond? If he was going to, then why hadn't he let me die in the first place?

After a second, he seemed to tear his eyes away with an effort, shaking his head and refocusing on my face.

"Lie down and rest," he rumbled. "And I'll tell you what happened."

"I don't want to rest!"

It sounded petulant and childish, but the thought of lying down next to him again made the panic well up again. My mate.

My fucking *mate*, and a dominant mate at that. I'd planned to mate someday, but I'd have been the one giving the bite. I didn't have a knot, but I'd have fucked her—probably her, or maybe him, who knew—and bitten her neck, and claimed her.

Only now I'd been fucked, and knotted, and bitten, and claimed, and owned.

Fragments of what we'd done in the cell flashed through my mind, jagged rents in the disturbingly normal room around me. His teeth rending my flesh. His knot forcing me open.

His hands cradling me, his lips pressing softly against my skin, cherishing me.

Lying to me with his touch, because he needed me compliant and I'd asked him to do it, to pretend, to make me feel like he cared about me before he tore me apart.

And he expected me to lie down next to him and…no. Just no.

I blinked myself back to full reality, feeling chilled again.

Calder was still waiting for an answer. I shook my head at him.

Calder frowned at me, but then he shrugged and settled himself more comfortably against the pile of pillows at the head of the bed, as if he didn't give a fuck one way or the other what I did, or whether I stayed near him.

"The bond tied us together and wouldn't let you die," he said finally. "I pulled everything through it. Everything you had to give. I drained you. Until I had enough to get out of that fucking collar." His hand moved, an aborted gesture perhaps indicating how much of *everything* he'd taken. "But you didn't die."

Cold sickness gripped my stomach, tightening my chest too. Apparently it would've killed him to sound even marginally happy about that. "Sorry to disappoint you," I managed through clenched teeth.

He stared at me levelly, but his body went tense. "If I'd left you there, the bond wouldn't have been strong enough, with the distance between us. I felt it fading whenever we weren't touching. I could've abandoned you to die on the floor alone."

But he hadn't. Maybe he hadn't given a damn, not really — but he'd kept his word. And that must have been…difficult. To put it mildly.

Calder was being kind of an asshole, but shame crept over me anyway. He'd kept his word. I was alive, and safe, and he'd been the one to do it.

"How did we get out?"

Calder shrugged, those massive shoulders shifting. "I followed the plan. Killed them all."

Screams, and thuds, and pain in the darkness. I shuddered at the memory, but sharp, brutal triumph welled up in me, warm and soothing in my chest.

"Good," I spat, sounding almost as vicious as I felt. "I'm fucking glad. I'm sorry I didn't see it. I'm sorry I didn't get to do any of it myself."

"There were three other prisoners there. One of them helped. The other two weren't in any shape to do it."

Oh, fuck. I'd completely forgotten about any other prisoners—and I'd known there were some. How selfish could I be? I hated myself in that moment.

"I'm glad you got them out too," I said, my throat horribly tight. I'd been useless, a burden—and he'd rescued all of us. "Where are they? Are they here with us? And where is here?"

"They went their own way. One of them had somewhere to go, and took the others with him. I got their names. A place they meant to go. One of them was a werewolf, with a pack in Idaho." He shrugged. "If you want to check up on them later. I thought maybe you would."

"You could have told them where we were going. I mean, I have a pack. It's easy to find."

"Not safe," he growled. "I don't know them."

Which probably explained why he'd ditched them as quickly as possible. It didn't sound like he'd gotten their info so he could follow up with them—but for me, and it kind of shocked me he'd figured out I'd want to.

But later. I wasn't even in a position to take care of myself quite yet.

Which reminded me. I needed to call the people who were.

"Where are we? I need to—fuck," I said, running my hands through my hair. "I need to call my cousins."

And the heavy weight of that felt like enough to pull me down through the floor.

"The Oregon coast," he said. "Right over the border from

Washington." Anticipating my next question, he said, "I broke into an empty vacation house."

I stared at him in disbelief. "We're not criminals, Calder! We're not—on the run. We didn't need to break and enter, we could've..." I realized I didn't know what else we could've done after all, since I'd been unconscious and unable to call anyone I could maybe ask for help. It wasn't like we had any money. But apparently we'd had a car, or we wouldn't be here. A stolen car? "How did we get here? And couldn't you have, I don't know, lifted the guards' wallets or something? Get us some cash?"

"So you're not a criminal," he said. "So what. Now you are. Also so fucking what. I wasn't exactly focusing on picking pockets when I ripped them limb from limb. I took one of their cars. That's how we got here."

"But—"

"Picture me trying to check into a hotel carrying your bloody, unconscious body, Jared," he snapped, showing a rare moment of actual emotion. Of course that emotion had to be annoyance.

But okay. Yes. That would be a one-way trip to jail—or to a bloodbath massacre when they tried to arrest Calder—and human authorities wouldn't be all that sympathetic to our wild-sounding story, one of several reasons why neither he nor I would have even considered going to the police in the first place.

All right. We'd broken and entered. We had shifter senses; if anyone showed up here, we'd be able to get out before we were caught.

So being a criminal, in this small sense, I could live with.

But on the run?

What the fuck had happened to Jonathan Hawthorne,

anyway?

I looked up at Calder and found him examining me, a strange look in his eyes. It cleared as soon as I caught him at it, and that hard, neutral mask dropped back into place.

"Do you think anyone's coming after us?" The thought chilled my blood, but we had to consider it. "There was another warlock. Hawthorne. I knew him before—before. He's the one who kidnapped me and put me there. Was he the one who brought you—"

"I don't think anyone's after us," he said, running over my questions like a bulldozer. Okay, message received. No questions. Although I was wildly curious. "We got away clean. No one was monitoring from a distance, I'm pretty sure. Or one of the other prisoners was pretty sure. A fairy. He seemed to know his stuff. And we didn't leave any fucking witnesses."

I mulled that over. "Hawthorne might still be out there, though. And he knows me. He knows where I'm from, my family." I went still, the realization hitting me like a ton of bricks. Hawthorne knew me. He knew my family. If he went looking for me…or in the two years since I'd been gone…fuck, fuck, *fuck, anything* could've happened. "Oh, gods," I choked out. "What if he—what if they—I have to call them. I have to call Ian *right now*."

I scrambled off the bed, throwing the blankets aside, heedless of my nudity and that I didn't have a phone and didn't know where to find one.

"Easy," I heard Calder saying from behind me, sounding startled. "You're not up to much—"

I ignored him, barreling out of the bedroom and into a cozy living room, with plush seating and a TV and a bookshelf decorated with tchotchkes. The normality of it had me reeling, falling against the doorframe and barely catching myself with one hand.

Or maybe that was starvation, dehydration, blood loss, and the aftereffects of healing a mortal wound.

Calder's hands landed on my waist, and I jumped a foot in the air, stumbling away from him and catching myself on the back of a floral-print couch this time.

"I'll find a phone, if there's a landline," he said from behind me. Sounding more resigned this time, and maybe with an undertone of...concern? Christ. I was hallucinating now. "Wait a second."

I didn't have much choice, since I was leaning on my arms, head hanging down, swaying like a drunkard.

He was back a moment later, and something warm wrapped around my shoulders. "I found someone's bathrobe," he said. "Come on."

I still didn't want his hands on me, or maybe I wanted them too much, but either way they shouldn't be there...but through the terrycloth it felt like something I could let myself bear. Or let myself have.

He guided me across the room and through a doorway into the kitchen, another bastion of middle-class kitsch. A clock shaped like a chicken dominated the wall over the sink, catching my horrified eye the second I walked in.

Calder nudged me into one of the chairs at the kitchen table, and then went off somewhere, leaving me to contemplate the salt and pepper shakers, two ducks wearing jaunty hats.

My stomach rumbled. I needed to call Ian, urgency thrumming in my veins, but...I didn't have much else in my veins. I had to replenish my strength. Not just from what I'd been through in the past couple of days, but in general. I hadn't had the chance to look in a mirror yet, and I wasn't looking forward to it. At least I didn't have a prisoner's long straggly beard.

Hawthorne had done some kind of magic to stun my hair follicles, and I hadn't grown any facial hair in years. They'd probably done something similar to Calder, but his stubble showed that it hadn't worked very well.

What had happened to Ian and Matt, to the pack, while I'd been gone? If anything had gone wrong, if they were... Ian and Matt could already be dead.

Nate could be dead, and that would almost certainly be partly my fault.

All of it would be my fault.

I shied away from it, shuddering. I couldn't bear the thought. They had to be okay. They simply had to be. And if Hawthorne was coming after them, I'd warn them in time. I had to believe it, or I'd go crazy. Crazier.

Calder came back into the kitchen, and I looked up to see he'd found a pair of sweatpants, clearly meant for a much shorter and fatter man.

Despite everything, I choked down a laugh. Gods, we were a pair. Both starved, fucked-up, gaunt and desperate, me in my mint-green bathrobe and Calder in those sweatpants that were more like capris on him—and that he'd had to triple-knot to keep from falling down.

But he had a phone in his hand, a cordless landline. He didn't give it to me.

"Can you trust them?"

I blinked up at him. "Trust them?" I repeated in disbelief. "*Trust* them? They're my family. My *pack*."

His expression grew more pinched, his brows drawn together. "Your family, your pack, who didn't bother looking for you for however long you were in that cell?"

"You have no idea if they looked for me or not! Of course they looked for me." That had kept me going, for months and months after I was first taken. The idea that Ian would never give up on finding me. That no matter what I'd done, he'd never allow someone to kidnap and torture his own blood and a member of his own pack, either out of loyalty or out of pride—or maybe that he'd want to rescue me so he could have the pleasure of beating the shit out of me himself.

That any day now, he'd bust through the door, claws dripping with the blood of my captors, and take me home.

He never came. Obviously. I'd stopped thinking about it after a while. Something terrible had happened to Ian, or despite everything I knew about him and the way he thought and felt, he'd stopped giving a fuck about me after all.

I couldn't stomach either option.

"Of course they looked for me," I said again, unconvincingly even to my own ears.

Calder let out a grunting scoff. "Sure. Can you trust them?"

I swallowed down the lump in my throat. Jesus, I needed a drink of water. I should've gotten that. Standing sounded hard. "Can you grab me a glass of water? And yes. If they take my call at all, I can trust them. They're pack." He still eyed me skeptically. "And they hated Hawthorne. The warlock who hasn't been around for a while," I reminded him. "Worst-case scenario, they don't give a shit about me. But they'd never work with him. Or anyone like him. And I need to warn them, in case Hawthorne's still out there. Besides, we need help."

"Maybe *you* do." With a last slow, doubtful perusal from those glowing silver eyes, he handed over the phone and turned away to the sink.

He set a glass of water down in front of me as I was staring at the keypad, trying to get up the courage to dial, my fingers heavy and reluctant despite my underlying panic. I knew Ian's number by heart; I'd called it so many times over the years. So many times every day, practically. I knew he'd have the same number, because Ian hated change the way some people hated colonoscopies.

I didn't know if he'd want to hear from me.

I drank the whole glass, set it down with a thump, and called.

It rang four times. Unknown number, of course he might not answer. I bit my lip. *Come on, Ian. Come on. Please.*

On the fifth ring, he picked up. "Yeah?"

That one, gruff syllable brought tears to my eyes. I struggled to catch my breath, probably sounding like a prank caller of the prurient kind. Ian's voice. My cousin's voice. The person I'd always loved more than anyone else in the world, even though I'd shown it by fucking, and fucking over, the guy he'd wanted for himself and working with someone Ian had thought was human pond scum.

Ian spoke again before I could get it together. "Look, I don't know who the fuck you are, but if you call this number again I swear I'll track you—"

"Ian," I rasped. "It's me."

The following silence set all my teeth on edge. "Who the fuck is this?" Ian demanded. "Who the fuck—*who the fuck is this*?" He sounded furious, murderous, with an undertone of raw pain and misery.

"Ian? Who do you—it's me. It's Jared, who do you think it is? You don't even recognize my voice anymore?" I couldn't keep the matching pain and misery out of my own voice. He didn't recognize me? He thought—what, that I was a prank caller after all? But would he have sounded so angry, so upset, if he didn't recognize my voice, and think I was an imposter, or something? I didn't get it. "Ian, it's me!"

"No," Ian said, his voice rough and hoarse. "No, that can't be."

"It's me, it's—fucking hell, Ian, come on! You, shit, you can't eat cheesecake. Ever. After that time at the county fair. Or, that time we both slept with that girl at the same party—" I cut off abruptly, remembering the girl's wavy dark hair and dark eyes, and slim body, and how she could've been Nate's female twin. And how I'd slept with Nate the first time, seducing him even though I didn't care about him. And how Ian had looked at me, full of silent, grim misery and betrayal, after he found out about it. That had been how I'd realized Ian's feelings for Nate went deeper than simple lust, and I'd never forgotten his face in that moment. "Ian, it's me," I said quietly, wondering if he was remembering the same things.

Another long silence fell. I could hear Ian's rough breathing, and practically hear the gears turning, too. Why was this so hard?

They thought I was dead, after all this time. That had to be it. But wouldn't Ian want to know I was alive? Wouldn't he be *relieved*? Even if I'd...betrayed his trust, his friendship, his love for me...

"Where the fuck are you?" he asked me, his tone hard. Untrusting.

Can you trust them? It looked like it might be the other way around. I deserved it, I did.

But not like this. Not after crawling out of hell, through a fresh hell, to get to this little fucking vacation kitchen with the chicken on the wall, wanting nothing more than to be safe. Actually safe, home, with my pack. Somewhere I could curl up in a ball and whimper without waiting for the other shoe to drop.

"The Oregon-Washington border," I said, since that was all I knew. I looked up to find Calder leaning against the kitchen sink, massive arms crossed over his bare chest and his face as skeptical as before. I gestured at him, in a *Come on, give me something* sort of way. He pushed off the sink and left the room again. Okay, thanks a fucking bundle. "In...some kind of...house."

"Some kind of house." Ian sounded like he wanted to reach through the phone and throttle me. "Could you be a little less specific, maybe? Because it's going to be way too easy to find you, and I like a fucking challenge."

I heard something in the background, a voice, raised in some kind of strident protest. Not clear enough for me to make out the words, but the tones made me grip the phone so hard the plastic creaked.

Nate. That sounded like fucking *Nate*.

"Who's there with you?" I whispered, through lips gone dry and numb. I didn't know whether I wanted to laugh in relief that he was okay, after all I'd done to make that less likely, and after what his father had put him through...or cry a little.

Or a lot. I'd been imprisoned, suffering and experimented on and tortured and alone, for fucking years. And Nate and Ian were...my mind whirled, and I leaned my elbow on the table and my head in my hand.

"None of your fucking business," Ian said briskly. "Where the fuck are you? I'm hanging up in five seconds if you don't give me something, here. Five. Four. Three. Two—"

A stack of papers flopped down on the table in front of me, and I jumped enough to rattle the chair and knock my knee into the table. "Ow, fuck! Ian, wait, hang on, fuck—" I scrabbled frantically at the papers. They were advertising mailers, sent to the 'current resident.' And addressed to the house we were in, presumably. I read off the address quickly, stumbling over the words, hoping Ian hadn't already hung up. "Ian? Did you get that?"

"I got that," he said grimly, and repeated it back, adding, "Map that for me?" to whoever was there. Nate. To Nate, probably.

I nodded, and realized how fucking stupid that was. "Yes," I said, sounding pathetically eager. "Yes, that's right. That's where I am. Ian, please don't hang—"

"It's about nine hours," he said. "We'll be there early tomorrow. Don't go anywhere. And no tricks. Whoever this is, you will fucking regret it."

And he hung up.

Chapter 6
You'll Never Be Hurt

After a couple of years of wiping down in a tiny sink and occasionally being allowed to stand under a cold spray for a few minutes, watched by colder-eyed guards, the vacation house's criminally-acquired shower felt like...well, heaven, and not reality at all.

Even with those awful little seashells on the shower curtain. Hell, after ten minutes of hot water flowing in luxurious, unthinkable quantities through my hair and down my back and around my legs, I could've kissed the fucking seashells. And whoever had hung the shower curtain. And whoever had built the shower.

I'd set the phone down, stood up, and gone straight to the bathroom, ignoring Calder's glare and mentally telling the rest of the world to fuck off.

I needed some space.

I needed some time.

I needed to feel clean for the first time in years, washing off whatever residue was left of my prison and also the knowledge that Calder had already washed me.

More than anything, I needed to have a little breakdown

where no one could see or hear me.

Tomorrow morning, probably, I'd be seeing my cousin. The chicken clock had told me it was about three in the afternoon, although on what day, I couldn't even hazard a guess.

So eighteen hours, maybe?

I leaned my forehead against the tiled shower wall, letting the water keep rushing down for as long as the water heater could keep up.

Everything around me felt unreal. I hadn't even seen the outdoors yet, and part of me suspected that if I tried to walk out the front door of this place, it wouldn't be there. I'd find myself back in my cell, or in some kind of blasted hellscape out of a nightmare, or in an endless void.

Anything but normal sunshine, trees, the wide blue sky.

I wasn't sure I could handle any of those options—starting with the sunshine.

At last I climbed out of the shower, a little shaky but a lot calmer.

I could do this, dammit. The real world. I could do it. First thing, I'd find some actual clothes and open an exterior door. Maybe I wouldn't step out right away, but I'd open it. Just to prove it wasn't locked and wasn't a trick.

Calder wasn't anywhere in sight when I stepped out, but I could hear him moving around in the kitchen. I dug through the dresser, finding another pair of sweatpants and an ancient t-shirt bearing the logo of a seafood restaurant. I stared at it for a long few moments, contemplating a world in which people went to restaurants.

Two years didn't seem like such a long time, until they were.

I found Calder in the kitchen as I'd expected, setting two bowls of soup on the table. He'd located the canned goods, apparently, and steam rose from generous servings of something that looked like chicken and barley.

I couldn't believe the question hadn't occurred to me yet. "Will this—normal food, is it enough for you?" I tried to make it sound casual, but the answer had anything but casual meaning to me.

"If the blood has the right type of magic in it...it's not the blood itself that sustains me. Not like a vampire. It's the magic in it that can feed me when I need extra strength, or when there's no real food available." He sat down in front of his bowl. "I won't need more. Not under normal circumstances." He glanced up at me. "I listened, while they did what they did to me. And that's how it feels, too. I'm not craving it."

He sounded confident about that, and...yep, that was enough for me.

I had food in front of me. And I wasn't going to get drained again. Good enough.

I dropped into my chair and fell on the soup without a word, and I wouldn't have bothered with a spoon if Calder hadn't already put one by my bowl.

His disappeared even more quickly, and when I looked up from my empty bowl, he was already leaning back in his chair and watching me. Those eyes caught and held me, just the way they had when the guards shoved me into his cell, and the way they kept doing every time I let myself meet his gaze for too long.

The mate bond thrummed between us, no matter how hard I tried to ignore it. It'd settled down a bit now, though, no longer frantically working to keep me alive.

And that...I didn't know more about shifter mating magic than the average werewolf, but I hadn't thought bonds would do that. Act independently, making their own judgments on how to balance magic and life itself between two mates. The bond had given Calder the strength to break free of the chains and magic that bound him, sucking my inherent werewolf magic out of me and pouring it into him, along with the strength he drew from consuming my blood. But then it had apparently, what, pulled some of that strength back? After he'd broken free, and he didn't need every drop of that power anymore. Kept me alive, drawing from him. It hadn't sounded like he'd done that himself.

But what if he had? What if he'd brought me back, sending his own strength and magic back to me through the bond? Saved me at the last moment, for no other reason than...what? Mercy? Compassion? Kindness?

If so, why hadn't he admitted it?

And looking into those hard, cold eyes, it didn't seem likely.

But I couldn't tear my gaze away. My heart beat faster, and my limbs went weak, nerveless. Passive.

"You need to go back to bed."

The words fell heavily into the silent kitchen, silent except for the ticking of the clock, which made the quiet all the more noticeable.

"I'm not sleepy." I had to force the words out.

His eyes didn't waver. I couldn't see anything else.

Calder hadn't been suggesting I go to sleep, I realized.

He hadn't been making a suggestion at all. He'd been telling me what he expected from me.

No, dammit, no, I didn't fucking play that way. I'd never wanted a dominant mate, probably not even a male mate, and I wouldn't have chosen this fucked-up bastard even if I had. I'd tell him where to jump off.

Any second now, I'd tell him. That I might have ended up

mated to him, and he might have put his bite on my neck, but that hadn't made me his property, his thing to use whenever he had an erection or simply got bored.

My cock twitched in the stupid borrowed sweatpants, and my ass…those muscles tightened too, like they were anticipating being loosened up by his cock.

Instead of telling him he could go fuck himself, but definitely not me, I found myself standing up, leaving the kitchen, walking to the bedroom on wobbly legs. He followed me, a looming presence at my back. The bite mark on my neck tingled and throbbed. The scent of him enveloped me, thick in the air, dark and searing and cold, so cold.

I turned as I reached the bed and found him standing just inside the doorway. Silver-mirrored eyes. My fingers still felt too thick and heavy, but I pulled the shirt over my head and dropped it on the floor. Untied the string of the sweatpants, fingertips fumbling, and dropped those too, stepping out of them and lying back on the bed.

Calder walked away, into the bathroom. I stared at the ceiling as I listened to drawers opening and closing, and then he was back, setting something on the nightstand. I knew what it was without looking. Lube, or lotion. Something he meant to use to take me again.

It felt inevitable, and I still couldn't open my goddamn mouth. The mate bond had to be doing this to me, but I didn't know how or why…it had to be the mate bond, because this wasn't me.

And it sure as fuck wasn't *him*. One time getting fucked, with his lips so hot on my skin, his body around me, making me feel like something he treasured as he split me open…

My cock hadn't hardened all the way, but I could feel that hot, weighty anticipation building in the pit of my stomach.

The need to open my legs for him became nearly irresistible, a twitch in my thighs, but I didn't move. Taking action apparently wasn't a part of whatever this was, not for me—or at least not when he hadn't told me what to do.

He wouldn't kill me this time. Would he? Not after saving me the first time. Not after carrying me out of hell, destroying everything in his path, ripping them to shreds and still managing to get me out at the same time. He'd opened the other cells. Dealt with our fellow prisoners. He'd said I'd have died if he got too far from me. Had he held me close the whole time? Cradling me in those massive arms while they broke out, stole cars, probably set the place on fire, if they'd had half the rage in them as they escaped that I would have, if I'd been conscious and able to wreak my vengeance?

It didn't matter anyway. I wasn't moving.

Calder lowered himself down over me, naked now too. My cock might not have fully joined the proceedings, but his had. Huge and hard and flushed, it hung between his legs, too heavy to stand upright. His arms caged my head, hands resting on either side. He wasn't even breathing hard, and it seemed so unfair. He leaned down until those eyes filled my vision again, until I had to close my own eyes or drown. My lips parted. I didn't move.

He kissed me, long and deep and slow. His knees settled between my thighs, nudging them apart. I lay splayed like an offering, legs akimbo, arms spread out, as he kissed me, his tongue lazily opening me.

One hand lifted up and found my chest, fingers teasing over a nipple. Pinching, but so gently that my flesh rose to meet him, hardening under his touch, begging for more of it.

He kissed me, and played with my nipple, until it felt too sensitive to take any more, swollen and aching. Until that gentle, repetitive pinch and release built into the agony of pressure with nowhere to go. I moaned into his mouth, and I moved at last, lifting my hands to grip his forearms. I tried to still his hand and failed. His fingers squeezed my nipple again, so gently, the caress too much to take.

"Please," I whispered in that fraction of a second between one kiss and the next. "Please, please…"

He let go at last, and the tension rushed out of me, my head swimming. He put his hand down, lifted the other, and that thumb and forefinger found my other nipple, pinching and squeezing.

It went on and on, until I was almost sobbing under him, his mouth muffling the sounds.

Calder stopped kissing me and lifted his head. I blinked away the water in my eyes, and he blurred in my vision. He lowered his head to my chest.

"Please!"

He ignored me, working my puffy nipples over with his mouth, back and forth, sucking, licking, flicking with his tongue, until my chest heaved with the sobs I tried to keep in. I couldn't feel anything but my slick, tingling lips and my too-hot, swollen tits, and the deep, heavy ache between my legs.

I couldn't even tell if my cock had hardened or softened. It didn't seem to matter.

I moaned in relief when Calder stopped at last, just as I couldn't take a second more of it without screaming, without exploding. My hands twitched, the urge to bury my fingers in his hair and drag his head back down to my chest nearly overwhelming. Back down? No, no more, no more…he laughed, very low, his breath brushing over my chest and making me sob again, just the passage of air over my too-sensitive skin a delicate agony.

He reached for the nightstand, kneeling up between my legs. I forced myself not to look at him by squeezing my eyes shut so hard I saw stars.

"On your back or on your stomach? Choose wisely, because this is going to take a while."

My belly clenched, and I moaned. "On my back," I whispered without opening my eyes.

It took a while. More than a while, an eternity. He didn't bother with fingers first, simply pushing my legs as wide open as they would go, holding my cheeks apart with his hands, and working his slick cock into me one massive inch at a time.

Slowly. So fucking slowly that I could've screamed in frustration.

Distantly, I knew I shouldn't have been frustrated by the glacial pace of his entry. I didn't want that cock buried in me again, filling me so deeply I couldn't breathe.

I pressed my knees down against the bed, keeping myself spread for him.

At last he was all the way in, my body impaled on him.

Calder lowered himself down on top of me, his weight crushing my chest and pressing me down into the bed, holding just enough of it on his elbows that I could breathe. He buried one hand in my hair, fingers wrapped in the strands, holding me still—as if he needed to. He buried his face in my hair, too, breathing me in.

And then he moved.

He fucked me with his whole body, his bulk moving like a piston, cock hardly withdrawing at all before it pushed back into me.

Chest hair rubbed over my still-swollen nipples, making me squirm, but I had nowhere to go. I couldn't move so much as an inch in any direction, stuck on his cock and pinned down.

I wanted to relax into it, give in to the repetitive motion of him moving inside me, moving me, rocking me along with his hips. Feel nothing but that thrusting inside me, the possession of his cock.

I couldn't. How could I, not knowing what came next? In the cell, at least what came next had been crystal-clear. And I'd had a purpose. Get Calder out, at least, even if I couldn't. Get word to Ian and Matt. Accomplish something with my death the way I hadn't in life. Get my revenge by proxy.

There was no purpose to this, no planned-out reasoning behind it.

Calder had looked at me, and he'd told me to go back to bed.

And I'd laid myself out for him like a slut.

He kissed my hair and then shifted down a little, the movement changing the angle of his hips. His cock hit that same perfect, singing place inside me, and sweet, horrible tremors went up and down my spine.

It also put his face lower, against my neck.

And I tipped my head for him, trembling, but giving him my bare throat. Because it was his.

"Don't," I murmured, breathy and weak. "Please, not again."

Calder kissed the hollow between my collarbones, his tongue flicking out and tasting the fine sheen of sweat there. "Never again," he growled into my skin. "I told you. Never. You'll never be hurt again."

My arms came up, wrapping around his back. The muscles shifted under my fingers as he kept up that steady, rolling rhythm, claiming me all over again. Did I have anything in me but him? His cock felt like it'd filled every inch of my skin.

I moaned. Another thrust, this one nudging my whole

body up the bed.

You'll never be hurt again…

It came back to me, in hazy recollections between his thrusts, between the building of ecstasy deep in me, what he'd said before he told me his name. That I wouldn't hurt anymore either way? Had he meant whether I lived or died? Life meant pain, always, no matter how careful you were. It didn't make any sense. He latched onto my neck, sucking a mark that didn't hurt at all, and the heat of his mouth arrowed down to join the heat between my legs.

"Oh, gods," I whimpered. "Calder."

He groaned, fucking me harder now, starting to slam into me with every thrust.

The heat went molten, and I couldn't tell which of us finished first, or if we finished at all, since it seemed to go on and on: the spilling of my come between us, his flooding me, his knot stretching me open and forcing its way inside, the glow of his eyes and the glow of the bond and the heavy pressure of his body holding me down, keeping me locked away from everything else. Everything that could hurt me.

I cried out, clutching at him, and the concept of hurt vanished, swept away in a tide of sensation, nothing but Calder around me and in me.

His knot stayed hard for a long time, probably. Maybe? It felt like a long time, even though it couldn't possibly have been long enough. At some point, he rolled us to the side, taking his crushing weight off of me. I almost missed it. I'd gone so long without any human contact at all, unless you counted the guards hitting me and the warlocks tying me down and hurting me—which I didn't. That had been inhuman, by definition. Being covered, sheltered, completely enveloped in another warm, living person felt like drinking a glass of water after a long run through the woods, or sipping a cup of coffee when you'd had the mother of all hangovers. Bliss.

But nestling into his arms, lying on our sides with his cock still buried inside me, wasn't so bad either.

I'd never wanted to be fucked.

And this still didn't feel like being fucked. It felt like a natural state of being. Wrong, if I thought about it, but perfect when I didn't. I'd been hollow, alone, and now I was stuffed full of him, so warm inside, my thighs spread awkwardly to fit him in between, the slight discomfort of the position only making it better, somehow. Highlighting that I'd had to adjust my body to accommodate him.

Gods. Much better not to think about it.

His hand wrapped around the nape of my neck felt wrong too, or should have. The hand, too big; the grip, too possessive. Casually possessive, even. Like he wasn't asking, but assuming. The way a man might rest his hand on the gearshift of his car, using something he owned in a way that felt most comfortable to him.

I melted into that hold like my bones were made out of wax.

And I very carefully didn't think about that either.

But my brain, temporarily offline after my orgasm had shut it down, fired back up again and wouldn't leave me alone.

Ian would be here in the morning. What the hell would he make of Calder? Ian was one of the few people I'd ever known I might give decent odds to in a fight against the man who'd become my mate—but not even odds. If Calder had an off day, maybe Ian could take him down.

Either way, if one of them said the wrong thing, or if Ian thought Calder had hurt me—which of course he had, and Ian wouldn't stop to listen to extenuating circumstances—a fight wasn't unlikely. And that fight would be ugly and brutal.

If Ian cared. Which he might not.

He didn't seem to trust me, maybe didn't even believe I was who I said I was.

I'd have loved to convince myself that he wouldn't be coming if he didn't believe me, but I knew that was bullshit. He'd come half because it might be me, and half because if it wasn't, then someone was fucking with him unforgivably, and that person needed an immediate beatdown. That was Ian's way. Ask the bare minimum of questions, and then kick someone's ass.

Calder's knot finally went down, and his cock slipped partway out of me, softened but still feeling impossibly thick and heavy as he shifted his hips and withdrew.

I'd missed this part before, unconscious and dying.

I grimaced against Calder's chest, wincing as he pulled out all the way, tugging on my insides.

And leaving me horribly, unbelievably empty.

I hadn't had actual *space* inside me before, had I? Waiting to be filled up? No, of course I hadn't. Which meant he'd created that space. And now it was waiting to be filled up again.

Gods, no, fuck that. I tried to clench my muscles. That only got me so far. He'd stretched me out. I'd go back to normal, what with shifter healing. And regular old humans did this too, right? All the time. I'd fucked my share of guys. Their asses hadn't looked like bomb craters the next day.

Of course, I had a normal cock. Calder didn't.

I clenched again and felt his come trickling out of me, slicking my thighs.

I shoved myself up and rolled out of bed, tearing myself out of Calder's arms. "Shower," I choked out, and fled for the bathroom.

Chapter 7
That Isn't How Mating Works

I thought I'd found a safe haven, with the door shut behind me and that stupid curtain drawn, but no sooner had I relaxed a little, the hot water running down over my ass and thighs and mingling enough with his come that I couldn't feel it anymore, than the bathroom door opened and closed.

A moment later, Calder drew the curtain aside and crowded into the shower with me. I wasn't a small man, and the addition of his massive bulk to the little space made it as claustrophobic as a clown car.

Gods, he was tall. Towering over me, just like I towered over half of humanity. He'd have had to bend his knees and duck to get under the showerhead.

Not that I was giving him the chance. My shower. My hot water. He could stand there and freeze.

Although with his alpha shifter metabolism, he might be warmer than the water on his own. My front felt as warm as my back, anyway, once he stood in front of me, mere inches separating us.

I looked up at him, wary and irritated, and trying not to pay too much attention to how his cock was already at half mast again and looking like it was heading straight for me.

The water sluicing over my skin, and the surprise, the humiliation-pleasure-discomfort, of feeling his cock sliding out of me and his come leaking out after, had shocked me out of the fugue I'd been in when I went and lay down on the bed. When I let him fuck me again, when I lay still while he sucked and plucked my nipples into the hot, swollen buds they still were, too sensitive for the heat of the shower.

I didn't know what had come over me, but it sure as fuck wasn't going to come over me again. So to speak. And I was going to make sure he knew it. I hadn't been able to speak up before, but I wasn't going to be so passive again.

"That wasn't an invitation," I snapped.

He shrugged. "I didn't think I needed one."

Reaching past my head for the soap on its little shelf, he started to wash up, completely unconcerned by my slack-jawed stare of disbelief.

He didn't think he needed one? To just...barge in on me? In the fucking shower? Was *nothing* sacred anymore?

"You always need an invitation! It's a *shower*, Calder!"

Another careless shrug, and he didn't even bother with a verbal answer. He rubbed soap onto his chest, the bubbles snaking down over his muscle-ridged abs and starting to pool around his cock. It'd risen a little more, the head now pointing directly at my groin.

I pulled my gaze up again by force of will, away from my horrified contemplation of how the ever-loving fuck that thing had fit inside my body. My ass muscles clenched in response to the thought. I still felt open, oddly conscious of a part of me I rarely thought about.

Or *had* rarely thought about. If I kept rolling over like a bitch every time Calder looked at me, I'd be thinking about it a lot more.

And wasn't that a disturbing thought.

It wasn't going to fucking happen.

"You might as well turn around," he rumbled, his voice deep and echoey in the shower stall.

"What? I—*what*?"

"Turn around," he repeated implacably. "I don't know how many times you like to shower in a day, but I'm going to fuck you again, here or back in bed. If you don't want to end up in here a third time, you might as well turn around and spread your legs."

"No fucking way!" I sputtered. "What the fuck, Calder? You don't just—tell me to—" I stopped, my mouth opening and closing. He *had* just told me to, hadn't he? A few short minutes ago. And I'd let him. Moving on, quickly. "This isn't how being mated works. We're going to get the bond broken anyway, as soon as we can find a halfway competent shaman."

The words felt strange on my tongue, tasting bitter and rough. I hadn't given it any conscious thought yet, but of course we'd be breaking the mating bond. It wasn't an easy or pleasant process, but it could—and clearly should—be done, in this case.

But mating bonds, as I'd learned, had their own brand of semi-sentient magic, and mine gave a quiver at the words and the thought behind them.

I quivered too. Probably in reaction to the bond.

Calder went very still, the bar of soap clenched in his fist. "No," he said. I opened my mouth to protest, but he went on with, "That isn't how mating works."

Oh. Shit, I thought he'd meant that he didn't want to break the bond. My stomach dropped miserably. Of course he wanted to break the bond too. Why the hell wouldn't he?

Neither of us had wanted this. And he hadn't wanted *me*.

And I hadn't wanted *him*, much more to the point, obviously!

"Okay, then what the hell is your—"

"That's how I work." His lips quirked a little. Patronizing fucking son of a bitch. "And that's how *you* work. Apparently."

"How I—you're out of your fucking mind." I glared up at him, standing my ground. Yes, I'd acted like a slut earlier. His slut, lying there and taking it. Spreading for it.

So I'd had a traumatic day. Year. Life. Whatever. I could be excused for taking a little comfort in something I usually wouldn't want. For shutting down and going with the flow instead of telling him straight-up that I didn't want to have sex with him, and that I wasn't his plaything.

Calder *looked* at me, his eyes glowing pale silver.

His cock stood out straight, now, rock-hard and straining. I could smell his arousal, scenting the air with enough pheromones and hot, spicy alpha musk to overpower the steam of the shower. My hole felt hot too, still wet with his come, still stretched from his knot. Ready to take him.

I couldn't look away from his eyes, and my own eyelids drooped. My body went lax, all the resistance draining out of me.

What the fuck was happening to me?

I turned around, braced myself on the wall, and spread my legs, my head hanging down and my eyes shut, while my mind raced like a hamster in a wheel.

Calder pressed up behind me, his cock sliding into the crease of my ass like it belonged there. He pushed it against me, back and forth, rubbing over my hole.

"Tell me how you want it," he said.

How I wanted it? I *didn't* want it! I'd never wanted to be

fucked before, and I still wasn't…like that. Submissive. Bending over when another man told me to.

I stuck my ass out further, pushing it against his cock.

Like my body wasn't in my control at all.

Maybe I couldn't say no. Maybe the bond was making me obey him, even though I'd never heard of that happening—bonds could and did nudge mates into *wanting* to please the other, but they couldn't force you to do anything. Emotions were a bond's playground, not actions. And I didn't feel any differently than I had before.

Okay, maybe not. But I still couldn't make myself say no.

Still. That didn't mean I had to go along with whatever fucked-up game he'd decided to play. I wasn't going to beg for his cock.

I forced the words out. "Just take me and get it over with."

"That's how you want it, then? Fast and rough?" He sounded painfully neutral, to the point of being strained. I almost craned my neck to try to catch a glimpse of his face, but there wasn't much point. I wouldn't be able to read anything there, anyway.

"I don't care if it hurts. I mean, it's going to hurt. I haven't had any time to heal. Just do it, if you're going to."

Calder pulled back a little, letting his cock slide out from between my legs. I couldn't feel him at all. Even the swirling steam seemed to still for a moment, holding its breath like I was holding mine.

"I told you. I wouldn't—" He broke off with a low growl that made every hair on my body rise. "I keep my fucking word." A hand replaced his cock, the sudden touch making me jump. He probed my hole with his fingers. "You don't need to heal," he said, sounding oddly defensive. "I didn't injure you."

I huffed a laugh. "Of course you did. I'm—all open."

"Yeah," he said, low and husky. "Yeah, you are." Two fingers pressed inside, easily, meeting no resistance at all. "But that's not the same as hurt. And I won't even need to slick you up again. You're still wet."

If my face got any hotter, it'd burst into flame. A shiver ran through me, and anger welled up…even though my cock had gotten hard again, as eager as the rest of my traitorous body. When Calder reached up and took one of my nipples between his thumb and forefinger again, my cry echoed off the tiles and my ass clenched around his other hand. And when he leaned down and kissed across my shoulders and neck, I thought I might come just from that.

"I think I could make you come without fucking you at all," he said, like he'd read my goddamn mind. He kissed the nape of my neck. "With kisses." He suited the action to the words, mouthing at the curve of my neck below my ear. His fingers started to move in and out of me, slowly and gently, and he swiped his thumb over my nipple, back and forth, so softly I almost couldn't feel it. Whisper-soft. "Just touching you. I don't think I will fuck you again. Not until you beg for it."

"What's—the point, then?" I choked out. "You're hard, you're an alpha, you're my—mate. For now, anyway. You want to fuck. So do it!"

Calder growled again, pressing up behind me, pulling his fingers out of me and wrapping his arm around my chest, tugging me up so that my body was plastered to the heat and strength of him. My head fell back against his shoulder. That arm around me lay hard and heavy over my collarbones, pinning me in place, and the other hand still teased at my chest, moving from one side to the other, plucking and stroking.

My cock stuck out in front of me, the water of the shower

pounding down on it and almost, almost providing enough stimulation. But *not* enough, I needed...I didn't touch myself, though, instead reaching up to hold onto his forearm, my fingers digging in.

I couldn't even really feel the mate bond. Not as strongly as I'd have expected. Gods, if this wasn't a bond gone wrong, gone weird...it was me.

Calder bent and tucked his head into the curve of my neck. His cock pressed into the small of my back, and he shifted his hips, letting it rub against my skin. His hand started moving down, tracing delicate patterns, fingertips trailing over my ribs. He got almost down to my cock and then moved back up again, and I moaned, bucking my hips into the empty air.

"You don't want it rough," he murmured, and kissed me again, right on the mating bite. "You want me to make love to you. Like you asked for."

"I didn't ask you to...make love to me," I gasped, feeling a little sick. I hadn't asked for that. I would *never* ask for that. How pathetic did he think I was?

"Not in so many words." He stroked me again, from where his arm lay against my upper chest all the way down to my groin. He teased his fingers up my inner thigh, and I thought I might scream. So close. So fucking close. "But that's what you want. And I'll give it to you. Do you want me to tell you how beautiful you are?"

Humiliated, furious tears leaked out of the corners of my eyes, not lost quickly enough in the water of the shower. Not nearly quickly enough for me to pretend they hadn't been there. My lower torso went heavy, with every muscle tensed.

"That's fucking stupid," I whispered.

"So beautiful," he whispered back, his hand splayed over my belly, rubbing in slow circles. "My fragile, beautiful little toy."

What? Not a word of that was remotely true, but he followed it up with the softest possible ghost of a kiss to my mating mark, and my whole body convulsed, my knees giving out as I shot every drop of come in my body onto the shower wall. I hung in his arms, shuddering with aftershocks.

He loosened his arms and turned me around, clutching me around the waist and working his other hand between us, grasping his cock. Calder's mouth came down on mine, and he sucked all the breath I had left right out of me, kissing me endlessly as he jerked off against my stomach.

He grunted and shook, and his hot come dripped down my abdomen, onto my spent cock.

Fuck it. I just couldn't.

I leaned on him and gave up, letting him wash us both, soap and then rinsing, my cock and balls and between the cheeks of my ass, under my arms and over my chest and belly. He held me up with one arm while he washed himself. I barely had the will left to stay on my feet, and I weaved and drooped as he shut off the water and pulled us both out of the shower.

When he rolled me into bed and then pressed up behind me, wrapping himself around me, I let him.

***

I didn't sleep, but by the time a few minutes had passed and I'd roused myself enough to pay attention to anything but the drift of my own half-formed thoughts, the room had darkened, the window a black square reflecting the ambient glow of the light we'd left on in the bathroom.

To my werewolf eyes there was more than enough light to see by, even fine details. Gods only knew what Calder could see. Alpha vision sharpened when their eyes took on that glow of magic, their inherent power intensifying at the same time. He could probably see in what an average shifter would consider pitch-black.

I wiggled around, turning myself in his arms, trying to pull back a little.

He allowed it, removing his arm from over my waist.

I settled on my side with a foot or so separating our faces. He regarded me calmly out of half-lidded eyes, a predator at rest, like one of those big cats sunning on top of a rock in a nature documentary.

Not much point in trying to sit up or get out of bed or run away, right? I might as well be comfortable, and I'd far from recovered from all the physical strain of the last couple of days, let alone the couple of years before. It'd take me a while to be really strong again, really fit. Practicality had always been a strength of mine, even though it'd been my weakness, too; what could be more practical than allying with someone who could help me achieve my goals, even if that someone was Jonathan Hawthorne?

But it'd stand me in good stead now. I wasn't impatient. I could regain my muscle mass and my good health in whatever timeframe I needed. My werewolf physiology would see to it, and all I had to do was eat and rest.

So it made sense to stay in bed. Even if it meant staying in bed with Calder.

Besides, if I scurried off like a scared rabbit, he'd only laugh at me.

Anyway, I wasn't scared. I was insulted and pissed-off. "You know how stupid that sounded, right?"

Thank gods, he didn't need me to spell it out. I didn't think I could've repeated what he'd said to me out loud. Hearing it once had been horrifying enough.

Of course, that meant he quirked that sardonic little smile and repeated it himself, the bastard. "That you're beautiful? And fragile? That?"

I bit my lip hard, my face going hot all the way to my hairline. "Yeah," I gritted out. "That. I'm not any of that. I'm not...beautiful," I spat. "And definitely not...look, I used to be one of my pack's enforcers. I don't know what the fuck you were talking about, but it's bullshit."

His smile widened a little. "It made you come."

"It did not! I don't know what made me come, but it wasn't you saying—saying—"

Calder shifted over on the pillow, putting his face so close to mine he could almost have kissed me. "Compared to me, you're fragile," he said. "And you are beautiful." My whole body tensed up. "Breakable."

"A Mack truck is breakable compared to you," I growled, at the limits of my patience.

He shrugged—not a move easy to pull off lying on his side, but he managed. "Okay, fine. So you're not beautiful. Not fragile at all."

I'd wanted him to say that, right? I opened my mouth and closed it again, at a complete loss, especially since the pit of my stomach had gone all tight with something disturbingly like disappointment.

"Objectively, anyway," he added abruptly. "To most people. Sure. But to me?" He reached up and stroked his fingers down the side of my face, trailing them along my jaw. "I could destroy you. But I'm not going to. I promised you. And I told you, a couple of times, even though apparently you didn't listen. I keep my word. Always."

I tried to remember exactly what he'd said, but what I

managed to dredge out of my memory still left me as confused as it had when he'd said it in the first place.

"Yeah, I know you told me nothing would hurt anymore, but that was because I was going to be dead. Nothing hurts when you're dead."

"I said nothing would hurt either way."

Yep, still confused. "I don't get it."

His hand tightened, holding my face in place, forcing me to look at him without flinching.

Those mesmerizing eyes flared brighter. His voice low and earnest, he said, "Nothing is ever going to hurt you again. Not even me. Especially not me." He swallowed hard, his Adam's apple bobbing, and hesitated. I wouldn't have interrupted him for a million dollars. "All I wanted was to destroy. Kill everyone in my path. Anyone, especially them, but everyone. But you asked me to take care of you. You asked me not to hurt you more than I needed to. And I gave my word, and you believed me." His voice had gone so low I wouldn't have been able to hear him at all if he hadn't been speaking inches from my face. "I took you out of that fucking place. I carried you out, and that makes you my responsibility, because I saved your life. I don't want to hurt you, and I won't."

That was...a relief. And more than that—but I couldn't even begin to process how much more. One thing more thing stood out, though, beyond the fact that I didn't need to be afraid of him every second. "I'm not your responsibility. We're mated—for now. But that doesn't mean anyth—"

"You are, and it has nothing to do with being mated. I promised," he repeated, his jaw setting mulishly.

Oh, Christ. He had to be a stubborn bastard on top of everything else. Just my luck. Okay, I'd leave that alone for now. Maybe the mate bond was fucking with him; maybe he'd been more shaken up than I'd thought by nearly killing me.

I had to shy away from anything else it sounded like he meant, because if I really believed he meant to protect me against all comers for the rest of our lives? Prevent me from being hurt, in any way, ever?

Well, that sounded like it could be moderately terrifying.

But I also ached for it, so deep down I could hardly even feel it. Pressure, building up under the defenses I'd erected around my real feelings, when I couldn't feel anything but pain and had to push it down or explode.

I had to remember it wasn't real. I wasn't even sure the promises never to hurt me again were real. We'd see how that worked out if he ever had a choice again between hurting me and getting something he needed, like freedom or revenge or his own life.

So forget that, for now. I'd deal with it later.

But there was something else there too, something I couldn't quite formulate clearly. "Not hurting me doesn't mean…treating me like that, though. Calling me those—things. Your toy." My face went all hot, and my lower body felt…heavy. Like I needed to move, or needed something else. I didn't want to think about what else. "Fragile. You don't have to treat me like that. I don't want your pity, or, or whatever else. Your—it's like you're making fun of me, somehow. Because I asked you to go easy on me, before."

Calder smiled. A real smile, the first one I'd seen on his hard, emotionless face. It showed his sharp teeth, but they didn't look like a threat this time. "I don't have to treat you like that. But you want me to. You asked me to. And I gave my word, Jared."

"I don't—I didn't ask for—I don't want that. I *don't*."

The smile went as sharp as his teeth, his eyes gleaming

with more than their alpha glow. "Fine. You don't want that. You can prove it tomorrow. Right now, we need something else to eat, and then sleep. Your cousin's getting here in the morning?"

What the...okay, now I had whiplash. Prove it tomorrow? What the fuck did that mean?

The mention of food took first place, though. That bowl of soup had been good, and we'd both needed to start a little slow, easing into normal caloric intake after near-starvation. But my body felt primed to devour a steak—or for that matter, a whole cow. Cooking optional.

And then there was the question of Ian. My heart tried to leap and sank instead. Fuck, I didn't know what to think, I just knew that the idea of seeing him again nauseated me more than my gnawing hunger.

Calder was already rolling out of bed, stretching his back—and okay, maybe I didn't want to be mated to him, and I didn't know what the hell I *did* want, but Christ, the muscles in his back and shoulders, and his ass and legs, were worth a lecherous stare or two—and looking like he was heading for the kitchen.

"I guess you could hear him through the phone, too?" Calder nodded, leaning down to pick up his stolen sweatpants off the floor.

It didn't surprise me—my own hearing was keen enough that I'd have heard at least part of that conversation from across the small kitchen. And his had to be sharper than mine. He would've picked up every word Ian said, and maybe even Nate in the background. But knowing he'd heard and *knowing* he'd heard were two different things. And having Calder privy to my own cousin's suspicion and mistrust made it even more painful than having only heard it myself.

"Then you know as much as I do," I said. "It wouldn't surprise me if they scoped out the house first, instead of just driving up and knocking on the front door. I think Ian suspects it's some kind of trap. I don't know why, though, unless it's just that I've been gone for so long without any explanation. And that's the kind of thing you explain in person. Even if he'd given me the chance to tell him over the phone, which he didn't."

Calder nodded again, tying the string on the pants. "I'll know when they're nearby," he said, without the slightest trace of uncertainty. "I can sense other alphas. Even when they're hidden with magic. And your cousin's an alpha."

My eyebrows rose. "You could tell that over the phone?"

"Yes."

He left the room without another word.

I slowly crawled out of bed and found my own makeshift clothing.

Well, dinner was likely to be had without much sparkling conversation, but judging by the rattling and thumping coming from the kitchen, at least the man was willing to cook. That was something.

Chapter 8
I Buried Him Myself

Calder woke me at the crack of dawn, a hand over my mouth and his massive body looming over me in the near-darkness. "They're here," he said quietly. "Not close enough to hear us talking at a normal volume, but close enough to maybe hear if you made some noise."

My heart jumped into an instant gallop, my chest tightening, a wave of nausea rising up.

Ian. They were here. My cousin, my family…I was going to see them again. Now that it was imminent, I could hardly believe it. What if they hated me, which I richly deserved? What if they satisfied themselves that this wasn't some kind of trick, and then…just left again?

Fuck. But Calder was tilting his head at me, raising his eyebrows.

I nodded behind his hand, and he pulled it away, apparently satisfied I'd keep quiet.

"We don't need to be careful of them," I said, propping myself up on my elbows and trying to get my brain jumpstarted. I'd never been a morning person. Even a jolt of overwhelming adrenaline wasn't enough to make me truly alert, only jittery and miserable. "They think they need to be careful of us, that's why they're sneaking around. They're no danger to either of us."

"I don't know them," he growled, getting up and grabbing his clothes.

Well, those ridiculous pants. Not that he looked all that ridiculous in them. I had a feeling there was no garment on earth that could've made Calder less than intimidating as hell, and that included Hammer pants, or clown shoes.

Strike that. Calder in clown shoes would've been downright *terrifying*.

I blinked that image away. Shit, I hated early mornings. I hated the way I couldn't control my own thoughts, hated that they were nothing but a cascade of absurd images and gut-clenching anxiety.

"I know you don't know them, but I do. Calder, look at me."

To my great surprise, he turned, pants dangling from his hand, and gave me his full, glowing-eyed attention. "What."

Well, at least he wasn't being polite about it. That would've made me run screaming, sure the world was about to end.

"I took your word. Remember? Without question. It's your turn. I give you my word. My cousins, my pack, they're no danger to you. I mean, okay, I doubt you're actually afraid of them. What the hell would you be afraid of? But they're not going to try anything shady. They'll defend themselves if necessary, but they're...honorable."

He blinked at me. "Why would you think I wouldn't be afraid? Of course I am. How do you think I ended up in the same place as you? I'm not invulnerable, and I'm definitely not infallible." That came out sounding distinctly bitter. "And even if they can't hurt me, they could hurt you."

I fidgeted uneasily, plucking at the edge of the sheet. "They would never hurt me. Unless you count telling me to fuck off and die, and they wished I'd never come back. They could hurt me that way. But not physically."

I made myself stop fucking talking, because I couldn't believe I'd actually said that shit out loud, the secret fears I'd been keeping bottled up pretty much the entire time I'd been held captive—and which had only grown in force and intensity since I'd talked to Ian.

Calder scowled, and his eyes darkened, his face so ferocious that I almost shrank back against the head of the bed. "They'd better not." Before I could come up with any answer to that, he said, "I'm going to do a little recon."

And he vanished into the front room of the house, moving much more quickly and silently than anyone that big had the right to.

I got up and dressed as efficiently as possible, and slipped into the bathroom to take a piss. I'd just shaken off and decided against flushing the toilet, mindful of Calder's caution about noise—maybe I wasn't worried about Ian and whoever had come with him hearing me, but it seemed wisest to not irritate Calder too much when he was already on edge—when I heard a deep, guttural cry from the other end of the house.

Calder. Fuck. I yanked up my pants and ran, skidding through the living room and into the kitchen, where I thought the cry had come from. If I could've shifted, my claws would've been out and my fangs lengthening.

The loss of my wolf nearly had me howling, except that I couldn't do that either.

I slid to a stop next to Calder, who'd opened the back door a few inches and had clearly been peering out and scenting.

Except that he'd fallen against the doorframe, gripping it so hard his claws were half-buried in the wood, and he looked awful, his eyes wide and his whole face set in something between terrified joy and desperate, hopeless longing.

"Arik," he gasped. "Arik."

Arik? There was no one in our pack named Arik, and what the hell could've made him abandon his caution like that...I heard a shout from outside, a deep, familiar voice.

Calder yanked the door the rest of the way open, letting it crash into the wall, and I crowded in next to him, craning to see over his shoulder.

For a moment I couldn't focus on anything specific. Too many scents hit my nose all at once: pine sap, sea salt, squirrels, damp earth, the faint fragrance of roses, rotting wood, a thread of car exhaust. And true outdoor light shone in my eyes, unfiltered by a window or any barrier at all. The sun, peeking through overcast.

The *sun*.

It all set my senses reeling, set *me* reeling, and I bumped into Calder as I staggered.

Then the foreground caught up with me. The scent of pack—Ian and Matt, warm and familiar, hearth and home.

And a man running across the lawn behind the house, not someone I knew, slim and pretty and dressed all in black, with a long blond ponytail streaming out behind him and a look on his face to match Calder's, hope and terror shining in his brilliant green eyes.

Behind him...Matt, chasing after him but without a hope of catching him before he reached the house, cursing and calling for him to stop, popping claws and with his face white and set.

Matt. Oh, gods. Matt. He looked almost the same, like the

years hadn't touched him much. Why should they have? He'd just turned thirty when I was taken. He'd only be thirty-two now, not much older at all. It felt like he should've been completely different, the way I was.

Calder wrenched his claws out of the doorframe and jumped down to meet the blond, bypassing the steps down from the door completely.

The blond barreled into him. I stood frozen. Calder would rip him to pieces.

Calder wrapped his arms around him and buried his face in that long blond hair. I could see his shoulders shaking even from the doorway, tremors running through his huge frame. The other—Arik?—wrapped his arms around Calder, his knuckles white with the force of his grip where his fingers dug into Calder's bare back.

Matt skidded to a stop a couple of feet from them, his mouth open in shock. He'd obviously thought Calder was going to kill...who was this guy to Matt? And now he didn't know how to react, now that the two of them were plastered together like they were never going to let go.

Calder's reaction was anything but hostile. I was pretty sure I had the same expression on my face that Matt did.

But he still hadn't looked at me.

"Matt," I said hoarsely.

After a second, he tore his gaze away from the embrace.

We stared at each other, equally frozen. "Ian!" Matt shouted. "Get your ass around back."

He looked back at Calder and presumed-Arik, like he couldn't pay attention to anything else, even his long-lost cousin. There was a strong scent of magic on the air, now that I could focus enough to pick out details. From Arik? Yes, I thought so. Although Calder's scent had intensified, along with Matt's, thick alpha pheromones drowning out everything else.

I dared to venture out of the shelter of the door, putting a foot on the top step.

Pounding footsteps came from my right, and Ian popped around the side of the house, claws out and fangs bared. He stopped dead when he saw the tableau. "What the fuck is—" He looked up at me and went abruptly silent.

Calder and Arik still hadn't moved.

Matt stared at them.

Ian stared at me.

My breath came in quick, painful little bursts.

Of all the reunions I'd imagined, this wasn't it.

"Jesus motherfucking Christ," Ian finally choked out. "Nate! I need you, hurry the hell up!"

"Make up your fucking mind," drifted around the side of the house. Nate. Bitching. Well, that hadn't changed. I felt like I'd stepped through the looking glass. "First you tell me to stay in the car. Then you tell me to hide. Now you're yelling at me for not—"

Nate appeared at Ian's side, saw me, and stopped dead too.

"Don't fucking move a muscle," Ian said.

"Look, you told me to hurry—oh, you mean him," Nate said. Our eyes met, and I wished I could sink down through the ground and disappear. Again. The look in those dark brown eyes could've chilled an ice cube, but behind that...hurt. And betrayal. He knew what I'd done. And he'd been perfectly happy not having me around. He shifted a step closer to Ian, and Ian's arm shot out and wrapped tightly, protectively, around his shoulders.

Yep, no doubt about what those two were to each other.

Nate had his jacket collar turned up against the damp chill of the early morning, so I couldn't tell if he had a mating bite.

But their mingled scents, not to mention their body language, told their own story. If Ian and Nate weren't mated, they were the next best thing.

I looked at Ian instead, and that wasn't much better. Maybe there was something like hope in the depths of the chill pale-blue of his eyes, but mostly I just saw wariness, in his expression and the hard tension of his body. His sharp scent held nothing but mistrust.

"Ian," I whispered, my throat too dry to really speak. I was trembling, and my hand shook visibly when I reached out to him. "Ian, it's me. Please."

"Sit down on the steps," Ian said. "Hands out where I can see them. Nate's going to figure out what the fuck you are."

What the fuck I was? "I'm your cousin, Ian!" That came out a little stronger, but still pathetic and desperate. My eyes had gone all hot. I was going to break down crying, right here on these weathered steps, with their splinters digging into the soles of my feet and the mist off the sea sticking tendrils of my hair to my temples and making me shiver. With my own family looking at me like I was some kind of monster.

"No," Ian said hoarsely. "My cousin's dead. I buried him myself."

He believed it. He really believed it, I could hear it in his voice and in the certainty of his strong, steady heartbeat, familiar enough to me that I could pick it out of the background noise.

I dropped down on the top step with a tailbone-bruising thump, my knees gone all watery, and buried my face in my hands. He didn't even believe it was me. A long time ago, I'd have been embarrassed to have Ian see me cry.

Now I didn't care about bullshit like that, but he thought I was a stranger. An imposter. Some*thing*, not some*one*. I didn't want him looking at my face at all.

A commotion broke out somewhere in front of me, Matt's tense anger and Calder's low rumble, another voice arguing and explaining. I thought I heard that other voice saying something about a brother, and Calder, and it almost got through my head, but I didn't fucking care anymore. I'd escaped, I'd made contact, I'd done my part to get home. All I'd needed was one little shred of welcome. Anything.

Ian had rejected me.

Matt had barely looked at me.

Calder, who'd said he'd take care of me, had forgotten I existed to cuddle some gorgeous blond.

And Ian's words kept echoing in my mind, bouncing off my skull and growing louder and louder.

I buried him myself.

They hadn't just assumed I was dead. They hadn't given up on me without a reason.

There had been a body.

My body. And maybe they hadn't had any forensics done, but they wouldn't have needed to. Werewolves could identify their own, through scent and the low-level bond that formed between pack members, who spent so much time together that their inherent magic mingled. That magic left a trace.

Ian and Matt wouldn't have been fooled by another person's corpse under an illusion spell.

The body had been mine.

Somehow, the body had been mine, and that made me...my gorge rose up, bile sour and sharp on my tongue and searing my throat, and I leaned over the side of the steps and threw up, my eyes watering and my nose stinging, wave after wave, until I was wrung out. I hung there, panting and dry-heaving.

The commotion had stopped.

I managed to look up.

All five of them were staring at me with varying degrees of disgust (Arik), concern (Nate, bizarrely), and shock and horror (Ian and Matt). And total impassivity, of course (Calder).

But when black spots swam in my vision and I started to topple over, it was Calder who darted forward and caught me before I could fall, his strong arms the only things anchoring me to the world. I let my face lean against his bare chest while I tried to keep from passing out.

The dizziness cleared a little after a minute, and Calder pulled me to my feet. I felt it rumble in his chest as he said, "I'm taking him inside. You can come in if you want. Don't touch him."

He didn't need to spell out consequences for ignoring that command. His tone said it all.

Of course, he was dealing with Ian. "The fuck are you to tell me not to—"

"Shut up, Ian!" The one voice I didn't know. Arik. "Don't start your usual—"

Calder started maneuvering me through the door, bearing most of my weight. I kept my eyes closed. I was pretty sure if I opened them I'd throw up again.

"That's not my—Jared, it's not him," Ian snarled, "but that doesn't mean whatever he is, isn't our problem to deal with—"

"He's my mate," Calder said, low and deep and with quelling finality. "He's mine to deal with. Arik, come help me. The rest of you, mind your fucking manners."

Calder's arms tightened, and I clung to him. His mate.

Whatever I was, some revenant or magical construct or thing Jonathan Hawthorne had created, a copy or a clone, Calder had claimed me. *This* body, with *my* consciousness—mine no matter if it was the real Jared's or not—inside it.

I might not have a family anymore. At least for now, though, I had a mate who was willing to speak up for me, to half-carry me into the house and lay me out on the couch, like he was currently doing.

Even though whoever Arik was, he was clearly important to Calder—almost certainly more important than I was. But Calder had some attention to spare for me.

I'd take it. Any crumbs anyone was willing to give, at this point, because the thought that I might not even be *me*...

Calder let go of me after easing me down onto the cushions, and the nausea returned. I squeezed my eyes shut and held perfectly still, willing my stomach to stop turning itself inside out. It still churned, but nothing more came up. Sick dizziness made everything spin, though.

A chorus of clumping booted footsteps told me the whole parade had followed us into the living room.

Oh joy. They could watch me try not to vomit all over the floor again, and maybe discuss all the ways they weren't happy to see me. That conversation could take a while, from how they'd reacted so far.

"I want an explanation." Matt, sounding like he'd gotten his shit together, with a pack leader's authority ringing in his voice. "From the beginning. Is he—Jared—up to it yet?"

"That's not Jared," Ian muttered. "It's not fucking Jared." His voice broke a little on my name.

Okay, maybe that made me feel a little better. Not much, but a little. At least Ian had mourned me, even after all the things I'd done, even though I *was* me, wasn't I? ...Okay, okay, not going down that road again. My esophagus convulsed, and I swallowed hard. My throat stung and burned.

"Whoever he is, he needs to talk," Matt said.

More footsteps, these a little lighter. "Um, I got him some water." Nate. "You, uh, want to give it to him? Or I can—"

"I didn't see you pour it," Calder said. "Arik, will you get him another?" His voice changed when he said Arik's name, when he spoke to him, a yearning, incredulous softness that made my chest clench up.

"What, you trust him but not me?" Nate sputtered, his voice going high and annoyed. "He's *my* ex, not Arik's, and even if he is supposedly your brother, which sounds like bullshit, Arik's a freaking necromancer—"

Arik cut him off with, "Fuck you, Nate!" But I almost didn't hear it under two deep, menacing growls. Calder's. And Ian's. I'd have known those growls anywhere. Nate let out an "Eeep!"

I cracked my eyelids enough to see Ian shoving Nate behind him, the glass of water spilling everywhere, Ian's face nearly as red as his hair. Arik had squared off with his arms crossed over his chest, and Calder was standing over me with his claws out.

Matt stepped between Ian and Calder, his eyes glowing and his lips pressed in a thin line. "Everyone sit down," he said, his voice snapping like the crack of a whip. "Ian, in the corner with Nate. You—" He looked at Calder.

"Calder," Arik said, in a tone of annoyed reminder.

"Calder," Matt almost-growled. He moved a step closer to Arik. "Next to him," he gestured at me, "if you insist." Matt took Arik by the arm, and I thought for a second he'd pull away. He glared at Matt, but he didn't move. "Arik, please stand over here with me," Matt gritted out, tugging Arik over to the entertainment center, where he propped himself on the edge and pulled Arik down beside him, setting the example of de-escalation for everyone, like the competent pack leader he'd obviously become in my absence and without my interference. "And we're going to figure out what the ever-loving fuck is going on here. Without any claws involved."

After a beat, everyone actually did what Matt told them. Even Calder, sort of, though he just crouched down next to me, right by my head. Ready to spring back up and into action, if necessary. He did retract his claws. Ian, grumbling and still red-faced, let Nate tug him over to the armchair in the corner—and subsided into silence when Nate pushed him into it and perched on his lap. Nate leaned over and whispered something into his ear that cleared Ian's expression a little.

I had to look away quickly.

"I'm going to get him that water," Arik said unexpectedly, with a sweet smile for Calder that made me wish I had the strength to growl too, and headed into the kitchen. Calder's brother? They looked nothing alike. And Nate thought it sounded like bullshit...while Matt seemed to be having issues of his own with their little reunion scene.

Calder let me take the glass from Arik's hand, and I propped myself up enough to get it down, feeling like a freaky zoo animal with all of them staring at me. *Watering time for the undead monsters, kids! Don't miss the show.*

I set the glass down on the coffee table, and Arik resettled next to Matt—not without brushing his hand over Calder's shoulder as he retreated, something that wasn't lost on Matt by his deep frown. The tension between Arik and Calder was almost thick enough to touch, like they couldn't wait for all this bullshit with my death and resurrection to be over so they could...I didn't know what. Talk, maybe, hopefully, and not more clinging. That embrace could've been brotherly, I guessed, although…it wasn't any of my business, though, was it? Calder was my temporary mate. He didn't belong to me.

Even if he was the only person in this room who seemed to give even a passing fuck about me, and wasn't that ironic.

"Okay, let's hear it," Matt said. "From the beginning."

I took a deep breath, and I pulled myself up so that I could sit and face them, at least.

And I told them.

Chapter 9

A Second Chance

I didn't leave anything out. Maybe I should have. Maybe it would've let me keep a little of my pride to skip over the fact that I couldn't shift anymore, or that I'd given up hope, or that I hadn't resisted what Hawthorne and his people had done to me in stoic silence, or with dry, cutting, sophisticated commentary à la James Bond.

And maybe it was more than a little petty of me, that I took a horrid, vengeful pleasure in watching Ian's eyes widen and his fists clench, claws extending even though he was clearly trying to keep them under control. To see Matt grow grimmer and grimmer, his shoulders so rigid they were like boulders. To see Nate turn away, swiping under his eyes to try to brush off the tears.

I didn't want their pity; it made me sick. But their guilt, their remorse? I *really* wanted that, so much that it made me even sicker.

Maybe I wasn't Jared—their Jared. I felt like I was, and I wanted to scream at them that I was, that they were wrong. Instead, I told them everything that had happened to me, all the pain and horror, while I was alone and abandoned. And no matter who I was, it made them as sick as it made me.

I didn't leave out anything that had happened before Hawthorne kidnapped me, either, although I didn't get into the details of how I'd slept with Nate partially at his father's behest—that would be implicit. And they probably already knew I'd worked with him. Even if they didn't, they deserved to, whether they blamed me or the version of me they'd almost certainly buried way up in the hills, in an old graveyard we used because even though it wasn't on our pack lands, it had an ancient oak on it that some fairy had given to one of our ancestors in a treaty, and it was tradition.

My body was lying under that oak, rotting away.

I had to swallow again, desperately, as more bile rose up. I kept it down this time, barely, and Calder handed me the water glass without a word. I drained the last of it.

"There's not much more to tell," I rasped after I'd handed the glass back. "Calder needed a boost to get us out, so we mated." I was leaving out some details of that episode, so sue me. I couldn't go there, not with this particular audience. My cousins. My ex, who was with one of the cousins. Calder's…who the fuck knew what, who was clearly with the other cousin. Calder himself. Fuck. "He used our combined magic, got us out. Killed them all. And here we are."

Arik's green eyes narrowed to slits. "That last bit's a little sketchy."

"It's the truth," Calder said.

To my great surprise, given how intimately he seemed to know and trust my mate, that didn't instantly smooth Arik over. He cocked his head, looking from me to Calder and back again. "You could both be imposters," he said, sounding like the words were being dragged out of him. "You don't—you're not the same. You could be…fuck," he said, and rubbed at his temples. Matt's arm around his shoulders tightened, Matt's fingers stroking over Arik's upper arm.

"No, I'm not the same," Calder said. That yearning colored his tone again. He was looking at Arik, not at me. He'd stayed right next to me the whole time I was talking, but he'd been looking at Arik. "They had me longer than they had Jared. Much longer. And whatever they did to me…I'm different. But I'm the same individual."

His phrasing was clearly very intentional. Maybe they'd changed him, but there was only one of him.

Not the case for me.

At least my duplicate was dead, and I didn't need to fight him to the death for my place in the pack, or something, like in some crappy movie. Or share my life with him.

His life?

Fuck.

"It is sketchy," Matt said. "You come to us with this story. Claiming to have, what, left this mysterious prison in ashes behind you? When for all we know, you're brainwashed, or enchanted, and this is some kind of trap. We shouldn't have come in the first place," he added heavily. "But—" He gestured with his free hand, indicating…what?

"But what?" I demanded. "If you think this is a trap, that I'm trying to get you killed, lure you in for Hawthorne, why the fuck are you here?"

Ian started to say something, but Matt put his hand up, a sharp, quelling gesture that Ian actually obeyed. Matt's eyes never wavered from my face, dark-blue gaze sharp. He wasn't quite as tall and broad as his massive younger brother, and his dark brown hair didn't stand out as much as Ian's flaming red. He shouldn't have had as much presence. But he'd grown into the alpha he'd always been meant to be. I couldn't look away.

Whether he acknowledged me or not, he was my pack leader, and I couldn't deny his authority over me. I craved it, actually, because maybe it'd mean they'd accept me again.

"You think we think you're working for Jonathan Hawthorne?"

I blinked at him. "Well, yeah. I mean, I used to be. Sort of. Working *with*," I said, stressing the word. "Not *for*. Not that it's a lot better. So I understand your suspicion. Seriously, I get that part. What I don't get is—" I swallowed hard. "I don't understand how there were…two of me. I don't understand any of it."

"Why Hawthorne, specifically?" Matt pressed. He'd gone even more rigid, leaning forward a little. I glanced at Ian and Nate out of the corner of my eye. Nate's face had gone white, and Ian looked like he might explode with tension. "When was the last time you saw him?"

All my hackles went up. This question was massively important to them, but I had no idea why. "Well, I mean, Hawthorne was the warlock holding me captive who we all know, so that's why. I honestly don't know for sure how long ago I saw him last," I said slowly. "Time kind of—I didn't have any way to keep track, and I was unconscious or drugged at intervals, which made it even harder. But it was a long time ago. I think maybe a year? Or even more. He spent a lot of time with me when I was first there, but then he wasn't around anymore. And one of the other warlocks took over. I figured he was off doing something horrible to someone else."

"He was," Nate said, sounding choked. "He was trying to kill us. But we killed him instead. Ian killed him." Nate shifted a little in Ian's lap, looking like he was trying to burrow into him.

"We killed him," Ian confirmed, and pulled Nate closer.

"About a year ago."

I looked back and forth from Ian and Nate to Matt. Some of the tension had gone out of Matt—finally. He sighed, a long, gusty breath of relief. "Which means we already know you're not working for Hawthorne," he said. "And you're unlikely to be working for his associates, either."

"How does that follow?" Ian demanded.

Nate rolled his eyes, but I noticed he had his face turned so Ian couldn't see it. I frowned. Was their relationship one-sided? Nate had always seemed to dislike Ian, snapping at him when they spoke, ignoring him when he could. Had he hooked up with Ian out of some kind of expedience? If Nate was doing to Ian what I'd done to Nate...that would be the worst, most fucked-up kind of karma.

Nate stopped making faces and answered Ian's question. "Because if they were, then they'd know—he—was dead. And they'd know we knew. They'd have come up with some other story that accounted for it. But they didn't know, so whatever my fath—um, *his* associates knew, they don't."

Ian digested that for a second, and Matt shook his head and laughed a little. "Thanks for the super convoluted explanation, Nate, but yeah, that's what I meant. If you were working for them, I'd have expected you to show up trying to tell us how happy you were he was dead, or something along those lines, to gain our trust. Not thinking we still suspected you of working for him."

"*With* him, temporarily," I gritted out. Even through my relief that a little of their mistrust had maybe been done away with, that rankled.

"You haven't answered Jared's question," Calder said. "And I was sketchy about our escape because it's none of your fucking business how I killed them. You weren't there in that place. That was my revenge. Mine, and Jared's. Not yours. Don't ask again."

"Fine," Matt said. "Fine. The details don't matter that much, as long as the outline's true." He sighed again. "And I haven't answered Ja—his question because I don't have any fucking idea." He looked up at me, meeting my eyes steadily. Because he was a good pack leader, even if I wasn't his pack anymore. Because he always faced things head-on. Gods, if I could've gone back in time, given him the loyalty he deserved, that he'd earned from me…but I couldn't. "We buried a body that I'm sure belonged to Jared Armitage. I'd swear to it. And I wish I could tell you what that means for you, but I can't."

"We could exhume the body," Arik put in, sounding pretty damn cheerful about it. "I could cut him open—"

"No!" The word burst out of me, nearly bringing what was left of my guts up with it. "No, fuck, no."

"Ignore him," Nate snapped. "He's a necromancer, of course he always wants to dig up bodies. It's like fucking *Christmas* for him."

I looked up, panting through the last of my nausea, to see Arik had gone bright hot-pink from his neck up to his hairline. Matt was rubbing a hand over his lips. Hiding a smile? What the fuck was funny about that? Ian didn't even try to hide it, letting out a bark of laughter that almost brought tears to my eyes, it was so damn familiar, and I'd thought I'd never hear it again. "Low blow," Ian muttered.

"Screw you," Arik said weakly.

Gods, what had I missed in two years? For one thing, Hawthorne was dead.

That really sank in. Ian had killed him. He was fucking dead, and even if I hadn't gotten to do it myself, an Armitage had. That was nearly as good.

Apparently there was something about Christmas I'd missed.

I'd missed two Christmases, with all the little wolf pups running around and yipping for pie.

Matt said, "Arik, can you let the zombies go for a sec—"

"Revenants!" Arik snapped, his face still flushed.

"Revenants," Matt said soothingly, although the effect was a little spoiled by how he still sounded like he was trying not to laugh. I really, really wanted that story. I doubted I'd ever get it, though. "Anyway, look. We do need to figure this out. And it seems like it'd be better taken care of at home. We can't stay here for long—am I right in thinking you two appropriated this house without asking the owners?"

Home. Matt had said we'd go *home*. A little sound came out of me that almost bordered on a sob. Home.

"I broke in, yeah," Calder said bluntly. "Not much choice. You're suggesting we go back to your pack lands. What are the terms?"

"The terms?" Matt repeated, his eyebrows going up. "We'll figure out what's going on with…Jared." Damn him, for the way he seemed so reluctant to call me by my name. It *was* my name, even if there had been another one of me. It wasn't like I had any other to claim. "Arik and Nate's magic ought to be up to the job of figuring this out."

"It's safe, Calder," Arik said. "I promise you."

Calder nodded. "I believe you," he said, more gently than his usual rasp. "But that's not exactly what I meant." He fixed his eerie gaze on Matt again. "I only lead a pack of two. But I expect a formal issuance of safe-conduct. Jared is my responsibility, not yours. If he consents to whatever magical examination you want to do, he can revoke that permission at any time."

I blinked at him, and noticed Matt looked just as nonplussed. A pack of two? And had he gone to pack-leader negotiation school or something when I wasn't looking? How old was he, anyway? Not much more than a few years older than me, I wouldn't have thought. And I wouldn't have been able to pull all that out of my ass.

"He's not under your authority," Calder went on. "Not in any way. If Arik trusts you, we'll come with you in good faith. But we're another pack, and the instant you overstep that, I won't give you a second chance."

"Jared Armitage is the responsibility of the Armitage pack," Matt said, annoyance giving his words a snap to them that I knew would raise Calder's hackles.

I was right. "You're saying he isn't Jared Armitage," Calder shot back. "Until you admit that he is, stuff it up your ass." And he stood, turning back to Arik, dismissing Matt from his attention completely. Matt looked like someone had smacked him across the face and he wasn't sure what to do with it. "I need to talk to you alone," Calder went on, speaking to Arik—and not Matt. Very clearly not asking Matt's permission.

Arik stood, and Matt with him, pressing close to his side, even looming a little.

Matt did *not* look happy about the idea. I wasn't either. That meant leaving me with the other three. The people I should've been able to think of as my family, the people I should have wanted to be left alone with.

I tensed up as Calder and Matt squared off, with Ian starting to rise in the background. Fuck, I didn't want them to fight. Especially not over Arik, when none of them had seemed all that interested in fighting over me. Calder had claimed me as his pack, but...maybe that was as much for him as for me. Leverage. Authority. Having someone under him, no pun intended, gave him more of a place in the shifter world than a lone alpha could claim. If he had a pack, he had the right to negotiate as a pack leader.

But it was Arik, not any of the alphas, who spoke first. He lifted his chin, a gleam in those poison-green eyes that told me clearly it wouldn't be wise to fuck with him. "We'll be out in the back yard," he said. "Maybe the rest of you should bring the van up to the house and get ready to leave. Come on, Calder."

And he tugged his arm out of Matt's grasp and sailed out of the room, every inch a pack leader's mate who made his own goddamn decisions.

No one stopped him, because obviously no one would dare. I kind of wished it didn't make me like him a whole lot more.

Calder looked down at me, his face completely blank. "I won't be far," he said. "One shout from you, and I'll be back. Immediately," he growled at Matt.

And then he followed Arik through the kitchen and out.

The back door shut, and I was alone with my family.

Matt stared after Arik and Calder for a minute. "They're adopted brothers," he growled. "Not blood."

"Don't be an asshole, Matthew," Nate said with a sigh. "He's *your* mate. And people are allowed to love more than one person. You love Ian, right? And the pack, too. You have all kinds of people you love, in addition to Arik. Don't be a fucking hypocrite. If you can't take the idea of not having Arik all to yourself, then resign as pack leader, never see your brother again, and move up to the mountains like your parents did."

Matt flinched, visibly, his fists clenching and unclenching at his sides.

"Jesus, Nate," he muttered. "Tell me how you really feel.

But you're right. Obviously, you're right. I'm being an asshole. I just don't trust him. There's something not right there. And if he's Arik's brother, then where's he been for the last—I think it's been like fifteen years since they've seen each other? And Arik hasn't told me very much about him. Not very much, as in less than a few sentences."

Hello? I was right here, their best possible source—and in fact only possible source—of information about Calder. His fellow-prisoner. His fucking mate. Not that I knew much about him, but more than they did.

But they trusted me even less than they trusted him, this total stranger—this very menacing, stone-cold killer who'd already threatened them a couple of times.

I stared down at my bare feet, my uneven toenails, the hem of the sweatpants I'd stolen because I didn't have anything in the whole fucking world.

"Nate, why don't you come with me to get the van," Matt said. "Ian, stay here? Keep an eye on things?"

On me, he meant. And maybe on Arik, too, although I had to give Matt credit for leaving the house and not hovering himself.

I kept staring down as they all agreed, and as Matt and Nate went out the front door, Nate already starting some kind of argument about who was sitting where on the drive home. I suspected the basis of it would be, 'who has to sit next to Jared, because it's sure as fuck not going to be me.'

All the air felt like it'd been sucked out of the room, replaced with a heavy, ominous silence. Ian didn't say a word for a long time. I couldn't look up at him. I'd lose it completely. We'd been like brothers, born only a few weeks apart, inseparable since birth. Matt, a few years older, had always been groomed as a future pack leader. Ian and I had run wild together. We'd been our pack's enforcers together, since the council thought that was the best use of our tendency to get in stupid fights; we might as well get in stupid fights when they told us to, instead of randomly. Also, we were really damn good at getting in stupid fights *together*. We were a seamless unit, and no one could ever take us down.

Until Nate. Until my ambitions got the better of me. Until I got delusions of grandeur, and decided that boring, serious Matt wouldn't be the pack leader we needed—and why shouldn't it be me? My father was Matt and Ian's dad's older brother. I had just as much of a right. I had better ideas. I'd deal with the Kimball pack and their posturing once and for all, like a boss. Everyone would look up to me.

I'd been young, to be fair, but that didn't excuse selfishness and arrogance and stupidity and betrayal.

"Can you stand up for a second?" Ian asked abruptly. "I want to—can you just stand up? Look at you. I want to look at you."

No, I couldn't stand up, dammit, and it was weird that he wanted to look at me, but I found myself rising anyway, still not able to actually look back at him. I stuck my hands in my pockets and stared down at the floor. Ian didn't say anything else, and curiosity finally won out.

I looked up at last.

Ian had his eyes fixed on me, his gaze hungry and lost and full of so much goddamn hurt.

"You look like Jared, and you smell like Jared," he muttered. "I can't fucking—"

And then he lunged at me, so quickly I couldn't react, couldn't try to get away. His arms wrapped around me in a bear hug that nearly squeezed the breath out of me.

He was a few inches taller, but he slumped down, leaning

until he rested his forehead on my shoulder. And his own shoulders were shaking, his chest heaving. Crying. I was pretty sure Ian was crying.

I grabbed him back, fiercely, hanging on for dear life, inhaling him greedily. I'd have given my right arm for a single breath of my cousin's familiar scent when I was locked up alone and in pain. My own eyes stung. Fuck, I wanted this to be real, I wanted to really be me…

Ian lifted his head and fixed me with a wild-eyed, bloodshot gaze. "You're a fucking asshole," he growled. "Nate. Everything. Fucking Jonathan fucking Hawthorne, Jare. What the hell were you thinking?"

"I wasn't," I choked out. "I'm sorry. I didn't—I'll never—it's me, Ian, it's me, please, it's me, whatever you buried, that wasn't *me*—"

Ian grabbed me close again and crushed me in his arms, my face smooshed into his shoulder this time. "Don't ever do that fucking bullshit again," he said in my ear. "Fuck. I missed you so fucking much."

Not for the first time in the past couple of days, or the past two years, I didn't think I could break any more than I'd already broken.

Wrong again.

I sagged in Ian's embrace, resting my face on his shoulder, and I howled. Only with my human throat, but it still felt like all the pent-up misery flowed out of me, finally finding something like its proper voice.

Ian held me tight, and I could've stood there and cried on him for hours.

The back door banged, and heavy footsteps pounded through the kitchen.

I looked up to find Calder snarling in the doorway, his

hair flying wild around his shoulders and his eyes glowing like twin supernovas, his claws out at the ready. Ian spun and shoved me behind him. The peace and contentment I'd started to find ebbed right back away again, but...*Ian had shoved me behind him*. Protecting me.

He'd wanted to protect me. He cared enough.

I didn't really want that, though. I wanted to be equals again. I didn't have my claws, I couldn't shift.

But I could still stand shoulder to shoulder with him.

So I did, stepping forward until I was even a couple of inches in front of him. After all, it was my enraged mate he was confronting.

"He didn't hurt me," I told Calder, looking him in the eyes steadily. "Not physically. Not the other way, either." I hoped he'd remember what we'd talked about that morning, and that I wouldn't need to spell it out.

Apparently he did, because he eased back, his posture loosening and his claws retracting a little. "Don't protect him from me," he said. "Being your cousin doesn't give him the right to touch—"

"The right to what?" Ian demanded. "Hug him? I'm pretty sure I'm allowed if he wants me to!"

More footsteps, and then Arik popped up behind Calder, peeking around his giant upper arm and looking ridiculously tiny next to him, even though he wasn't actually all that small—taller than average, even. I couldn't help noticing he got a lot closer to Calder than anyone else would have dared, what with him looking like he might commit murder any second. Arik didn't seem to have any sense of personal space where Calder was concerned.

And for a moment, as Arik glared at us, I could almost see a family resemblance. It wasn't in their features, unless you counted Arik's very light blond hair and Calder's white-blond tangle. Something in the way they held themselves, though, and the way they stared people down without a trace of concern. Like Arik had grown up modeling himself on Calder, the way a kid tries to imitate his father.

And then it disappeared, as Arik rolled his eyes and shook his head, an almost Nate-like display of annoyance. "They're allowed to hug, Calder. We're allowed to hug. Fuck it, let's all have a group hug, if you're done posturing. Are we done posturing?" he asked, in a tone like you'd use with preschoolers who'd been misbehaving on the playground.

Calder and Ian both grunted something that could've been agreement. Christ, but I could see why Matt had chosen Arik as his mate. Aside from Arik being completely fucking gorgeous, someone I'd have tried to fuck a few years before.

Arik nodded sharply. "Then let's pack up and get the fuck out of here, okay? This place gives me the creeps. What's with the fucking chicken on the wall, anyway? It looks feral."

We didn't have anything to pack, although Calder ducked into the bedroom for a minute and came back holding a pair of socks, which he held out to me. "It's cold," he said. It was, and I refrained from pointing out he still didn't have a shirt on. I stared down at the socks for a second before I put them on. No one had given me anything in…he'd thought about my feet, in the cold.

A car engine and the whisper of tires on asphalt sounded from out front, and we all headed out, Calder, to my shock, bothering to turn the lock in the handle of the doorknob as we left.

Chapter 10
A Place Here

Calder nudged me awake as we passed the *Laceyville: Population 19,229* sign, and I blinked as it whipped by. Well, went by at a normal pace, really, since Matt had taken the wheel when we left and hadn't relinquished it since. Ian and Arik, strangely, had been allied in their vociferous complaints about that, with phrases like 'drives like my grandma' thrown around.

Even more strangely, I'd been the deciding vote.

"I doubt this van even goes over a hundred, Ian," I'd cut in, when Nate started to get involved in the argument too—standing right next to Matt and backing him up, of all things. "So why would you even want to drive it? Besides, I'd rather not start puking again."

Ian had shot me a death glare that warmed me all the way down to my toes, since it was exactly the way he'd used to look at me when we all squabbled and I didn't take his side immediately.

Anyway, he'd given in, mumbling a couple more insults about Matt's Prius, Arik had made a bid for the keys that'd been shot down by everyone in a chorus, and we all piled into the old blue van that'd clearly been resurrected from the Armitage junkyard. Arik took shotgun, and Nate and Ian climbed in the back, leaving me and Calder in the middle seat. If having Ian breathing down his neck bothered him, Calder didn't show it. He settled in silently.

Everyone settled in silently.

Matt pulled into a fast-food drive-through after a little while and sent the place into a flurry ordering sixteen animal-style double-doubles. The cute little human girl taking our order would've been even more startled if she'd seen how quickly all of them vanished.

Meat. Real meat, and cheese, and onions…and meat. I tore into my burgers like a feral beast, dropping the trash into one of the paper bags and flopping back in my seat, feeling like an anaconda.

And then I fell asleep, my head tipped back and my whole body as heavy as lead.

I woke up curled into Calder's chest, his arm around me and my face pressed to his bare skin, his heavy, steady heartbeat echoing in my ears, with no idea how or when I'd moved. When I levered myself off of him, he didn't even twitch, just laid his arm along the back of my seat to let me go. I wiped the drool off my chin—and how had he not even reacted to that, Christ, how fucking embarrassing—and sat up just in time to see the Laceyville sign.

Then I was fully awake. More than awake. Panicked.

We'd be home in a few short minutes.

The last time I'd been on the Armitage pack lands, I'd been leaving them to meet Jonathan Hawthorne, creeping down the long driveway late at night with my headlights off, hoping no one would notice me leaving and want to know where the hell I was going—just like I'd been doing for most of a year before that, when I went to fuck Nate.

I was nearly vibrating out of my skin by the time Matt turned the van off the narrow highway and onto the road leading through the pack lands that would end at the pack house near the center.

And I felt it. The subtle change in the air, in the quality of the ether, that told me we were on our own ground. Everyone else did, too, except for Calder; Matt, Ian, and even Nate and Arik all let out a little sigh as we made the turn and crossed our territory boundary.

I *felt* it. That had to mean something. It had to mean I was *me*, didn't it? Jared Armitage, the prodigal cousin, coming home at long last, in his actual real body and everything.

Arik rolled his window down, and the cool breeze hit my face, a wall of the scents of home. Redwoods and water, grass and mushrooms, rocks and dirt. All of it smelled exactly the way I remembered it. Night had fallen as I slept—and I couldn't believe I'd crashed that hard, after having slept all of the night before, but maybe nearly dying could really take it out of you—and the forest on either side of the long driveway lurked in total gloom, only picked out by the faint light of a setting quarter-moon. An owl hooted in the distance as we rumbled along the road. Nothing looked different, even though I practically plastered myself to the window like a kid coming home from a long summer vacation. And nothing smelled different. It looked so similar to the night I'd left home for the last time that it felt like a dream.

No one came out to greet us when we pulled up in front of the pack house. In fact, the whole place seemed eerily quiet for a normal evening. I cleared my throat. "Where is everybody?" My voice sounded thin in the silence.

"I called ahead," Matt said, obviously going for

nonchalance but missing by a mile, tension infusing every word. "They're having a run out at the other end of the territory. You know, down by the stream near the southern boundary? I think they put all the little kids to bed a while ago and a couple of parents volunteered to stay behind and hang around the cottages to keep an eye."

I did know, and I could picture it all too clearly. The pool we all used to jump in, with a tire swing hanging out over the middle, so that someone had to make the first leap for it and swing it back to the giant boulder before anyone else could use it. A lot of the time that person missed, and we all laughed. A lot of the time, it was me missing, and I laughed as much as anyone when I went splashing down, my hands scrabbling for the swing and not quite making it. Everyone shifted back and forth from human to wolf, depending on whether they were swinging, or swimming, or singing, or telling a story, or running around chasing critters in the underbrush. Even in this chilly weather, some of the younger guys, at least, would swim, coming out with their hands over their groins to hide their cold-shriveled dicks.

Werewolves didn't have a lot of modesty. I'd skinny-dipped plenty of times with the whole pack, including my great-aunt and a bunch of kids, and never thought anything of it, just like they didn't. Nudity in human skin or in fur didn't bother anyone. But no guy wanted everyone seeing his junk after immersion in forty-degree water.

They'd have thermoses of coffee to pass around. Luke, Ian's and my other closest crony, would always have a bottle of cheap bourbon.

"Anyway, the pack house is pretty empty tonight, and almost everyone's moved into the cottages lately anyway. Let's get settled in, yeah?" And with that, Matt shoved his door open with a creak, clearly done explaining.

Maybe because he didn't want to say straight-out that he'd gotten everyone out of the way so they didn't see me, even though we both knew that's what he meant.

Ian had hugged me. Ian had...forgiven me? I doubted it'd happen that fast. But it had seemed like he meant to try. Maybe he was regretting that moment of affection he'd shown me, and maybe he wasn't. But he'd *shown* it. I held on to that as we all got out of the van and headed up the front steps of the pack house. Matt wasn't ready to trust me, but I had to believe Ian would have my back, like he always had. There were a few new gouges on the porch railing, and the steps sagged slightly more in the middle. Paint peeled off the front door. Christ, they hadn't done much maintenance while I'd been gone, had they? My fingers itched for a hammer and a paintbrush. Ian would have my back. Maybe he'd help me paint the porch. Normal. I could go back to normal.

That little flash of optimism evaporated as Calder prowled up the steps right behind me, wariness in every line of his big body, looking at everything suspiciously with those silver eyes.

No, I couldn't go back to normal. I couldn't forget or deny what had happened to me. This wasn't a normal homecoming.

"Come on, let's go upstairs," Matt said, sounding incredibly weary. I tried not to take it personally. He'd done an eighteen-hour round-trip drive in a shitty van, and that'd make anyone fucking tired, even if the circumstances had been otherwise ideal. Which they hadn't. "Do we have extra sheets?"

Nate sighed heavily. "Gods, this pack. I'll deal with the bedding. Arik can help me. He knows where everything is in this house."

At least the bustle of going upstairs, Nate and Arik

rummaging through a hall closet, and Matt and Ian digging through another closet for clothes, made it impossible for anyone to try to talk about anything. Or have to avoid talking about all the things none of us wanted to acknowledge, either.

They'd given us a room way at the end of the hall, one that had its own bathroom. I tried not to think of it as another prison, another space I was expected to stay in until allowed out. I very deliberately didn't ask about my own old room, or where my stuff had gone. No one volunteered the information, either.

Like the rest of the pack house, our assigned room had seen better days—those days being sometime around 1975. Matt and Ian's dad had really, really liked orange at some point, and the curtains in our room wouldn't have been out of place in a cheap highway motel, stains and all.

Still. It smelled like dust, mildew—and pack. I could live with it.

But I couldn't live with the way they were all moving around me, working like a well-oiled machine while I stood there useless and extraneous. Separate.

I muttered something that didn't even make sense to me, and escaped into the bathroom, flipping on the shower as high as it'd go to drown out the sounds of their voices. It didn't work, though. I washed mechanically, listening to Ian's footsteps coming back in the room, his grumbled explanation to Calder of what he thought might fit him in the clothes he'd brought. Matt went in and out, saying something about sandwiches.

I turned off the shower, and I heard the bedroom door shut at almost the same moment.

With an old scratchy towel wrapped around my hips, I stepped back out into the bedroom.

Calder and I were alone with the sandwiches, the old clothes, and the orange curtains.

I stood in the middle of the room, blinking at the closed door, at the dented brass doorknob. Like if I looked at it long enough, it'd open again, and one of my cousins would pop in and say, "Hey, just kidding! Get changed and come downstairs. We can catch you up on everything you've missed."

A glance at Calder showed him standing by the bed, also staring at the door.

Looking as bereft as I did, in fact.

Christ, I hadn't even considered, until this moment—because I was an idiot, obviously—that Calder might feel the same way I did. All the extra sleep had finally cleared my mind out a little, and for the first time in gods only knew how long, I could really focus it. Calder had just escaped too, after even longer in his cell than I'd been in mine. Even longer away from the real world. And Arik was his *brother*? Where had he been, while Calder had been imprisoned? He'd run to Calder when he first saw him, but now he'd retreated along with my family…

Oh, shit, and that hit me like a body blow. Not *my* family. *Arik's* family. Arik was far more a part of the Armitage pack, of the Armitage family, than I was, now. The pack leader's mate, and probably the pack shaman, too, or close enough, or maybe sharing that set of duties with Nate. Either way, he had Matt's love and trust—and a place here that I didn't.

And Calder had never had one at all.

I cleared my throat awkwardly. "So Arik's your brother?"

Calder started a little and turned to me. "Yes."

I resisted the urge to pinch the bridge of my nose like I'd always made fun of Matt for doing, since it made him look like an old guy.

"I was hoping for a little more than that. Like maybe *how* you're brothers, since I heard Matt say you're not related by blood. Or how long it's been since you've seen him. Or maybe what the fuck you two talked about when you went out back alone. Or maybe why he doesn't seem as happy to see you now that he's had a chance to think—"

I stumbled back a step, accidentally biting my tongue and cutting myself off, as Calder lunged at me, looming over me with an expression on his face that told me he'd had *enough*.

My back hit the dresser, knocking it into the wall with a thump and rattling the plate that held the sandwiches. I tasted blood in my mouth from where I'd bitten my tongue as I tripped. When I pressed my hands back against the dresser drawers, my sweaty palms slipped on the wood.

Calder loomed over me, mouth a hard, flat line, the heat and bulk of him penning me in.

He'd promised never to hurt me. He'd promised. I had to remember that, even as my heartbeat started to gallop and skip.

"We talked about this pack," he rasped. "About how he trusts them, and doesn't believe they'll fuck us over. We haven't seen each other in nearly fifteen years, and no, he's not my brother by blood, but that's the easiest way to describe what we are to each other. And I'm not sure he trusts me anymore, even though he was happy to see me and know I'm alive. Because I'm not the brother he remembers. Is that good enough? Any more fucking questions?"

Maybe I'd gotten better at reading him, or maybe he simply couldn't keep his mask in place with his emotions running high, or maybe that realization—that he felt the same loss and confusion and longing and betrayal that I did—made it easier to interpret the harsh lines of his face and the tension radiating from him, pent-up violence and anger with nowhere to go.

I could give it somewhere to go. I could be the lightning rod for his aggression, and suddenly I wanted to be, with a fierce ache I couldn't control. My cock leapt to life, draining all the blood from my head and making me dizzy.

I reached up and grabbed hold of Calder, burying my fingers in his thick tangles of hair, and yanked his head down, mashing our mouths together and thrusting my tongue inside.

Calder took over within a millisecond, fucking me with his tongue like he owned my mouth, his hands gripping bruises into my waist, thrusting me against the dresser with his hips grinding his cock into my belly. I moaned into his mouth, trying to get a leg up and wrapped around his thighs, arching into him like a bitch in heat, desperate to get him between my legs and on me, in me. To have him fill me up and pound the frustration and sadness out of me, give me something else to replace the yawning misery gaping in my chest.

He wrestled me around and dragged me to the bed in two quick strides, tossing me down and landing on top with enough force to knock the wind out of me. He bit at my lips, sucked my tongue, shoved his tongue into me, and I moaned again and writhed under him, digging my fingers into the muscles of his back.

Fuck, yes, this was what I needed, to have him fuck the thoughts right out of my head. Bruise my body, a different hurt from my aching heart and mind…

Calder stopped, lifting his head, his chest heaving and his eyes wild. "No," he said hoarsely, like he was trying to convince himself as much as me.

"Fuck, fuck…" I tried to force him back down. Yeah, that didn't work. I shoved my hips up and he lifted further off of me, leaving me fucking the empty air between us. "Come on! Fucking...what the fuck are you *stopping* for?"

He sucked in a deep breath. I glanced down. Yep, that massive cock was sticking out in front of him, looking like it might rip right through his pants. He wanted this as much as I did.

Wanted *me*. At least someone did, and I needed him to *show* it by using me until I broke again.

He sat up enough that I had to let him go, but before I could reach for his cock, he gathered up my arms and shoved them over my head, pinning my wrists against the bed with one hand.

Easily. I didn't have a chance.

When Calder bent down and kissed along my collarbones, I tried to buck up again. His other hand landed on my hip and pinned the rest of my body down with the same humiliating ease.

And then he bent further, taking the edge of the towel still covering my hips between his teeth. He ripped it off, tearing it away in two jagged strips.

Calder spat out a few threads and looked up at me, baring those sharp teeth in something like a grin.

The breath stuttered in my chest. The sound I made couldn't be called anything but a whimper, and I hated myself for it a little bit.

His mouth pressed to my sternum, furnace-hot, his hair brushing over me and sending shivers up and down. And he kissed me, open-mouthed kisses with his tongue trailing over my skin, burning where he touched me and leaving me damp and cool in the chilly air of the unheated room. Back and forth, nuzzling down my sides to lick at my ribs, at the dip of my waist. He kept his body angled so that my cock still didn't have any friction, not even the head bumping against him as he moved.

Calder was almost going to make me come like this, just from his mouth caressing me and his hard grip around my wrists. The pressure built and built, my balls drawing up.

It wasn't enough, though, and he had me so close to the edge that I wanted to scream.

"Why are you doing this to me?" I sounded wrecked, helpless. Just the way I felt. Except that I was angry, too—furious, even, underneath. I'd shown him what I wanted, and he'd ignored me, dismissed me, like everyone fucking else.

He lifted his head. "Kissing you? Why am I doing that?"

I squirmed again, and his hands tightened. "Why are you holding me down and *just kissing me*," I gritted out.

Calder raised his eyebrows. "You trying to prove it?"

Prove it? What the…and then I remembered. "I don't have to prove anything to you."

"Yeah?" He bent and took one of my nipples in his mouth, sucking it hard and then pulling off with a pop. I squeezed my eyes shut and gasped in a breath. I'd been trying to get off, and now I desperately needed to keep from shooting off like a rocket. If I did, while he was…this wasn't how I wanted to get off. I didn't need to be treated like something fragile. Something soft. He looked up at me again. "I say you do. So prove it. Don't come."

I remembered something else. "You said you'd fuck me when I begged for it." His tongue circled my nipple again, sending sparks straight down to my cock. Fuck, fuck…I'd never wanted someone to play with me like this. And I hadn't wanted to find out how much I loved it. At least if he was pounding me, okay, that wasn't what I wanted either, right? But at least it was something that could make a normal person come, unlike being pinned down and kissed. "So fuck me, please. I'm begging." My tone couldn't have been drier. I knew he'd tell me that wasn't what he'd meant.

Calder laughed against my chest. "All right," he said. "I'll fuck you, since you begged."

And he sat up, let go of me, and then flipped me onto my stomach before I could try to take advantage of my freedom.

I craned my neck, peering over my shoulder at him wide-eyed, even as my gut clenched with want. "What the fuck, Calder?"

He smiled, his real smile. For a second he looked a lot younger, and frighteningly hot instead of just fucking scary. But his eyes didn't lose that predatory gleam. "I believe in the letter of the law," he said. "I told you to beg. You begged." His smile widened and showed some teeth to match the look in his eyes, and I shivered. Oh, shit. "You said you didn't want me to treat you like that. Now's your chance to show me. I'm going to fuck you. If you don't come before I do, you win, and I'll fuck you again, and I won't be gentle."

My cock pulsed under me, and I dropped my forehead to the bed, breathing hard, unable to meet that heavy gaze anymore.

I didn't have anything to prove.

But gods fucking damn it, I'd prove it anyway.

Chapter 11
Didn't Prove a Goddamn Thing

He'd said he'd fuck me.

So naturally, that's what I expected him to do. I lay still, thinking any second I'd feel the harsh burn of his huge cock stretching me open.

Instead he moved down, shouldering my thighs open so that I had my ass tipped up in the air and my knees spread wide like I was presenting myself to be mounted. He pressed his face between my cheeks, stubble brushing over the sensitive inner curves.

I let out a yelp, and he chuckled.

Right against my hole, his hot breath tickling over that delicate skin.

Fuck, and now I was thinking of myself as delicate. Or at least that part of myself.

I wasn't, and he needed to get the fuck out of my head.

For a few long moments, he just breathed on me, hot and soft and making me squirm. And then his tongue flicked out, drawing little circles. Clockwise. Counterclockwise. Tracing my hole, getting it wet. Heating my skin. Big hands massaged my thighs, working my muscles into jelly. Christ, that felt good, and I could've melted into the bed if my cock hadn't been so hard the mattress was in real danger of getting a hole drilled in it.

"You taste sweet, Jared," he rumbled against me.

I let out a high-pitched sound I'd deny to my dying day. Gods. My name, in that deep voice, and spoken right against my hole...

And he hadn't stopped talking. "So fucking sweet." He traced another circle. "Soft. Even softer inside." He suddenly thrust his tongue into me, and I started to shake, helplessly. Every word strung me tighter. Every touch.

Calder pressed an open-mouthed kiss to my hole and slid up again, kneeling between my calves. A click. Had he brought that bottle of lube with him in his pocket? Apparently so. Christ. And then the slick sound of a hand on flesh, getting himself ready for me. He leaned down, covering me with his body, warm and heavy. But not too heavy, not enough to make me feel trapped or crushed.

Enclosed. Protected. Cut off from a world that didn't know what the fuck to do with me, and that I didn't understand anymore. He leaned his elbows on either side of my shoulders and rubbed his thick cock over my ass. No need to hold me down, anymore, or keep me in position. My ass rose up to meet him. He wouldn't hurt me. He wouldn't ever let me be hurt, even though everything and everyone else seemed hell-bent on it.

As long as he was on top of me and around me, nothing would ever hurt again.

The head of his cock pressed inside, and I pushed back to take him in.

Slowly, inch by inch, he filled me, until his hips hit my thighs. He nuzzled my throat, kissed the mating bite, slid a hand under me and cupped my pec, thumb stroking softly over my nipple.

He didn't move. He didn't need to. Speared on that cock, covered by his strong body, I didn't need anything else. The world vanished, narrowed down to the way he'd filled every hollow place in me.

I shook, and I tightened around him, milking his cock with the force of my orgasm. My fingers curled into the sheets. Above me, Calder groaned, the first involuntary sound he'd ever made when he took me. He started to thrust, and I took that, jolting with every one of his movements. It wasn't long before he felt thicker inside me. His knot, already swelling and pushing inside.

"Fuck," he growled. "Jared." His knot caught on my rim, and he shoved it in. "Jared," he whispered, low and rough, and came in spurt after spurt. I felt each one, hot and deep.

He rolled us to our sides and wrapped me in his arms, his face buried in my hair, his chest heaving against my back.

I reached up and laid my hand over his before I'd realized what I was doing, and jerked it back. He moved too fast for me, though, grabbing it again and pressing it against my chest, with his over it.

And then he laced our fingers together and kissed my hair.

My eyes popped open, and I stared wide-eyed at the opposite wall, my body going a lot stiffer than I would've thought I'd be capable of after coming my brains out.

"Easy," he said. "Easy, Jared. I'm still inside you. If you get too tense and squeeze those muscles around my cock, I'll stay hard all night."

"You're holding my hand." My voice went up a whole octave, and I had to clear my throat. "Why—you're holding my hand."

He shrugged, jostling me a little, and I winced as his knot tugged on me. Another kiss, this time to the top of my ear. "You're holding my hand too."

I looked down. Yeah, I was. I'd wrapped my fingers tightly around his in return. Our forearms lay pressed together across my chest.

Beyond that, my cock lay soft and sated against my thigh. I'd come first, and from nothing more than having him inside me. Apparently my whole body had decided to get in on the 'make Jared look like a pathetic idiot' plan.

I wished I hadn't slept all night and then all afternoon and evening, because I couldn't have slept again even if someone drugged me. No escape that way. I had to lie here and listen to Calder's heart thumping, feel his knot buried in me, and deal with the fact that we were holding hands and I didn't want to let go.

It also meant I couldn't get out of saying what had to be said. Maybe Calder stuck to the letter of the law and always kept his word—although the combination seemed to verge on malicious compliance. Or at least 'get the better of Jared' compliance, which felt the same to me. Maybe I wouldn't have been so annoyed if he hadn't laughed at me. Either way, I couldn't let him show me up. We'd made a deal, and I'd lost the bet.

Which meant I had to be a man and admit it, dammit.

"I guess I didn't prove a goddamn thing," I muttered.

I expected him to laugh at me again, or gloat about it. He'd seemed to find my attempts to get my way kind of amusing so far.

But he only gave my hand a squeeze and sighed, his breath ruffling my hair.

"I'm glad you didn't." He paused, and his chest rose as he drew in a deep breath, like he was bracing himself. "I would've kept up my end of the deal. Fucked you without holding back. I didn't want to."

Because he didn't think I could take it? Did he see me as that weak—as pathetic as I really was?

"You were willing to kill me. You didn't give a fuck if I lived or died." His fingers felt good between mine, thick and strong, like his cock inside my body. I hated that I couldn't make myself let go. "And now you're obsessed with this idea that I'm your—responsibility." I spat the word, because it tasted awful. "A pack of two. Because you're in a better position dealing with other packs, with other shifters, if you're not a lone alpha—"

"I didn't give a fuck if anyone lived or died, least of all me," he retorted, cutting me off just as I started to build up a good rant. "I hadn't seen another living thing in six years that I didn't want dead. Do you fucking understand? *No one.* And I was never exactly the kindest person to begin with. Then they threw you in my cell. You smelled like prey. You were probably there to spy on me, or…some new way to fuck with my head. If I'd protected you, gotten attached, they'd have tortured you to death in front of me."

My head spun, everything I'd thought and felt about the way he'd treated me when I first landed in his cell reorienting dizzily.

It made sense, it made such horrible sense. They would have, I could imagine it vividly. And his total unconcern over whether I was dead or alive, lying next to him on that filthy pallet…as long as he treated me like an insignificant plaything, like something to use and abuse, the guards wouldn't give a fuck. They *hadn't* given a fuck. Their lack of concern had ultimately allowed us to escape.

And then he'd killed them all, without mercy, while he

carried me out of that place, keeping me safe from any further harm. Probably risking his own life to do it, because it would've been a fuck of a lot easier and safer for him to take on several guards and at least one fairly powerful warlock without having to protect my deadweight at the same time.

And he'd rescued the other prisoners. Three other beings were safe and alive and able to go home because of him.

It was my turn to squeeze his hand back, because I didn't think I could've forced words out through my tight, scratchy throat if my life depended on it.

Six years. He'd been there three times as long as I had.

Six fucking years, oh my fucking gods. And he'd still had the presence of mind and the strength of body and of will to save me. That place had drained all the life out of me, all the fortitude. And he'd come out the other side even stronger than before.

"I know you think I think you're too weak to take me," he went on at last, again with that uncanny ability to read me.

I couldn't be transmitting that much through the bond, could I? Emotions could bleed through when bonds were strong, and there were legends of shifters hearing their mates' actual thoughts, sometimes, in moments of high stress. But I couldn't feel him like that, and bonds were almost always even in terms of the mates' senses. They allowed you to glimpse your mate's mind, or they didn't, and that cut both ways.

"I don't think you're weak," he said. "You survived there. You still wanted to live. You wanted to escape. You're so fucking brave—Jared. I didn't want to kill you. You almost died, and I was holding you in my arms when I ripped that collar off, feeling your life slip away." He stopped abruptly, his arm tightening around me. "You're the bravest man I've ever met," he added quietly, and for once that deep, menacing rasp sounded nothing so much as comforting.

"I could take you." I swallowed hard.

Fuck. That wasn't what I'd meant to say. Not at all. I could've thanked him for the compliment, or denied that I'd been thinking that at all, or any one of a number of things. *I could take you*. Christ. Like I was begging for his cock and his knot after all—begging for real, this time.

Finally a little tremor of amusement went through him, the ghost of a laugh. He took some of the sting out of it by ducking his head to kiss my shoulder. Gods, that felt good. How could a mouth that terrifying feel so incredible, caressing my skin?

"You're weirdly insistent on that for someone who'd never gotten fucked before I put my cock in you." That amusement carried through into his voice, and my eyes burned. All that bullshit about how brave I was, and how I wasn't weak, and he was laughing at me for being a needy little bitch.

Well, fuck him.

"It's the mate bond," I said, desperately spinning my wheels, looking for an out. And it had to be the mate bond, right? That, and... "And I'm feeling...off-balance, okay? My family thought I was dead. They *still* think I'm dead, even though I'm right fucking here, except maybe Ian, and I'm wondering if he's so desperate to get his cousin back that he'd sort of try to overlook it if I'm some kind of creepy magical construct. I never wanted this before. I won't want it after we break the bond, either."

A heavy silence fell. "Arik's a shaman now," Calder said at last, sounding neutral again, without a trace of the emotions he'd been letting show so freely—freely for him, anyway. "He could probably break the bond. The other, Nate. He smells like magic too. Between the two of them I doubt it would be an issue."

I swallowed hard. Breaking the bond...I'd suggested it. It was logical.

"Nate's a warlock. He's fairly powerful, I think, even though he didn't have much training, because his—" I cut myself off, realizing it hadn't been spelled out explicitly in our conversation back at the house where they'd found us. No one had bothered to explain, because all of us were all too aware, and we'd forgotten Calder didn't have the same background. And I couldn't hide it, even though I wished I could. "Jonathan Hawthorne was his father."

The silence after that went from heavy to crushing.

When Calder broke it, his voice could've cut through steel.

"Nate said you were his ex." I stayed silent, and I could almost hear him thinking, putting the pieces together. Some of his emotions were seeping through the mate bond after all, now that I was focusing on it, and they weren't pretty. I shied away from looking at them too closely. Shame and guilt coursed through me as I thought about what I'd done. And Calder was going to despise me as much as I despised myself, once he thought it through. "You were working with Hawthorne against his own son? Your lover?"

"Yeah." Further explanation wasn't possible. I didn't have a good excuse.

Sure, I hadn't realized at first how truly horrific Hawthorne was. When he'd told me Nate was a dilettante with no control over his own magic and no desire to learn, and that Hawthorne was using his own abilities and also Nate's magic to protect them both, I'd believed him. He'd convinced me that Nate would be better off with a boyfriend who didn't mean him any harm, as opposed to the many predatory assholes who'd be only too happy to fuck and use a pretty boy like Nate for his body and the magic that ran through his veins. Between hindsight and what Hawthorne had revealed while sneering at me, taunting me, when he had me at his mercy in that lab, I was sure he'd already been using his own magic, and the magic he'd stolen from his son, to influence my mind.

But it probably wouldn't have worked on me if I hadn't been willing to believe it. Willing to believe anything, because Hawthorne was so complimentary about my abilities, about how I'd be the right leader for the Armitage pack—and so confident that he could help me take control. Without actually fighting Matt, of course; it'd be bloodless, best for everyone.

And by the time my doubts kicked in, it'd been too late. Hawthorne had his figurative claws in me. If I'd gone to Matt and Ian for help, I'd have had to come clean—and I was too afraid they'd tell me to go fuck myself and get out of the pack forever.

I would've deserved that, actually. And Calder had to agree, because any reasonable person would. But he hadn't pulled away. He hadn't ripped his knot out of me and gotten as far from me as the confines of this room would allow. He still had his fingers tangled with mine, his face resting against my hair.

He'd gone a little stiff, but he hadn't pulled away.

"How old were you? When this started."

I stared at the wall and licked my dry lips. "Twenty-four."

He digested that for a moment. "You were too young," he said. "You still are. And you've paid for it. Paid more than enough."

And he said it with complete finality, no doubt, no hesitation.

No contempt or blame.

He shifted his hips, rubbing his knot over the perfect spot

inside me to have me gasping. The mix of incredulous relief at—not his forgiveness, since he wasn't the one I'd hurt, but maybe absolution?—and that intense pleasure, had me squirming in his arms, not sure whether to laugh or cry or just beg him to fuck me again.

It turned out I didn't have to beg. His knot didn't shrink, and he kept rotating his hips, pressing deeper with every pass, fucking me without even pulling out to thrust back in again. Every tug of his knot at my hole had me seeing stars, until I was holding onto his hand with a death-grip and releasing little punched-out moans with every motion.

I didn't come again, exactly. My cock hadn't had the time to get hard, even if the conversation had been the type to allow me to be aroused that way. But white-hot sensation radiated out from where he filled me, and I clenched around him, again and again, gasping with the overwhelming pleasure of it.

Calder did come a second time, growling in my ear as he pumped me full again. He never let go of my hand for a second.

This time we didn't speak afterward. I didn't sleep, but I drifted, not needing or wanting anything other than the sweaty, spent, perfect sense of peace that'd settled over me.

At long last his knot started to go down, and his weight shifted, like he was getting ready to let go and pull out of me.

I clutched his hand desperately, needing to say one thing before he wasn't holding me close anymore. And before I lost the little bit of courage I'd dredged up while we lay there.

"Can we wait to break the bond until they figure out who I am? I can't—please, can we wait, and do that first?"

"There's nothing to figure out. You're Jared Armitage."

That hadn't answered my question, and maybe he wanted to reassure me, but I couldn't quite believe it. And right at that moment, I belonged to Calder. I might or might not belong to my pack anymore, but at least I had that—that piece of identity, that anchor to other people in the world. If it turned out I truly didn't have my pack, and I'd already broken the bond...I'd be nothing, no one, with no connections. Isolated, a single flickering spark floating through the darkness and starting to fade. And I needed time to come to terms with that, if it had to happen.

There might or might not be enough time in the world, but I'd worry about that later.

"Maybe, maybe not. I feel like I am. But—can we—" I couldn't bring myself to ask again.

"Breaking the bond isn't a pressing priority right now," was all he said, still not fucking giving me a straight answer. "I need a shower. You going to join me?"

"Not right now." I couldn't look him in the eye after all of that.

Calder grunted some kind of agreement and disentangled himself from me, carefully but efficiently. The bed dipped as he rolled off.

A minute later the shower turned on.

And footsteps in the hall alerted me to someone coming our way. And then that someone knocked.

Chapter 12
I Wasn't Dead

Werewolves' casual disregard for nudity notwithstanding, I did *not* need anyone seeing me naked and dripping with Calder's come right at that moment, so I jumped out of bed like I'd been electrocuted and started yanking on some of the clothes Ian had left for me. "Just a minute!"

"Sure," came through the door. Arik. That didn't surprise me. The footsteps hadn't been heavy enough for Ian, and Nate or Matt would've announced themselves, since Matt was thoughtful and Nate couldn't shut up ever. I hadn't been able to figure it out by scent. They'd all been in and out of the room too many times for me to pick out who stood at the door.

And anyway, the room reeked of sex and pheromones. That muddied everything. Arik was going to get a treat when I opened the door; he could probably already scent it from the hallway.

I opened the window before I crossed the room to let him in, for all the good it'd do.

Arik's nose wrinkled as I pulled the door open. "Huh," was all he said, in a tone that could've been disapproval, or just lack of interest. He shrugged and strolled inside, the gesture and his total indifference to any kind of invitation making him look like a skinny, green-eyed mini Calder.

They might not be blood, but Calder had raised Arik, or had a large hand in it; I'd have bet money on it. People unconsciously copied their parents, whether they wanted to or realized it or not. Something tight in my chest loosened up a little—leaving only twenty other causes for anxiety behind. Still. Better.

"Where's everyone else?" I asked. "Talking about me?"

"Too tired," he said evenly, not responding at all to my challenging tone. It deflated me like a pricked balloon. "Nate and Ian went to the Shack of Solitude, and Matthew's taking a shower."

I choked on a laugh. "They went to what?" That was the perfect, perfect description of Ian's run-down bachelor cabin—although apparently it wasn't inhabited by a bachelor anymore. "Who—Ian lets people call it that?"

Arik quirked a wry smile. "He doesn't have much choice. When his little fucker of a mate names things, the names tend to stick."

Of course. Of course that was a Nate-ism, and all I could do was shake my head and laugh a little more.

Arik didn't say anything else, leaving us standing there awkwardly. I'd already shot my wad as far as trying to start a conversation. What the hell was he doing here? Looking for Calder, probably, but the shower kept on running. Calder's senses were all sharper than mine; he'd probably known Arik stood at the door before I did. And he had to be listening to every word. So that explained why he hadn't burst out of the bathroom with his claws at the ready, but it didn't explain why he wasn't hurrying the fuck up.

Calder didn't do much by accident, I'd started to realize.

So if he'd decided to linger in the shower and leave me and Arik alone, he had a reason.

Maybe he wanted me to broach the subject of breaking the mate bond after all, but he wanted me to do it myself, without his interference?

But I didn't have it in me. Not yet.

Arik wandered over to the window, looking out at the stars—or maybe getting some fresh air. He didn't seem to be in any hurry either, frowning at the sky and ignoring me.

Okay, enough. "Do you want something? Because we're going to bed."

That was an outright lie. I doubted I'd sleep at all that night, and my circadian rhythms were going to be fucked for days. Not that it'd make much difference. I'd had a fucked-up sleeping pattern for years, now.

Arik drummed his fingers on the windowsill, lifted his hand to look at his fingertips, and brushed them together to get rid of the dust, still frowning. "You know, one of these days we need to organize a better cleaning rota. Fuck, this place would give a dust mite allergies."

I tried not to laugh, I really did, but a little bark of amusement escaped me. "At least some things haven't changed around here."

Arik looked up at me sharply, his green eyes gleaming. "Yeah, and from what I gather, no thanks to you. I mean, things could've changed. For the much, much fucking worse. With that son of a bitch Hawthorne behind a lot of it."

Anger and grief welled up in me, seizing me by the throat. Part of me wanted to crumple defensively, roll into a figurative ball and plead my case. Another part of me wanted to rip his fucking head off. How long had he been a part of this pack, five fucking minutes? I'd been born into it.

But Calder's voice echoed softly in my mind. *You've paid for it. Paid more than enough.*

I straightened my spine and stared him down. "Things did change for me," I said. "For the much, much, *much* fucking worse. I don't know the whole story yet, but when I hear it…if I'd been here, I'd have been fighting side by side with my cousins. I wasn't here because I was locked up in hell, with your brother. Ask him if you think I'm exaggerating. And if all you came here to do was bitch at me, then get the fuck out."

Arik smiled sourly, tossing his head like an annoyed horse. His blond hair, loose now, flipped around his shoulders like a frigging shampoo commercial. Christ, he probably had Matt wrapped around one of those slim fingers, and here I was antagonizing him. Not to mention he was the one who was supposed to figure out who and what I was…and then I'd be depending on him to break my bond to Calder without doing either of us any permanent damage.

Nice going, Jared. Very fucking clever.

But I couldn't regret it. Fuck this. I'd screwed up. I'd paid for it. If I needed forgiveness, and arguably I did, then it wasn't from Arik.

And this was my home, my pack.

For the first time in years, I felt willing to really fight for something: for my home, for my place in the world, for myself.

And it felt good, like I'd started coming alive again. Buried in that prison, I'd been as dead as my lifeless doppelganger.

I wasn't dead. And that meant I needed to fight to get my life back.

Arik hadn't moved, but he'd opened his mouth like he meant to retort.

Nope, he'd said enough already. "I know everyone's tired tonight, but tomorrow I want to sit down and talk about what's next," I said, trying to project more confidence, more authority, than I really felt. Fake it 'til you make it, right? "You're going to be able to figure out how Hawthorne staged my death, right? You're a shaman, and it sounds like you're a necromancer, too. Fake bodies ought to be right up your alley."

Arik sighed and propped himself up against the wall, crossing his ankles and also crossing his arms over his chest. The t-shirt he wore showed the tattoos on his arms, and I didn't know a ton about magic, but…yeah, shaman. Those swirling runes and arcane patterns couldn't indicate anything else.

"I haven't told Matt this yet," he said slowly, thoughtfully. "I probably should've talked to him about this first, since he's my mate and the pack leader and everything." He rolled his eyes exaggeratedly. "Anyway. You have a huge fucking chip on your shoulder. I get that. More than you know. And your shitty attitude's tempting me to walk out and not say anything, by the way—"

"My shitty attitude? The fuck? I'm the one who—"

"Oh, shut up and listen for a second, will you?" he snapped. "Gods, you Armitages are so irritating sometimes. I know how it feels to be misplaced. Out of place. FUBAR. You know, fucked up—"

"Beyond all recognition, yeah, I know the acronym. Get to the point." My heart had started pounding, my hands shaking. I ended up crossing my arms too, so that it didn't show. Whatever he wanted to tell me…I was afraid to find out.

He seemed to understand, and he didn't snap in his turn— although he did narrow his eyes at me in a way that told me to really shut up this time, or else.

"The point," he said in an insultingly patient tone, "is that it's a lot easier to create a dead body than a live one. From a necromantic perspective, anyway. From any other perspective, either one would be close to impossible. But necromancy is fucking cool." He flashed me a bared-teeth grin. I didn't dare to disagree, and I didn't have the breath to even if I'd wanted. Because it sounded like he was saying...

"Bottom line," he went on, "I think the likeliest possibility is that you're you. Or...most of you. You missing a spleen? Or maybe your appendix? It's possible to make something out of something, but something out of nothing, not so much. Especially since the body convinced Ian and Matthew. Matthew's not stupid, and Ian—uh, Ian has good instincts."

"Ian's not stupid either," I said with automatic loyalty, even as my vision blurred a little.

He thought I was me.

"Sure," Arik said. "Whatever you say. The source is suspect. *Anyway.* I'm going to want to do a full examination on you, check for missing parts. And feel your spark, the life in you. You can't duplicate life and make a copy, unless you're an amoeba. And Jonathan Hawthorne was the lowest form of life there is. Not nearly evolved enough to be a fucking amoeba."

"No argument here," I breathed. "I'm—finding out he's dead, and not out there somewhere. Felt like a two-ton weight off my shoulders."

The bathroom door opened, and I jumped. I hadn't even noticed the shower turning off, or the sounds of Calder moving around in there, though he must have made some noise.

Arik's face turned toward him like a sunflower at dawn. I turned too, and found Calder looming in the doorway, dressed in jeans and a t-shirt, barefoot and with his hair dripping little dark spots onto the shoulders of his shirt. He looked almost normal. But I could see why he hadn't had a shirt on since I'd met him. The shirt had yet to be made that could fully contain his biceps. This one was making a valiant effort, though, and both it and the jeans had to belong to Luke, since he was the only one in the pack with measurements anywhere near Calder's.

"Arik," he said, that softness back in his voice—as soft as he could get, with that rasp that always underlaid his tone. "I'm glad to see you."

"Yeah. Me too. You have no—" Arik cleared his throat. "I'm—look, I'm having trouble believing…this feels too good to be true. Like some kind of trap. A trick."

I felt abruptly out of place and incredibly awkward. They were staring at each other like I didn't exist, and like they were about one second away from another goddamn hug.

"And I'm fucking pissed!" Arik said, abruptly and too loud, his face going red. "You weren't in that place for fifteen fucking years!" He sounded choked, like he was about to cry— like a little kid yelling at his dad, hurt and abandoned and lost.

Calder's face set, deep grooves around his mouth. The way he'd probably look in twenty years. "When I left, I had to go without you. I was in too deep. If I went voluntarily, without killing as many of them as I could before they took me down, they agreed to leave you alone. And they did, right? I made them take a blood oath."

I had no idea what he was talking about, not specifically, but I could imagine the possibilities. The supernatural world had as many gangs, criminal organizations, and underground shit as the human world, and it went even deeper and darker.

"They left me alone," Arik whispered, hugging his arms around his chest. "But so did you."

"But you survived," Calder argued, taking a step forward, one hand out like he was pleading—reaching for Arik and praying for Arik to reach back. "I taught you what you needed to know, and you learned and survived. And I'm so fucking proud of you." His voice broke a little. Calder. Breaking down. After everything he'd been through, this was what broke him, and it made something in my chest crack in sympathy. "I'm sorry. If I'd have tried to take you with me, or come back for you, you'd have ended up dead."

Arik took his own faltering step, and that was enough. Calder crossed to him in two quick strides and wrapped an arm around his shoulders, pulling him in, leaning down to rest his chin on Arik's sleek blond head. Arik turned his face into Calder's chest and closed his eyes—and I was pretty sure I saw a tear streak down his face.

Gods. I shouldn't be seeing this. I'd been jealous at first, when I saw the way Calder ran to Arik at the house in Oregon—when I saw the way he reacted to Arik's presence. Yeah, I could admit it, because the feeling might as well have been a big neon sign beating me over the head, and I didn't have much choice but to acknowledge it existed. Why should Calder and this stranger, who'd already taken over my family, get a big happy reunion when I got suspicion and mistrust?

Maybe envious was a better word, because I wasn't jealous of either of them, obviously. I just wanted what they had.

But seeing how wary Arik had been of Calder after his first overwhelming burst of joy, and how Calder had obviously been suffering for it…okay, no. I was done. Done being a petty, selfish asshole. That had gotten me into my current predicament.

And also? It sucked. For everyone around me, and mostly just for me. By the time Hawthorne had kidnapped me—and it sure was fucking nice to have hope that was the right description for it, instead of 'killed and duplicated me'—I'd hated myself.

Because of bullshit like being pissed that two other people

had gotten one decent break in what sounded like two lifetimes of even more unbearable bullshit.

And this wasn't something an outsider should witness.

I turned away.

"Don't go anywhere, Jared," Calder said from behind me. Like I had anywhere to go, but it still surprised me. "Sit down. Have a sandwich. Arik's going to get his shit together any second now."

"Fuck off," Arik murmured, sounding a little watery.

I turned back in time to see Calder give him a gentle cuff to the ear. "Watch it. Same rules, kid. Say whatever you want to those other assholes—"

"—but don't cuss out the asshole who cooks you dinner and keeps a roof over your head," Arik finished for him, with a soft little laugh. "Yeah. Only I made those sandwiches. And this is my roof now. So suck it up." Arik ruined the effect by pressing his face back into Calder's chest and wrapping him in a tight hug, squeezing him so hard his arm muscles went rigid. "I missed you so much."

"Yeah, me too," Calder said. "Come on. Let's sit down. I'm starving. Tell me some of what you've been up to for the last fifteen years, shit. And tell Jared the rest of your plan to prove he's him."

And that was how I found myself sitting cross-legged on the floor, with Arik on my left in the same pose and Calder sprawled on my right, and the giant plate of ham sandwiches on the floor in between us in easy reach of everyone, with Arik telling Calder tall tales of his adventures before he met Matt—tales that were a little too funny and a little too light on detail to be completely true, in my judgment. I thought he was probably hiding most of the worst of it, trying not to make Calder feel even guiltier than he did—but even the not-worst set my teeth on edge in some places.

The door opened ten minutes in, when we'd eaten about half of the sandwiches. Matt walked in and stopped, frozen and expressionless. And then his shoulders dropped, and he sighed.

"Figures," he said. He shot Calder a wary look, and me an even warier one, but when he looked at Arik, his lips twitched up in a helpless smile.

Shit, my cousin was whipped. Good for Arik. And, as I glanced back at the mate in question…good for Matt, too, because the light in Arik's eyes couldn't be anything but love.

"Come sit down," Arik said, patting the floor between him and me. "I saved you a sandwich."

"Bullshit, you just hadn't gotten to it yet," Matt shot back, but he came over to our weird little picnic area anyway.

And hesitated. Because of me, no doubt.

"For fuck's sake, sit down next to your cousin and chill the fuck out," Arik said. "I told him first, because I hate it when people talk about me when I'm not around," that said in a pointed tone, "but I was thinking about it on the drive. He's probably him. If he isn't him, physically anyway, then that piece of shit Hawthorne somehow transferred his spark from one body to another, which is, one, magic I want to get my fucking hands on, and two, way too much fucking trouble to bother with. Either way, maybe he's physically a weird clone, but I doubt it. And mentally he's almost certainly the same. So sit down and eat a goddamn sandwich."

Matt sat down, his knee brushing mine, and ate a goddamn sandwich.

Calder shifted position a little, casually leaning so that his arm was behind me. His hand landed on the small of my back, and he massaged in slow circles, his fingers dipping under the waistband of my jeans.

When I took a deep breath, it went all the way down to the bottom of my lungs, unconstricted, for the first time since I could remember.

Chapter 13

Who Needs a Spleen, Anyway?

"Yep, definitely a missing spleen," Arik said with—in my opinion, anyway—unnecessary satisfaction, taking his hands off of my bare torso and sitting back on his heels. "I think he took half your liver, too. That grew back," he added in response to my look of horror.

"Is the spleen growing back too?" Nate asked, from his perch on a mossy log a few feet away from where I lay on the damp earth getting chillier by the second.

We'd come out to the woods to do Arik's 'examination,' because he claimed the trees would help. That sounded nuts to me, but Nate hadn't argued—and Nate argued with everything.

Arik turned and shot Nate a condescending, disgusted look down his nose. "Do you even know what a spleen is?"

"It's an organ that—does—it's important to—of course I know what it does!"

"No, you don't. You don't know what it is, where it is, or anything about it. I don't know how a warlock can be so ignorant of basic anat—"

"You're the healer, not me!" Nate had a finger raised,

ready to shake it at Arik, and he'd sat straight up. Arik had his hands on his hips.

Christ, how did Matt and Ian live with these two?

"Who gives a shit what it does," I hurried to interrupt, "and no, Nate, it doesn't grow back. Right?" Because I wasn't even a hundred percent sure about that myself. My liver had, though…but they did that? Okay, I had no fucking clue either.

"No, it doesn't grow back," Arik said with a put-upon sigh. "The liver regenerates, yes, but it's the exception. Organs don't just magically reappear, and yes, haha Nate, pun not intended, shut the fuck up. Even werewolves don't grow things back that wouldn't grow back in a human. They just do whatever healing's possible a lot faster."

"Can I put my shirt back on before you finish the lecture?" We'd found a patch of grass between the trees, but it still had plenty of pebbles and redwood needles embedded in it, which were now partially embedded in my back. "No spleen. Got it. I'm assuming I can live without it, since here I am, right? I mean, who needs a spleen, anyway?"

"Keeping all of your originally issued organs is generally advisable," Arik said primly. "But yeah, you can live without it. And no, you can't get up," he said, planting a hand on my sternum. "I still need to look at your spark. Hold still. And no more stupid questions while I focus," he shot over his shoulder at Nate.

Behind his back, Nate stuck out his tongue and mouthed something that looked like 'I'm Arik, and I know everything,' his face scrunched up in a way that was probably supposed to imitate Arik's smugness.

I choked back a laugh. Fuck, I'd forgotten how much I genuinely liked Nate, when I'd had the leisure to appreciate him. I hadn't really enjoyed fucking him much, maybe because I'd been so guilty the whole time—even though objectively he ought to have hit most of my buttons.

My previous buttons, anyway. The Jared who'd owned his very own spleen had been all over topping cute twinks until they squealed.

This Jared apparently had other interests. Maybe that was what the spleen did?

Probably not.

And besides, Nate belonged to Ian now, and vice versa. It hurt my ego a little to know how quickly Nate had gotten over me, and how little he'd really cared about me. I'd thought he was kind of in love with me.

I schooled my face back to normal before Arik could notice my expression and closed my eyes, trying to let the kind-of-uncomfortable sensation of his magic creeping through my body wash over me instead of making me twitch.

Shit, maybe *Ian* had thought Nate was kind of in love with me.

My eyes popped open, all the calm I'd been cultivating fleeing in a hurry. Aww, shit. Ian hadn't seemed all that pleased when Arik airily announced that morning that he and Nate did *not* need anyone's alpha mates present during the exam, thank you very much, and that we'd see them in a couple of hours.

Matt had just shrugged and maybe looked a little relieved, and Calder had frowned and nodded. We'd been eating breakfast in the pack house's oddly deserted kitchen. Matt had probably told everyone to keep their distance for now, but it still felt wrong and lonely, without any kids running in and out or councilmembers bickering over their coffee. I had yet to encounter anyone but my cousins and their mates.

Ian had put down his own coffee cup, humphed, and left

the room, stopping only to grab Nate around the nape of the neck and plant a firmly possessive kiss on him before he stomped off to sulk.

Or possibly fix the porch. I'd mentioned it when we came downstairs, and Ian had gone all red and said something unflattering about my handyman skills. He'd want to show me up.

And sure enough, as Arik, Nate and I were filing out the back door, hammering and cursing drifted through the house from the vicinity of the front door.

"I'm glad you're back," Matt muttered as I passed him, a small smile playing on his lips. "Ian's always so productive when you get him all competitive."

That warmed me all the way into the woods, despite the chilly bite to the air and the gray overcast threatening imminent rain.

Anyway, Ian wasn't thrilled, and maybe it should've dawned on me sooner that he wouldn't be.

Christ.

"Hold still and stop freaking out," Arik said. "I'm almost there."

At least worrying about Ian had distracted me. But now that I tuned in again, I could feel the tendrils of Arik's odd, fizzy magic wriggling through me, like skinny, excitable little worms.

Oh, fucking *gross*. I swallowed down bile. Why the fuck had I put that image in my own head? The—not worms, they were *not* worms, not even a little bit, dammit—all seemed to converge on a spot right at the crown of my scalp, until my skull felt like it might pop off…and then they vanished.

Arik took his hands off of me again, looking immensely smug. A lot like Nate's imitation of him, in fact.

Dammit, I wasn't going to laugh. Arik was in the process of proving to my family that I really belonged to it, to them, and he deserved better from me.

On the other hand, that would make Arik my family. And family got teased.

Family. My stomach churned with nerves. I could have one again, if Arik made it so. I lifted up a little, as if straining to hear him would bring about the result I wanted.

"You're definitely you," he said, and I let my head thump back into the dirt, closing my eyes again. Savoring those words, and the Armitage earth beneath me, the life in the grass, the hush of swaying branches above me as the wind swept through, the goosebumps on my skin.

Alive. I was alive. And me. And free. And...home, for real.

"You're completely certain?" Nate, and I couldn't read his tone. Anxiety? Maybe. Disappointment? That had to be my own paranoia and guilt.

"Completely," Arik said, with reassuring confidence. "A life spark can't be split without leaving a clear trace. If your— that fucker had tried to make two Jareds, two real Jareds, and then killed one of them, this one would be—there's no technical term for it. Let's go with all fucked up. I can't explain the shifting thing, sorry," he said, anticipating my next question. "That'd take more work, and it may be out of my area of expertise, if what they did was chemical as well as magical. Anyway, Jared, you're whole, except for the spleen." To my surprise, Arik patted my leg, impersonal but somehow comforting. Like a competent doctor with a freaked-out patient. "And who needs a spleen, anyway."

"Good," Nate said after a pause, sounding a lot less confident. "That's a relief."

"Yeah," I managed to rasp through my tight throat. "It

really, really is."

"Okay then," Arik said briskly, and jumped to his feet. "My work here is done. Nate, anything to add? I'd understand if you wanted to check him out too."

Nate blinked up at him, looking a little startled by this display of professional courtesy. "I trust you," he said.

"Oh." Arik cleared his throat, his cheeks flushing. "Of course, I mean, you don't even know what a spleen is."

Nate rolled his eyes. "Whatever."

"I'm heading back to the house. Matthew has a council meeting later, and I need to catch him before that." The flush deepened. "We have some important stuff to discuss first." And with that, he strode off through the woods. "I'll tell him I gave you the all-clear, Jared," he called back over his shoulder.

And then Nate and I were alone. I grabbed my shirt and pulled it on quickly, the consciousness of being half-naked while alone with my ex, my cousin's mate, hitting me hard. Ian would kill me if he saw this.

"Important stuff," Nate muttered derisively. "I guess Matthew's knot in his ass qualifies as important."

Oh, gods. I choked, tried to cover it with a cough, and ended up red-faced and wheezing when that went sideways and made me have a coughing fit for real.

Nate eyed me, unimpressed, chewing on his lip. That might've turned me on a couple of years before. Now it just made me feel like pond scum.

Christ. I wasn't going to get another chance, not with Ian clearly feeling not so great about having me and Nate in close proximity. Trying to manufacture another opportunity to get Nate alone would only end up with Ian breaking my nose, or possibly rearranging my remaining internal organs with his claws.

I braced myself. This was going to suck, but dammit...Arik had confirmed I was me. That meant...gods, that meant I actually had to live with these people. Get along. Make my peace with everyone. Something that felt a lot like Arik's magic not-worms squirmed in my gut.

"I'm sorry," I said, still sounding a little hoarse. "Nate. I know you maybe don't want to hear this from me, and you don't owe me anything, like forgiveness. But I'm truly sorry. I fucked up. And maybe you want to hear this even less, but I really liked you. Like you. Not like that!" I added, when his dark eyes went wide and his eyebrows shot up. "Not anymore. Maybe not ever."

Okay, not helping, because now he'd gone all red and he looked pissed as hell.

"Maybe I did, for a while, you're really hot," I babbled. "I mean, not hot like I'm trying to hit on you. Hot like...it wasn't just because he told me to. But you're Ian's mate. And I respect that! And that's not the only reason I'm not hitting on you, I respect you too—"

I broke off, completely nonplussed, as Nate burst into laughter. Not just a polite ha-ha, or an awkward chuckle, but full-bore, body-shaking cackles. I stared at him, my face getting hotter and hotter, as he laughed himself out, finally subsiding with a few helpless guffaws and wiping at his watering eyes.

"Oh my fucking gods," he said, and laughed some more, shaking his head—at himself or at me, or maybe both. "Jared, you're such an asshole. I can't believe it. Even when you're trying to make nice and make it up to me and apologize, you are still just such a fucking bag of tools."

My face could've fried a whole carton of eggs. Lucky me, because I probably had a whole carton's worth of egg on my face.

Stiffly, I got up, brushed the detritus off my jeans, and gave Nate an awkward nod. Understood. Living with him in the same pack was going to be…fuck.

I turned to go.

And Nate's voice stopped me. "That doesn't mean I'm not glad you're alive."

I turned back, and I found his intent dark gaze fixed on me, completely serious.

"That's hard to believe."

He shrugged. "Believe what you want, I guess. But it fucking broke Ian when you…died. When he thought you'd died. When you were gone. You don't deserve to have him love you that much," he said fiercely, eyes blazing. "Ian's so loyal. He'd have loved you no matter what, and he *did* love you no matter what, and you treated him like shit. I don't even care about what you did to me. Whatever, I got some mediocre sex out of it." *Mediocre sex?* But I shoved down the flare of offended anger. I deserved whatever Nate had to dish out, even if I didn't deserve Ian's loyalty. And Nate was right about both. "And I got a mate out of it, sort of indirectly. A better mate than you'd ever have been."

Mediocre sex. Fuck my life.

He really was right, though, dammit.

"Yeah. I'm sure he is." Nate stared at me, mouth open. What, he'd expected me to argue? To say something snide about how if it'd been mediocre for him, how bad did he think it'd been for *me*? Probably.

But that was previous-Jared.

This was the new, spleen-free Jared, who didn't want to be a treacherous, selfish dick anymore.

And all new Jared could think was: I'd doubted his love for Ian. I'd been wondering if Nate's need for security and safety, for an alpha protector, had led him to take advantage of Ian's devotion.

I'd misjudged Nate, clearly. Disregarded him, used him, and now given him a lot less credit than he deserved. He loved Ian. It rang in every syllable he'd said to me and shone out of his pretty eyes.

"I was awful," I said, the honesty scraping my throat raw. "Awful to you. Even more awful to Ian, because he expected better from me, and you knew all along I wasn't the greatest. Awful to Matt. The whole pack, by extension. But I love Ian more than anyone. He's my best friend. I'm going to try to be his best friend again, too, if he'll let me. You're right that I don't deserve a second chance."

But no. *You were too young. You've paid for it.* I'd earned it, dammit. At least earned the right not to abase myself anymore, and to simply ask for what I wanted, apologize honestly, and let the chips fall where they may.

"Or at least, I wouldn't have deserved a second chance if I'd come crawling and asking for one a couple of years ago. But believe me. There's nothing you could do to me..." I swallowed hard. "I've done my penance," I gritted out. "If it's not enough, I'll accept it. But I want to come home."

That came out so plaintive and pitiful I expected Nate to laugh at me.

He didn't.

Nate just eyed me speculatively, the belligerence fading from his expression and his body language.

He stood, making a face as he tried to brush the moss off his ass. "This pack is kind of a magnet for hard-luck cases, isn't it?" he said ruefully, and I had to laugh. "Yeah. I mean, me. Arik. You. It was your pack from the beginning, but still."

"I'm never going to let any of you down again." I'd never

meant anything more in my life. "If you guys give me the chance to prove it, anyway."

Nate sighed and strolled across the little clearing to my side. "Like I have any say," he said. "Ian's trying to be a hard-ass and not just welcome you back with open arms, but we all know how that's going to work out. He'll have you back as his right-hand man in no time."

"I won't let him down," I repeated. "Or you. I'm really sorry, Nate. You have no idea how sorry."

"Yeah," he breathed. "My not dearly departed asshole father had a real way of making people fucking sorry for their life choices. Mostly the life choice of having anything to do with him." He shook his head. "Come on, let's go back to the house. I'm hungry. And I need more coffee."

Well, that I could get behind. I fell into step with him, and we wove our way through the underbrush and around the trees in shockingly companionable silence.

Jonathan Hawthorne, bringing people together in hatred of him since whatever dark day he'd been born on. What a guy.

"Do you think you could help me figure out the shifting thing?" I blurted out. "It was maybe partly what they injected in me, but there was magic too. Warlock magic. Your—his magic. You might be better at figuring it out than Arik would be."

"I'll do my best," Nate said dubiously. "No promises. What the fuck were they doing to you, anyway? To any of you. I mean, the way you described it, they were torturing you, and I can't figure out why. Last year..." Nate stopped and swallowed hard, looking shifty, and then sighed. "Fuck it. If you're you, and you're not working for anyone he was involved with, then there's no reason not to tell you this. Last year we heard a rumor that there was a group of warlocks, mostly, but some other supernaturals, led by my father, and they had some half-baked plan. To, like, take over the world?"

I stopped and stared. Take over the fucking *world*? One tortured werewolf at a time?

Nate stopped too, shaking his head. "Yeah, I know, it sounds insane. Even more insane than usual for that waste-of-oxygen bastard. But what they did to you must have been part of it. I don't know how, though. Obviously they were studying you, but—what were they trying to learn? What was it for?"

"You have no idea how much time I've spent beating my head against that particular brick wall." Weeks. Months. Years. Until I couldn't even care anymore. "Concrete wall, actually. If you want to get all literal."

"Ugh. That's—fuck, Jared. I'm sorry. I know that doesn't mean anything. But I am."

"It means a lot," I said, trying not to get all choked up. "It means more than you know." Nate was getting all shifty again, fidgeting and looking anywhere but at me, like he'd reached his limit on sappy emotions for the day—and I was right there with him. "Anyway, whatever they were doing, hopefully it's over now, right? He's dead. And Calder killed his associates when we got out of there. Whatever their plan was, it's got to be over now."

I hoped. Christ. *Take over the world*. Hubris, but...fucking terrifying hubris. Hawthorne and company might have been pretty fucking far from doing any such thing, but how much damage could a group of warlocks do on a smaller scale, working toward a goal like that?

Strike that, I knew exactly how much damage, because I'd been part of the wreckage left behind. And so had Nate, for that matter.

"I haven't heard anything else," Nate said, sounding a

little dubious. "But they're all dead, like you said," he went on, a bit too brightly. Like he wanted to convince us both. "Fuck it. We won. Let's go gloat somewhere with more coffee and less damp, cold, miserable natural beauty."

It was such a fucking Nate thing to say that it pulled a laugh out of me, and I waved my arm, gesturing at him to lead the way.

I followed, stepping over a fallen branch, and looked around. We'd made it almost to the edge of the forest, where it thinned out and then opened onto the huge garden behind the pack house. That was one thing they'd improved since I'd been gone, anyway. It looked amazing, full of vegetables and herbs and also weird flowers I didn't know the names of, a mix of practical and magical. I'd goggled at it on our way into the woods, earning matching smug looks from Nate and Arik, who were clearly responsible—and, oddly, a muttered comment from Nate about reanimated plants that had Arik turning all red.

"Well, like I said, I'll do my best to help with the shifting thing," Nate said abruptly, pulling me out of my thoughts. "You may be shit out of luck, though. What if *that's* what the spleen is for?" He peeked up at me mischievously and pulled a ridiculous face, and I cracked up, Nate leaning in to bump his shoulder against mine and laughing right along with me.

We stepped out of the trees, still laughing.

Ian and Calder stood a few feet away—not laughing. Ian had his arms crossed and a thunderous look on his face, and Calder was as expressionless as I'd ever seen him, but with his shoulders set and his whole posture rigid.

Well, shit.

Chapter 14
Your Shirt's Inside Out

"Hi!" Nate said brightly. "Hey! What's up?"

I winced. Calder's mouth tightened, and Ian was about to pop claws, I could feel and scent it in the suddenly thick air.

Nate trotted over to Ian and stretched up to kiss his cheek. "So Jared's actually Jared," he said, still way too cheerfully. "Good news, right? Arik double-checked. He's missing his spleen, though."

"I wouldn't say I'm missing it, exactly," I said, desperately hoping to lighten the mood. Nate laughed. The others didn't.

Fuck my life. What the hell did Ian think we'd been doing in the woods alone, anyway? For that matter, what did Calder think? Ian couldn't possibly believe Nate and I had been fooling around, and Calder...yeah, he might not trust any warlock at this point, but I'd come out of the woods smiling and laughing. It wasn't like Nate had been torturing me.

Ian glared at me. Calder just *looked* at me, and I didn't know which I hated more. Calder seemed to be waiting for something, one eyebrow slightly raised. What? Fuck, I wasn't a mind-reader.

I glanced at Nate, hoping he had more psychic ability than

I did. *Help me! Something better than 'Hey, what's up?'*

Maybe he got the message, or maybe he felt the tension as much as I did, but either way he grabbed Ian by the elbow. "Head back to the Shack of Solitude with me? There's, um, some important stuff to discuss with you." A hysterical laugh bubbled up, and as I fought to keep it in, Nate threw me a wink over his shoulder.

Ian actually growled. Fuck, Nate had no sense of self-preservation *at all*. Ian wrapped an arm around Nate's waist and started dragging him off without a word. Shit, Nate would be lucky to be able to walk after what Ian was going to dish out…and then Nate glanced back one more time, flashing me a self-satisfied grin.

Okay, so maybe he knew *exactly* what he was getting himself into.

I turned back to Calder, who'd gone even grimmer.

Heat pooled in my belly. Christ, this mating bond—or who knew, the loss of my spleen—had really done a number on me. He looked at me like that, and part of me wanted to bend over and beg. My cock being one part, but the muscles in my ass clenched involuntarily too. He'd fucked me so long and so deeply the night before that I shouldn't have wanted him again.

But the only thing stopping me was the idea of being stuck on his knot at the bottom of the garden, right when it looked like it might start raining any second. And knowing my luck, rain or not, half the pack would decide to come out and take the air. Matt might have told them to make themselves scarce for now, but I knew my pack. Their curiosity was a much stronger force than their obedience.

"So I'm me," I said, for lack of anything else that didn't boil down to 'take me now.' "Like Nate said, Arik double-checked. I'm definitely me."

"I didn't doubt it."

Okay, that didn't have quite the enthusiasm I'd been looking for.

"That means they'll trust me again," I said. "My family. I can really come home. For real."

Calder let out a little grunt. "Yeah, Ian really looked like he trusts you."

"Okay, not fair. Look, yeah, Nate and I have a history—"

"You fucked his mate."

"He wasn't his mate at the time!" Calder's eyebrow lifted a little more. Dammit. "Look, Ian liked him, I knew that. But it wasn't anything serious." Except that it had been. Obviously. I tried again. "It all worked out in the end."

Calder moved at last, stalking forward. Prowling. I stood my ground, but it wasn't easy. "It worked out. So much that you come tumbling out of the woods with Nate, laughing and winking at each other."

"Nothing—"

"And your shirt's inside out," he growled, looming over me, silver eyes flashing.

"Arik had me take it off for the exam," I gritted out. "I didn't—oh, for fuck's sake. You'd be able to smell it on me if I'd been getting up to anything with Nate. And why the hell do you care? You and Ian suddenly best friends now?"

"Anyone who had a hand in taking care of Arik when I couldn't is all right with me," Calder rasped at me. "And don't change the fucking subject."

The urge to take him by the shoulders, shake him, and scream in his face swept over me like a tsunami. Change the subject? *Change the fucking subject?* He was the one who couldn't answer a goddamn question!

Instead, I shoved him in the chest. "Back against that tree, Calder."

I had the satisfaction of seeing a look of total, startled surprise cross his face for a moment. "What?"

"Back. Against. The tree." I couldn't try to beat some sense into him. That might not end *too* poorly for me, what with the whole 'no hurting Jared' promise, but it wouldn't end well, either. It wouldn't work, at least.

And on top of wanting to slug him, I simply *wanted*. I couldn't deny it. But I was so fucking sick of only being allowed to want on his terms. On anybody's terms. If I made up with Nate, I pissed Ian off. How was that fair, that he'd get angry when I tried to get along with his mate? When he had to know better than anyone how much Nate loved him. And if I asked Calder to fuck me, I got fucked his way.

Never mind that I liked it too. More than liked it. Had started to crave it.

Fuck that. No.

Calder slowly took a few steps until he stood next to the large tree I'd pointed at, and he leaned back against it warily.

It helped that he'd done what I told him, but it wasn't enough.

The open-mouthed, wide-eyed look on his face when I dropped down on my knees in front of him came close to being enough, though. That felt good. Putting him as off-balance, for a minute, anyway, as everyone else had managed to put me.

As I unbuttoned and unzipped his jeans, it occurred to me that what I was doing could be seen, in the right light, as submitting to my mate to reassure him he didn't have anything to worry about, that he had no reason to be jealous.

It also occurred to me that I'd never sucked a cock before, and that starting with Calder's pro-level dick probably wasn't the best move. I needed something more…JV, like five or six inches. Normal.

I pulled Calder's cock out, and it was already half-hard and shiny at the tip. Definitely pro. Maybe even the Olympics. My large hand barely wrapped all the way around.

I'd had this fucking thing inside my body? In broad daylight, looking at it up close, the thought made me cringe and clench my ass as if I could retroactively keep it out of me. Except that I'd moaned and spread my legs and begged for it, hadn't I?

"You don't have to do that," Calder said, his tone gentle now, all of a sudden. I flashed back to saying exactly the same thing, back in his cell, when he'd lifted me up and said he was going to suck me before he fucked me.

Well, anything he could do, I could do better. Dammit.

And this time, I really didn't want gentle. Ian had dragged Nate off to have his way with him, and I knew Ian wouldn't be going easy on his flirtatious, mischievous, wayward brat of a mate. And maybe Calder was even bigger and more dangerous than Ian, but…Nate was only human, truly fragile and breakable compared to a werewolf like me. And smaller. A lot smaller.

Calder hadn't seemed concerned about Nate's safety. So why the fuck didn't I rate the jealous alpha treatment?

I wrapped my hand firmly around the base of his cock and went down on it, as far as I could go. The girth of him stretched my lips and filled my mouth, but I kept going, ignoring my gag reflex and my watering eyes and lodging the thick head into my throat. I swallowed around him, over and over, rubbing my tongue over the underside, not even bothering with pretending to have any kind of technique. Just choking on it until I ran out of air.

I pulled off, panting, and looked up. Calder's eyes were fixed on me like he couldn't see anything else, like I was all that existed in the universe, and he had his claws embedded in the tree to either side of his body. Lapping at the head of his cock, I sucked him back in again, the taste and scent of him and the obscene slurping sounds I was making and the heaviness of him on my tongue filling all my senses. Filling me.

It took real effort to pull off again, but fuck this. Calder wasn't moving at all. He held himself rigid against the tree, his hips still.

Fuck. This.

I let his cock go and watched it bob in the air in front of my face, flushed and wet and impossibly hard and thick. I'd had that *inside me*.

He stared in disbelief as I got to my feet, a little awkwardly, since my own cock had somehow gotten hard enough to press uncomfortably against my zipper.

"You want my mouth?" I demanded.

Calder frowned. "You're the one who wanted to suck me off, Jared."

I took a step forward, getting right in his face. Well, I had to tip my head up to do it, but it counted. "If you want my mouth, you'll have to fucking take it," I said, slowly and clearly. "Fuck it. Shove your cock down my throat. Pin me by the neck and pinch my jaw to keep my mouth open, choke me, make me swallow every fucking drop of your come, knot my mouth—"

With a savage snarl, Calder ripped his claws out of the tree, retracting them as he went, and grabbed the back of my head, jerking me into a brutal kiss that bruised my lips against my teeth. He bit more than kissed, savaging my lips, swallowing my desperate moans. I shoved my hips against him, his cock stabbing me in the stomach, and rode his thigh. He pushed his leg up and nearly lifted me off my feet, and I cried out, my balls drawing up.

Calder spun us, and the second my back hit the tree his hands landed on my shoulders, forcing me down to my knees again. Only this time I had nowhere to go. He took my chin in one big hand, massaging my jaw with his fingers.

"Open," he said.

I opened.

He slid his other hand behind my head, holding it in place and cushioning it from bumping into the tree trunk, and pushed his cock into my waiting mouth.

And stopped, the head of his cock just barely nudging into my throat. I couldn't get a full breath, I couldn't speak, I couldn't even moan. There wasn't anything except the hot, demanding flesh filling my mouth.

"Look at me." I had to roll my eyes all the way up, since I couldn't shift my head so much as a fraction of an inch. Calder stroked my cheek with his fingertips. "You want me to show you who you belong to? Is that it? Teach you a lesson, so you never go off into the woods with pretty boys like Nate again?"

I would've nodded—no, shaken my head. I'd have shaken my head, but I couldn't move. I didn't want a *lesson*, for fuck's sake. What I needed was to come, my cock almost hurting. I needed him to do what I wanted, fuck my throat and show me...show me...not that, not who I belonged to.

But when Calder thrust a little, choking me and drawing out a strangled, helpless little sound, I couldn't do anything but gaze up at him like an obedient, submissive mate.

"You're mine." He thrust again, not too hard, but hard enough to show me I couldn't do a fucking thing about it. "You belong to me." Still in that even, factual tone. "Only me. Mine,

Jared. I'd tell you to repeat it, but your mouth's busy right now."

He fucked into me a little harder, and his fingers flexed in my hair. I took it all, still gazing up at him, caught and held by his silver eyes. *His.* I couldn't say it, but I could hear it repeating over and over again in my mind.

"Are you going to come while I use your mouth, Jared?" Now he sounded a little rougher, a little less in control. Of himself, anyway. He had me completely subjugated. "Get yourself off. I want to see you come all over the ground while I'm fucking your pretty face."

I scrabbled at my fly, but I didn't even make it. By the time I had the zipper down, I was already coming, helplessly, all over the dirt and leaves at his feet, still pinned in place by the huge cock speared into my throat.

"Fuck," Calder gasped, and thrust harder, almost hurting me, making my throat achingly raw. And then he stiffened and pulsed on my tongue, shooting straight down my throat while I swallowed desperately, trying to get it all into me.

He didn't knot my mouth after all. Oh, gods, if he'd knotted my mouth I'd be stuck kneeling there, mute and helpless, moaning around it like a gag…one more spasm struck me, and my cock dribbled another small spurt of come. He waited until he'd softened a little, and then slowly dislodged his cock from my throat, dragging the head over my tongue. A few drops escaped, and I licked my lips, trying to catch it all. I'd tasted my own come—I mean, what guy hadn't?—so I knew what to expect. But it tasted better than mine. It tasted like mate, like Calder, like his magic and our bond.

He stroked my cheek as his cock slipped out from between my lips. "Yours," I said hoarsely, still unable to look away from his eyes. "I belong to you."

Without bothering to put his cock away, Calder slipped his hands down and caught me under the arms, hoisting me up and leaning me back against the tree, wrapping his arms around me.

And then he kissed me, long and slow and sure, tangling his tongue with mine and chasing the taste of himself in my mouth. I wound my arms around his back and let myself go pliant, kissing him back lazily, without any intent at all. We kissed because it felt good, because we wanted to, because feeling his warm, big body wrapped around mine was an end in and of itself, not a means to something more. He pulled back at last, sucking lightly on my lower lip.

"Better?" he asked.

I blinked at him. "I didn't—I wasn't—what does that mean?"

Calder smiled down at me, his eyes almost soft, as much as they could be with that ever-present glow. "It means you feel better."

Well, that didn't answer my question at all.

But it wasn't like he really needed to.

"Yeah," I breathed, giving up on pretending. "Yeah. I feel better."

"Good." He kissed me again. "We should go back to the house. I think we have some important stuff to discuss too."

Did he mean…? Yeah, apparently he had caught that byplay, because he raised an eyebrow at me suggestively.

"You're insatiable," I said, shaking my head. "Seriously. You just fucked my mouth." The blush I could feel heating my cheeks made me blush even more, in embarrassment for blushing in the first place. Fuck me.

"Which means your ass hasn't gotten fucked yet." He didn't show a trace of shame, damn him. "And that means you still want it. Come on, Jared."

Calder took my hand and tugged, easily pulling me after him as he walked away—not because I didn't resist, obviously, but because he was so big and heavy that his momentum was irresistible.

"I don't need my ass fucked," I muttered, even as heat built in the pit of my stomach and I felt that throbbing need between my legs that I couldn't ignore.

"Sure you don't," he said. "I'm going to do it anyway."

Well, I couldn't argue with that. I followed him into the house.

Chapter 15

If He Needs Me

It felt too damn easy.

That thought kept nagging at me for the month after Arik declared me officially alive and real, as I slotted more and more seamlessly back into my pack with every passing day, as I went to bed every night in Calder's arms.

The only time I didn't worry about it was those stolen hours in between a day spent with the pack and a night spent asleep, when Calder made me forget everything but him, everything but how thoroughly he owned my body and overwhelmed my mind.

I couldn't deny it anymore. He fucking owned me, and it terrified me—whenever he wasn't actively taking me apart. Which, to be fair, he did often. In the shower, kneeling behind me and eating me out until I muffled my screams against my braced forearm. In the bed, where he spread me out and sucked my cock and fucked me, or draped me over his chest and made me ride him until my trembling thighs wouldn't hold me up, knotting me so that I stayed splayed across him for hours while he fucked me again and again every time his knot started to go down. I'd given up on trying to make him get rough with me, even though I still wished he would. If he had, it would've let me believe he only wanted to release the pent-up need of years without getting laid.

It would've let me believe *I* only wanted to release the pent-up need of years without getting laid.

But he didn't. He kept handling me with care, like a package marked 'fragile—this way up.' Except that he turned me over and upside down all the time, so maybe not. But his fingers stroked me so tenderly, his mouth caressed me so softly…and I stopped fighting it. I lay under him and let him worship me, or something that felt perilously close to worship.

Neither of us brought up talking to Arik about breaking the bond. But that didn't mean I didn't think about it all the time, waiting for the other shoe to drop.

Because as well as I'd started settling back into the pack, Calder kept himself aloof.

The afternoon of the day Arik had pronounced me officially Jared Armitage, Matt passed the word to the pack that I wasn't off-limits anymore.

And boy, did they ever come out of the woodwork. In a literal pack, crowding into the kitchen and surrounding me, with pats on the back and rib-cracking hugs, and tears from my great-aunt Alice, who'd always had a soft spot for me and saved me extra cookies. I had to tell my story a dozen times—although I left out a lot more than I had when I'd spilled my guts to my cousins. Part of me wanted to punish myself by explaining everything that had happened before Hawthorne kidnapped me, but Matt pulled me aside after the first outpouring of wonder and surprise and relief.

"Don't tell them what you did," he murmured in my ear, low enough to evade werewolf ears. "There's no reason to. It's over. They don't need to know."

"But—"

"No," he said firmly. "Ian and I are over it. So forget about it." He squeezed my shoulder and gave me a little shake. "Forget about it, Jared. I'm going to. I'm never going to mention it again. Clean slate."

I'd always been closer to Ian, with Matt a little apart, five years older and more of an authority figure than a friend. Sometimes, even often, I'd resented him for it.

But in that moment, I couldn't possibly have been more grateful to have Matt telling me what to do, taking responsibility.

"Thanks," I choked out, and then Amy, a girl we'd all grown up with who'd mated the quiet nerdy guy who'd always had a crush on her and produced two gorgeous kids, grabbed me by the arm and yanked me back into the fray.

I held her new baby and congratulated her beaming husband, listening to him tell me about his older son's first steps until a couple of second cousins dragged me out back to show me the greenhouse they'd started building.

Ian grinned and handed me a hammer and a pair of work gloves.

And we spent the rest of the day…being a pack.

And the day after that, I woke up in the morning, staggered downstairs yawning and looking for coffee, and had one of the pack councilors ask if I still remembered how to repair a fence, and could I give her a hand.

I did and I could. And doing honest, physical work, outdoors in the free fresh air and surrounded by people I'd known all my life, healed me more than years of therapy would've done. I started to feel like a person again.

But Calder kept himself apart, and the more I reintegrated into the pack, the more distant he became. He'd retreated outside while the pack welcomed me, and when I admitted he and I had mated and the pack tried to go find him and get all congratulatory, he'd shut them down with polite but terse comments about how it was temporary.

Maybe he intimidated them, and maybe they just showed some unusual tact in the face of both of our brief, neutral responses to their questions, but after that they dropped the subject and everyone ignored the elephant in the room.

Well, the glowing-eyed, glowering shifter the size of a small elephant, anyway.

Calder spent time with Arik, sitting in the garden and talking in low voices.

He went into the woods alone for hours at a time, coming back lathered with sweat. But if he shifted for his runs, he never let anyone see. I still didn't know what he'd shift into if he ever allowed me to witness it, and I didn't have the courage to ask him or Arik.

He grabbed his own food when he needed it, and he appeared like magic when I headed upstairs for bed.

But otherwise, he might as well have been a ghost, except that no ghost would've been able to fuck me like that. He managed to keep himself out of the way to a degree that frankly astonished me, given how much he stood out.

And it felt too easy, too simple, too…uncomplicated. Weeks went by. Calder didn't cause any trouble, and he didn't interfere with my homecoming, with the time I spent catching up and fitting back in.

A month plus a few days after Arik's exam, I tried to bring it up. I was sprawled across Calder's chest, my legs spread awkwardly wide over his hips to accommodate the thickness of his knot lodged inside my body. My head rested just below his collarbones, and he had his arms around me, one hand dipping between the cheeks of my ass to feel where we were joined, and the other carding softly through my hair. I hadn't gotten it cut yet, and it hung nearly as long as Calder's. I'd used to wear it short, but he seemed to love running it through his fingers.

Anyway, I hadn't gotten around to it.

But this had to be a good opportunity to find out what he had on his mind. He couldn't possibly be planning to stay in this weird limbo forever…and he hadn't shown any signs of trying to become a part of the pack.

Which meant he intended to leave.

I snuggled against his chest, nuzzling his warm, sweat-sheened skin. He smelled so fucking good.

Any second now. Any second, I'd ask him to—my eyes popped open. *Ask him to stay*. That had been the thought on the tip of my brain.

Calder slipped a finger fully between my cheeks and traced the rim of my hole where it stretched to the limit around his knot.

I shivered, and he kissed the top of my head. "Stop thinking," he murmured. "You don't have any decisions to make. I'm going to fuck you again in a second. Slow and deep. Punching my knot into you until you can't think anymore."

Yes, please, yes…but no, dammit, no. I *needed* to think. I couldn't do this every night and then ignore the obvious all day, able to do so because Calder made himself so scarce I didn't have the chance to approach the subject.

"We need to talk, though," I gasped, as he started to shift his hips under me, doing exactly what he'd promised. Punching his knot into me. Slow and deep. My body moving up and down on top of him, limp and receptive to every thrust of his cock… "Calder, please."

He stopped moving, and I whined. Calder sighed. "Mixed messages, Jared."

I lifted my head and peered into his face. He didn't look angry that I'd stopped him from getting off again, but...that wasn't his happy face, either. Not that he had one to my knowledge. But he didn't seem calm.

He still had his hands on me, though they'd stopped petting.

"What are you planning to do?" The question fell heavily into the silence.

Calder frowned. "Pretty sure I just told you what I'm planning to do."

"You know, you really suck at answering questions. Just once, okay, *once*, it'd be great if you'd cooperate a little!"

"And just once," he growled, "it'd be great if you were specific."

I glared at him, and he bared his teeth at me.

Suddenly, it struck me as funny, and my laughter shook us both. "Ow! No, your knot, it's okay, I—baby," I said, batting my eyelashes, "are we having our first fight?"

Something happened. A rumbling sound. His body vibrating under me. Oh, shit, he was going to fucking kill me...

And then I realized he was laughing. Actually laughing, with his teeth still bared and his eyes still gleaming eerily, but...laughing. *With* me, not at me.

I was pretty sure, anyway.

"When we met, I almost killed you. And now you're—our first *fight*?"

I tried to keep it together, I really did. And then I collapsed back onto his chest, giggling helplessly, Calder shaking with his own laughter under me. I had to press my hips down to keep his knot from pulling too hard on my stretched skin, and then he got harder inside me, and then I was riding him again, until he flipped me over and fucked me on my back, kissing me and nuzzling my throat...and time went by in a blur of moans and grasping hands and his hot mouth suckling my nipples.

I didn't know how much time, only that eventually we were lying on our sides with my head pillowed on his bicep, and his knot finally slipped out.

"Ugh," I grumbled.

"I can always put it back in."

I opened my eyes and met Calder's serious gaze, his eyes fixed on me so intently I almost wondered if there was something wrong with my face.

"Not right now," I said—with regret. Every minute I didn't have that stuffed into me, I'd started to feel incomplete. But no. I'd already started this conversation once, and I wouldn't have the balls to do it again. Either that, or I'd get distracted. Again. "Calder, I need to know what you're planning to do. Big picture. You're not acting like someone who wants to become part of the pack, but you're not—" I stopped. I couldn't force the word out.

"Leaving?"

I nodded, hating the sound of it even more out of his mouth.

"I can go anytime you want me to," he said. Calmly. Like he hadn't just dropped a fucking hand grenade. "Arik's capable of breaking our bond whenever we want."

Okay, *what*? I popped up like a jack-in-the-box. "What the fuck? You asked him already? You never told me!"

Calder rolled over onto his back and looked up at me, still perfectly unruffled. Wait...no. That muscle in his jaw. It twitched. Just a little bit. "I assumed you'd want me to bring it up with him, since I know him better. And we'd already discussed it. How many times did you want to talk about it first?"

Betrayal. That was the feeling souring my stomach and making my chest and my fists clench up. But why? We had talked about it. We'd agreed. I wasn't one of those people who needed to talk every little fucking thing to death before making a decision. Obviously we'd be breaking the bond, because we hadn't mated for any of the reasons sane people mated. We didn't love each other. We didn't even know each other.

Except that I felt like we did know each other, maybe better than I'd ever known anyone else, and vice versa. No one else would ever understand what suffering in that hellhole prison had been like. No one else had seen Calder chained, starving, boiling with rage, desperate and ready to rip my throat out.

No one but him had seen me ready to have my throat ripped out if it meant an end to it all.

And he'd shown me mercy. Kindness. And he thought I was the bravest man he'd ever known. He'd said so, and I'd come to learn that Calder might dodge most questions and stay silent when he wanted to keep his secrets, but he didn't say anything he didn't mean.

But...but. He didn't want to stay.

Not for me, anyway.

"What about Arik?" I demanded. "He's your brother. Practically your son, actually, it looks like to me." Calder flinched minutely, but he didn't disagree. "I mean, you raised him, right? You were everything to him. And you're just going to leave him again?"

"He doesn't need me anymore," Calder said, his voice a little less even. "He has a pack. A home. He's safe now."

"Bullshit," I shot back. "Total fucking crap. My parents

walked out on me. Matt and Ian's parents raised me the rest of the way, and it's not their fault I came out the way I did. They tried their best. This pack raised me. I had so many people—but it didn't matter. The people who were supposed to put me first." I swallowed hard. I didn't think I'd ever said this out loud before. "They didn't. No one did. I was safe without that. But it still wasn't enough."

And Calder wouldn't put me first either, no matter how much I wanted—Calder wouldn't either. If he put anyone first, it'd be Arik. Not me. But I could take second place. Since I'd never gotten that blue ribbon of mattering to someone more than anyone else, it wasn't like I didn't know how to live with being a lower priority.

"You should stay for him," I said, willing myself to believe I meant it. "He needs you. And you walked out on him once. How can you do that again?"

"I didn't walk out on him," Calder gritted out, his eyes flashing. "I'm not walking out on *anyone* who needs me. But y—he doesn't."

I actually saw red for a second. "No? Then fucking explain it to me." Because that seemed to be what Calder did. Get someone to need him, and then walk the fuck away. How could he be so callous about it? So fucking casual? "Why did you leave him before?"

For a long minute I thought he wouldn't answer, and I sat there silently fuming, promising myself that if he didn't give me *something*, I'd walk away myself. Go take a shower, leave the room, sleep somewhere else. Somewhere I didn't have to lie in his arms and know he thought it was okay to leave someone alone, with no one who really understood him, because he appeared to have a whole family and pack to rely on. I couldn't—that is, Arik couldn't—fuck, it would hurt like hell for him to be abandoned like that.

"I found him behind a dumpster when he was maybe two years old," Calder said at last. "Shifted. You know how shifters keep their human age, translated into the animal equivalent, when they're in animal form?" I nodded. A two-year-old wolf would be practically an adult, but a two-year-old werewolf would shift into a pup. The human half dominated, in that regard. "He was a miserable, skin-and-bones, flea-infested bobcat kitten. The size of one of my fists. I smelled another shifter and had to dig through a whole pile of filth to find him. I stuck him in my jacket and he huddled there and cried. He didn't shift back to human for weeks. I had to feed him out of a bottle I stole from the drugstore. He lived in my jacket the whole time."

I could only stare at him, wide-eyed, my anger dissipating as quickly as it'd gathered. His cold, factual accounting had left out the most important part of the story: the kindness and compassion it would've taken to do all that. The dedication, the tenderness, the love.

"How old were you?"

"Twelve. But I looked more like eighteen. I grew up fast." A bitter little smile flashed across his face. "No one fucked with me."

Yeah, I'd bet no one fucked with him. He'd probably been twice as scary at twelve as most people ever got their entire lives.

And when he found a half-dead shifter kitten, he stole a baby bottle and kept it in his jacket.

"What was he doing there?" I had so many fucking questions I didn't know where to start.

"Never found out," Calder said with a shrug. "Any scents that'd been there were long gone by the time I found him.

Anyway, it doesn't matter. Anyone who'd leave him like that, he was better off without. It doesn't matter. I took him, and I took care of him the best I could. A couple of times I tried to leave him somewhere, like an orphanage, where they'd be able to take better care of him. But he cried so much and held onto me with his claws so hard that I couldn't put him down. So I kept him."

"And then you left him," I said, even though I was wildly, desperately curious about those years in between when Arik had been two, and when he'd been…I counted quickly. Arik was about thirty now, I thought, so if it'd been fifteen years… "He was a teenager. He wasn't grown up yet, right?"

"No," Calder said heavily. "Not nearly grown up enough. But—" He stopped, staring at me intently. "I'm going to tell you this, but you can't tell anyone. Not even Arik. Especially not Arik. Do you understand?"

I nodded. He still didn't speak. "You have my word," I said, catching on.

Calder blew out a long breath. "When Arik was nine, he started getting sick all the time. That's not normal for shifters. You know that. I found a shaman and a human doctor. Long story short, he had a rare blood disease that shifters get sometimes when they're too malnourished as infants. It would've killed him. It cost a lot to get the healing he needed. And I didn't have the money. I couldn't rob a bank, or something, because then what if I'd gotten caught or killed? Arik would've died."

He shrugged again, as if he hadn't just taken his story from horrific to worse. "So I found alternatives. The underground fighting pits paid better than my day job, but I had to take an advance against my winnings. A big one. The fuckers I was working for were into a lot more than that, hits and drugs and…it doesn't matter, Jared. The details really don't matter. You can imagine. I tried to work it off for years, but in the end, I owed the wrong people, I'd made too many enemies, and I couldn't get out. They threatened Arik. So I made a deal: they forgot he existed, and I'd work for them without trying to kill them. We both took a blood oath. And I walked away."

"Jesus fucking Christ," I muttered. "Fuck, Calder. That's—I'm sorry. That's not enough, but I'm really fucking sorry. But why shouldn't you tell Arik this? And doesn't he already know? I mean, he was sick. He doesn't remember all of that? You really think he'd think less of you for doing what you needed to do to take care of him?"

"He'd think it was his fault. He was a little kid. He remembers being sick. But I downplayed it a lot. I didn't want to scare him. It was just us, living in this shitty little apartment. His life was already hard enough. He didn't know how much it cost to cure him. We've talked about it since I've been here. But as far as he knows, I just fucked up. And that's all he's going to know. He doesn't need that burden."

And Calder did? It seemed like more than anyone should have to bear alone.

I wanted to lie back down again, take Calder in my arms, kiss him and comfort him…but he wouldn't welcome that from me. Or if he'd allow it, tolerate it…I couldn't stand that any more than I could bear the idea of him pushing me away.

Shit. He'd been, what, nineteen? With a dying little kid, and no way to take care of him. No way out. No one to turn to. Maybe he'd have needed comfort then, but it'd been twenty years since then. That nineteen-year-old boy was gone.

And Calder, hard-eyed and closed-off and cold, had taken his place.

"I—he still needs you," I insisted. "He doesn't want you

to leave."

"Doesn't he?" Calder's gaze stayed fixed on me, intent and predatory. Hungry. A shiver went down my spine. "He should tell me himself, if he wants me to stay. If—he needs me."

"Ask him," I whispered. "Ask him to ask you to stay."

Calder shook his head. "That's not a burden he needs," he said wearily. "I'm not a burden he needs. So I'm not asking."

I felt small and cold, still shivering a little, lonely and bereft. I wrapped my arms around myself, biting my lip to keep from saying anything fucking stupid.

Calder rolled over again and gently, carefully, pulled me down into his arms again, tucking my head under his chin and wrapping his big body around me. I melted into him, nuzzling his chest. He pulled the blankets up and over us both, cocooning me in safety and comfort, holding me close.

I blinked to keep the tears back. Fuck. That story. And…he'd be leaving. If not now, then soon.

"Go to sleep, baby," Calder said softly. "Go to sleep."

Maybe I'd been too wrung out by everything he'd told me—or too worn out by a day's hard labor and getting fucked twice within an inch of my life—and maybe I'd just gotten used to doing what he told me.

Either way, I fell asleep.

And I woke up alone.

Chapter 16

You Seriously Can't Go Fourteen Days?

Arik stood up from where he'd been crouched over some weird, spiky little plant at the end of the garden, jumping a step back as I charged him between two rows of trellised peas.

"Jared?" he asked warily. "What's going—"

"Where the fuck did he go?" I demanded, almost a shout. I knew I looked crazy: red-faced and panting and wild-eyed. But I'd woken up without Calder, and he rarely left the room before I got up. He might get out of bed, but he never went far. He hadn't been in the kitchen. I hadn't been able to scent him anywhere. And no one I'd talked to had seen him. Fear had a cold grip on my chest, and I couldn't quite get a full breath. "Where the fuck is Calder?"

"Um," Arik said, looking incredibly shifty, like only a fucking cat could. He didn't have whiskers in this form, but I could practically see them twitching anyway. "Look, he didn't want to wake you."

I took another menacing step. Arik stood his ground, his eyes narrowed.

Okay, maybe not so menacing to someone who'd been raised by Calder, for fuck's sake.

My lungs still weren't cooperating, so I sucked in as much air as I could and made do. "Where. The fuck. Is he?"

Arik sighed. "He had to go somewhere. No, shut up and stop yelling, I don't actually know any more than that. He borrowed one of those half-junker cars Luke and Josh and Jenna keep swearing they're going to be able to finish fixing and sell any fucking day now, and he left. He said he'd be back in a couple of weeks, max, he had something he needed to d—"

"*A couple of weeks?*" My voice had risen to a very not-menacing screech. "A couple of weeks—Arik, he's my mate, and he didn't tell me he was leaving. For a couple of weeks!"

Arik eyed me dubiously, one eyebrow raised. "Max. A couple of weeks, max. And he told me you two were going to be breaking the mate bond soon, anyway." He smiled, a superior little curl of the lips accompanied by a fucking maddening lift of his pointy chin. "You seriously can't go fourteen days without getting railed by my big brother?"

Oh, fucking—that condescending little prick.

"Can you go fourteen days without getting railed by my big cousin?" I snarled.

He went as red as the flowers on his strange, probably poisonous plant. "We're not talking about me!"

"Yeah, okay, so you'd rather talk about your brother's sex life? What the fuck is wrong with you, Arik?"

"Nothing's wrong with me," he snarled back, baring his teeth. "I'm happily mated and fucking staying that way. So of course I don't want to be separated from him. What's *your* problem, Jared? Make up your fucking mind what you want, but leave me the fuck out of it!"

And with that, he stomped off toward the house, more heavily than someone that slim should've been able to. No one did angry storming-off like a cat in combat boots, it turned out.

I stared after him, still not able to get a full breath, still furious, but also...cold again. Alone again.

I had my whole pack. I didn't need to feel like that. Shit, I even had Arik, despite our spat just now, because he was my pack too.

Calder had gone without a word. He'd snuck out and left me.

He had 'something he needed to do.' Something completely non-specific that happened to include ditching me as quickly as possible after actually opening up to me for once. Treating me like a real mate, and not a fellow escaped prisoner turned hole for him to fuck whenever he wanted.

I sat down, right there in the muddy earth in the shadow of the climbing peas, because my legs didn't want to hold me anymore and I didn't care, and I was just fucking *done*. Calder hadn't treated me like a hole, and trying to stoke my own hurt and rage by pretending he had didn't help anything.

Truthfully, I'd never felt so cherished by any other person in my whole life. He'd treated me like—something so precious I didn't even have a comparison for it. Never like just a sex object, not even that first time in the cell. Even then, he'd shown care for me.

But he'd told Arik we wanted to break the bond.

And then he'd left.

Which meant all that care, the kisses and the strong arms around me at night when I woke panting and afraid...it was all a lie.

He'd been humoring me all along.

Go to sleep, baby.

I dropped my face into my hands and groaned. The faster I went to sleep, the faster he could sneak out and leave me.

You seriously can't go fourteen days without getting railed by my big brother?

Fuck that. Of course I could. I lifted my head, wiping the moisture off my cheeks with my thumbs. Stupid damp weather, leaving condensation everywhere. Yeah, the sun was out right now, but it might start raining again.

Whatever. I didn't need Calder any more than Arik apparently did.

He could go do whatever he wanted to do.

I didn't need him.

***

"You're doing what?" Ian demanded, looking at me like I'd sprouted a second head.

"Going to Lancaster," I said, going for casual. Instead, I sounded grouchy and tired and defensive. To be fair, Lancaster sucked, and it was totally overrun by vampires.

"Lancaster," Ian repeated, crossing his arms and leaning against the wall of the garage like he meant to be there a while. "Because you want to go get a drink. Dude, there are bars in Laceyville. You know, home turf. No vampires hanging around sneering and talking under their blood-breath about mange and kibble."

"I thought we were getting along with the vamps these days." Working on Jennifer's fence with her, I'd gotten the lowdown on all the local gossip and the pack's more big-picture relations with our nearest neighbors. She was the best councilmember to pump for info, and always had been. Smart, no-nonsense, and willing to tell anyone what she thought it was important for them to know. "Fenwick's our ally, right?"

"I guess," Ian said. "I mean, he's all right for a vampire. But that doesn't mean you need to go all the way to Lancaster."

Yeah, except that I did, because I specifically didn't want any of the pack around watching me.

"The Kimballs hang out in Lacey—"

"Try another excuse, Jare," Ian said. "You know we're all buddy-buddy with the Kimballs now, too. Colin's not a fucking idiot like his dad."

"Story of our lives," I said, not able to help a grin.

Ian laughed, shaking his head. "No kidding. The only Armitage less competent to lead this pack than my dad was your dad."

Or me. But I didn't need to say that, and I didn't think Ian had been thinking it, either. He and Matt really had put the past in the past; I hadn't heard a word about it, like Matt had promised me.

"I just want to get out a little bit," I said, hating that I sounded like I was pleading. I didn't need Ian's permission to leave our territory. Granted, I did need his permission to take a car, but fuck, everyone in the pack used those crappy beater cars. They'd even let Calder drive off in one without batting an eyelash. "Get some air."

"We have a lot of air here."

Frustration welled up, and for the first time since I'd been back, I genuinely wanted to smack Ian upside the head like I had when we'd been younger. We'd tussled all the time. I'd always lost. Hadn't stopped me from starting shit the next time, though.

"Fuck off, Ian. I want different air. I was locked up in a concrete fucking box for two years. I want to drive a car and roll the windows down and stop somewhere for a fucking drink, okay?"

I almost felt guilty when Ian's face softened, his eyes going wide. Reminding him of how I'd been a prisoner was dirty pool. But I needed to get out. Get a drink. Five or six drinks. As many as necessary to get me plastered enough to pick up a willing woman and charm her into taking me home, enough to fuck her and enjoy it and not spend every second of every day aching for Calder's knot in my ass, jerking off until I felt raw, pinching and teasing my own nipples until they were swollen and sore, shoving two fingers inside myself and still not being able to get myself to come.

And he'd only been gone for three days.

Worst of all, I didn't know if any bar within fifty miles would have enough liquor to make me forget how it felt when he stroked my hair and smiled at me. That real smile. Or the way he'd started laughing at my dumb jokes part of the time. Or the way he'd told me about Arik's childhood and made me promise to keep it to myself—because he trusted *me*, and no one else. Or the way he'd told me he thought I was brave. That I'd paid for my mistakes. That I deserved to have a home, a family.

He'd come back, I didn't doubt it. He'd said he would, and Calder followed the letter of his own law. But he'd only be coming back to break the bond and leave again.

I had to be ready to bear that, when it came. That meant distraction, and detachment, and getting drunk and laid by someone else.

"I'll come with you," Ian said at last. "We can take my car. Like old times, yeah? Blast some Metallica on the way. My sound system's awesome, I upgraded it last year."

"Which of your internal organs did you have to sell to afford it? Are we both missing a spleen now?" The comeback felt a little mechanical, but Ian laughed and flipped me off, so maybe he didn't hear the echo of how hollow I felt.

"Fuck you. I hustled some pool in a bar in Lancaster,

actually. Ended up having to beat the shit out of the pansy-ass vampire who lost the money, and his two dickwad friends. So maybe we shouldn't go back to that bar," he added.

I didn't want him to go to *any* bar with me, that was the fucking point! Ian wouldn't let me get wasted and wander off with some chick, because he was all mated and monogamous and boring now, and he'd try to impose the same standards on me. Never mind that my mating couldn't have been more different from his.

"I'd rather just go al—"

"Come on, hop in," Ian said, totally ignoring me. He tossed his keys up in the air and caught them. "We can go to Laceyville. It'll be fun. That dive at the corner of Main and Walnut got a new jukebox. It's not all country anymore. And they have Bear's Head on tap now too."

I gave in to the inevitable and opened the passenger side door of Ian's Barracuda. He'd get distracted by arguing with some asshole about his jukebox picks, and I'd be able to down some shots and at least sneak off to that dark alcove down the hall from the bathrooms and make out with one of the girls who always hung around the bar looking to hook up.

And screeching around the corner onto the highway with the windows rolled down and the music blaring, Ian's driving as out of control as always, did feel pretty fucking good. My hair blew back and tangled around my face and the bass riff vibrated through my bones. I shouted along with lyrics I hadn't heard in years but still remembered word for word.

I turned my head and grinned at Ian, the expression almost feeling genuine, and found him grinning back.

Shit, it was good to be alive.

And Calder would be out of my system in no time.

Two hours later, I was drunk enough to almost convince

myself of it. A short, curvy redhead drinking with a couple of friends over by the dartboard had been eyeing me for a while. She'd do. She'd be great. I loved petite lovers, smaller than me. Large breasts. Slender arms, with small, soft hands that couldn't break me in half if they wanted, but instead would stroke along my inner thighs and cup my tits and…fuck. I grabbed the next shot off the bar, already poured and waiting for me, and knocked it back.

Ian's voice boomed over the cacophony of the rowdy bar, saying something insulting about Aerosmith. I glanced in the direction of the jukebox. The guy next to him started waving his hands around, getting in Ian's face.

Yeah, that wasn't going to end well. I thought about going over there and trying to defuse the situation, chat the guy up until I found a band he and Ian could agree on, get everyone to get along. Like I always used to when we were out for the night.

And then if it didn't work, I'd back Ian up in the inevitable fight. I'd always done that too.

I flexed my fingers, keenly mourning the lack of my claws. Although that guy looked human, and what scent I could isolate from the many people around us smelled human, too, with no trace of magic. Claws would be so redundant, especially since…Ian. He made most other combatants, and their various natural or carried weapons, redundant on his own.

Whatever. If I did intervene, it'd be for that rando's sake, not Ian's, and I couldn't bring myself to care. I had my own fish to fry, and with Ian distracted, I'd gotten my chance.

One more shot? No, I had all the liquid courage I needed. Any more and I'd pass out on the girl instead of getting her off.

I crossed the bar, dodging a couple of stumbling, laughing drunks, and made it to the dartboard. She looked me up and down, I shot her my best come-hither smile, and a few words later she was leading me down the hall, glancing coyly over her shoulder and letting the strap of her tank top slip down a little.

Women who knew what they wanted were the best, and I wanted...

But my stomach churned heavily, and my palms had gone all damp and clammy. Sweat trickled down my spine.

Fuck. My face felt too hot, my scalp tingly.

"Give me just a sec," I said hoarsely as we reached the end of the hall by the bathrooms. "I need a little air."

She eyed me for a second, hesitated—and then shrugged. "I'll meet you here in a minute," she said, and pushed open the door to the ladies' room.

Thank fucking gods. I hadn't pissed her off too much.

Or maybe I had, and when I came back inside she'd have ditched me and headed back to the bar. But I could...I'd figure it out.

The exit door at the back was supposed to be kept shut, but it always stood open, propped with a chunk of wood, because the smokers liked to go out the back instead of standing on the sidewalk.

As I pushed the door open, the piece of wood got dislodged, and the door slammed behind me when I let go of it.

Shit. I could go back around to the front, but the girl wouldn't be waiting that long.

Fuck it. My esophagus spasmed, and I leaned against the rough bricks of the wall by the dumpster, tipping my head back and sucking in deep breaths of garbage-tinged damp, closing my eyes against the spinning.

Something scraped in the alley.

I opened my eyes. Something sharp, something dark and

threatening and almost familiar, tickled my nose.
And everything immediately went dark again.

Chapter 17
Amplification

Coming around after being knocked unconscious by magic was the kind of thing that sounded like it ought to be a slow process of unpleasant discovery. *Where am I? What happened? Are these spelled manacles around my wrists? My gods, what's happened?*

Not so much. The instant consciousness hit, it hit *hard*, and all the details became painfully, instantly obvious.

I'd been taken captive by a warlock, although not one of the ones who'd worked me over before—I could smell his magic, that dark, sharp, ozone-tinged smell that had hit me in the alley, even if I didn't recognize the scent of him in particular.

The manacles had my wrists in their cold, heavy grip, and the rest of me sat and slumped on yet another fucking concrete floor.

The panic hit me simultaneously. I bent to the side as much as I could, vomiting every drop of the shots and everything else I'd ever consumed, it felt like, all over the floor and spattering my leg. My heart rabbited, and I couldn't feel my extremities.

I wasn't brave. I wasn't brave at all.

More spasms turned my stomach over again, and I retched and dry-heaved until my eyes watered.

When I pulled myself upright a little, the room around me had blurred.

It didn't matter. I knew what I was looking at. A lab, of sorts, the kind used by warlocks who wanted to hurt me. A big table, metal, with straps and chains in strategic locations. A counter full of herbs and bowls and syringes. Concrete walls, a large double door off to the side, right now propped open.

And a tall, skeletally thin man with stringy black hair and a manic light in his eyes, leaning against the counter and watching me.

I'd never seen him before.

Who the fuck…? Calder had killed all the remaining torturers. He'd been sure of it, and he'd told me that our fellow prisoners he'd released had verified the body count. Even if I'd somehow missed seeing him during my time in that place, one of them would've known to look for him.

So this was someone new.

They'd been planning to take over the world, Nate had said. Hubris, yeah. But also…maybe they'd had a little more of a plan, more of a network, than we'd so optimistically assumed.

Stupidly assumed, more like.

My head thumped back against the wall.

I refused to speak first. Fuck him, fuck this, fuck everything. If he thought I'd start begging for my life, he could be disappointed. Even though the screams were bubbling up in my chest and trying to force their way out. Even though my head spun and spun and my forehead throbbed with the pressure of wanting to know why, how, I thought I'd been safe, I'd *been* safe, oh gods, what the fuck had happened, where was Ian, why why why oh gods…

"Do you know where your mate is right now?" he asked, his voice a little too high, a little too thin, scraping at the inside of my skull. "Does he have a phone?"

My mate. Calder. At least if they were asking, that meant they didn't have him too. He'd left the Armitage territory before I had, made himself vulnerable…because we'd thought it was over.

After a minute, the man pushed himself off the counter and strolled over to me. "Just answer me. I can make you answer, but that's less convenient for both of us."

Even though I hadn't met this particular son of a bitch before, he knew who Calder was, so he clearly had a connection to the other sons of bitches, like I'd been speculating a minute before. And he'd brought me somewhere with the right equipment and supplies to do anything he wanted to me.

My mind raced. Did it matter if he knew I didn't know where Calder was, or if he had a phone? Probably not. He wanted to find Calder, obviously. Or try to use me against him, somehow. I might as well admit I had no idea…since I didn't. And maybe that'd keep me alive a little longer. Although what the point of that might be I didn't know, since I wouldn't get out of here.

I had to face that. I'd gone home, my family knew I was alive. They'd look for me this time. My captor or captors would know or guess they would, and they'd have to kill me this time around and then skedaddle before Ian and Matt and the rest of the pack caught up with them.

So maybe my goal ought to be dying without being hurt too much in the process, and without giving them anything they could use against Calder. He'd be fine. He could take care of himself. Clearly, I'd been the much easier target.

"I have no idea. About either," I rasped through my burning throat.

He smiled sourly. "Unfortunately for you, I believe you." He shrugged, his thin shoulders making him look like a scarecrow under his black coat. "That's fine. I'd prefer to do it this way, in any case. He'll be more likely to come if he can feel you calling for him through the bond."

Feel me...my stomach clenched, hard, and I nearly threw up again. "Bonds don't work like that." Shit, I'd all but admitted we had a bond. How the fuck did he know, anyway? "And, and we aren't bonded," I stammered. "There's no—"

"Don't play the fool, no matter how naturally it may come to you. You're bonded. Do you think I didn't do a magical examination of you already? I saw the bond, and I recognized that beast's magical signature at the other end of it, although I can't use it to pinpoint his location. And that doesn't matter in the slightest, because he'll pinpoint yours and come running."

"Bonds don't work like that," I gritted out for the second time. Fuck, I needed water. My hands were going numb, suspended to either side of my head on those too-tight manacles. I was the unarmed man in a battle of wits, and I couldn't even argue with his playing the fool comment, because when you were right, you were right, damn him. "You can't—you can't feel things through them like that. Shouldn't you know that?"

"I know more about it than you do. A little amplification will take care of that annoying hitch. It's an unpleasant process, unfortunately. For you, anyway," he threw over his shoulder as he crossed back to the counter of nasty-looking supplies. "I couldn't care less."

Suddenly, I needed to keep him talking. The longer he gloated, the longer Calder would have to...do what? Not know

I'd been kidnapped? He wouldn't come anyway, I was sure of it. He'd have to be suicidal. And Calder was a cynical, untrusting bastard—thank gods, because it'd keep him far away from here. He'd know that if he came and handed himself over to keep me safe, they'd just kill or keep us both anyway.

Did I want him to come running to my rescue? A tiny little part of me did, of course. The selfish part. The part of me I'd hoped to leave behind in my previous cell, but apparently hadn't managed to shed after all.

Because gods, I ached for him. His snarl as he broke the manacles and swept me into his arms...heat and safety surrounding me, and I'd never complain again about how gently he handled me. I'd never complain about anything again as long as he kept holding me close. I swallowed hard and forced that away.

I could keep that fantasy suppressed, because I had to for what was left of my own sanity. One thing I'd developed in my two previous years of captivity was a fatalistic ability to face reality. He shouldn't try to rescue me. And he'd learned the same lessons I had. He wouldn't.

But that didn't mean I was eager for whatever was going to happen to me next.

"How did you find me? How did you—who the fuck are you?"

"My associate and I were affiliated with the ones who were studying you before, but we had a difference of opinion and left the project," he said without hesitation, albeit with a tinge of bitterness.

Great. Not only did it not matter to him what I knew, which meant he'd definitely be killing me, he had a grudge against my previous captors. And they weren't around for him to take it out on—he just had me. I'd already gone numb enough that the thought didn't do more than send a little tremor through me, distant and unimportant. And distracting him wasn't even working. He'd started doing something with his magical supplies, the conversation not slowing him down at all.

"We had surveillance on their facility," he continued. "We'd been waiting for a chance to get in, get some of our research. And then you escaped and left the lab in flames, including all the data," he snarled, shooting me a ferocious, wild-eyed glare over his shoulder. Fucking great. He had a grudge against me, personally, as well.

And…data? Fuck. Him. Everything that had been done to me, reduced to something as impersonal as *data*. Hatred and fury welled up, overcoming any self-protective instincts I had left. "But what the fuck did you even want it for?" I spat at him. "What the fuck were you trying to learn? With all that—with that—" I broke off, panting, unable to even find words for what they'd done to me.

He paused in his work, setting down a sharp, shiny instrument that made my flesh crawl, and turned back to me.

His eyes glittered. "What did we want it for?" he demanded, sounding incredulous, and shook his head, laughing a scornful little laugh that made my flesh crawl even more, as if it was trying to get off my bones and scoot away somewhere safe. "You can't see the benefit, the possibilities, in creating your own invincible army? Creatures like your mate. Or in being able to prevent werewolves from shifting at will, with just a quick spell and a little addition to their water supply. A whole pack, helpless, all but human. In an instant. Desperate to do anything to get their powers back. Obedient." His lips stretched in a rictus grin. "I'm sure you know how that would feel, don't you? You were our test subject for that particular technique, after all. And then you set the results on fire when you escaped. Which means I'll need to do the research all over again," he crooned, sounding half furious and half...anticipatory.

Nope, my flesh couldn't crawl any further. I cringed back against the wall, hating the display of weakness but needing to *get away from him*. My tongue curled in my mouth, dry and frozen. I couldn't have spoken even if my life depended on it.

Maybe it did. But I doubted it'd matter much.

"We already had your name and origins from the files we did manage to appropriate when we left the others," he went on, calmer now. Very fucking unreassuringly calmer. He turned again, going back to work, that shiny little knife flashing as he chopped something on the counter. "It wasn't any challenge to find you, and then wait for you to leave your warded territory, leave the protection of that thing you allowed to mate you. Losing him was a blow, and now we'll have him back again. He's too much of an achievement to waste."

He finished, setting down his tools, adding something else to a bowl with a little puff of indigo smoke.

He turned to me, bowl in hand. "At any rate, the past is the past, and it's unimportant. You're here now. And you're going to bring him here too."

***

I resisted. At least, I tried. I screamed a lot, anyway.

It all blurred together.

The bond stood out, though. Amplification, he'd called it. Through my haze of pain, searing agony lighting up each of my nerves individually until I felt like it must be visible through my skin, jagged lightning patterns—through all of that, I heard him telling me. How magic functioned like any other kind of energy, how it had a wave pattern. How that pattern could be amplified, the frequency the same but the power of the energy output increased.

That energy crackled through my bones and electrified my teeth, my back arching and my lungs raw from the shrieks it tore out of me.

My pain, my terror, my despair rode that energy, flying out through the ether and arrowing its way to Calder, far away but not far enough.

I knew it wasn't far enough. He could've been on the moon and he'd have felt me.

And I could tell when it reached him. Rage, deep and fierce and dark, like a black hole at the other end of the bond. Overwhelming, cold, burning fury.

"Tell him he has to come alone," the warlock said, his voice reverberating in my head with agonizing force. "Alone. Or we'll kill you. And we'll know. We have our own defenses here."

I tried not to, I tried until I felt like my limbs would snap and my spine would torque into a corkscrew, but he repeated himself, over and over again. I sent the message.

And then he released me from whatever compulsion he'd put on me, and I slumped against the wall, wrung-out and sobbing. My sweat-soaked skin felt like ice wrapped around me. Helpless shivers shook my body.

I'd called for Calder. I'd summoned him into a trap.

Gods, I prayed he'd ignore that summons.

But prayer hadn't done much for me in the past.

Two voices rose and fell in the periphery of my feeble consciousness. One belonged to the bond-amplifying asshole, while the other was new to me. His co-asshole, no doubt, the other one of his 'associates' who'd been working with him.

A few words floated through my soup of misery. *Bond*, and *barrier*, and *collar*. Enough to tell me more or less what would happen next, although not when. How far had Calder gone from the pack territory before he got my involuntary message? Did he have a phone? Would he be contacting Arik? For that matter, what would Ian have done when he realized I'd gone missing? And where had they taken me? It couldn't have been that far, could it? Although I had no idea how long I'd been unconscious. But I'd still been vaguely tipsy when I woke up, and with the speedy way my werewolf metabolism processed alcohol, we couldn't have been more than a few hours in transit.

A little bit of hope bloomed deep within me, no matter how I tried to squelch it. When I'd hoped before, the last time this had happened to me, it'd only led to more crushing disappointment. Hope wasn't my friend.

But I couldn't help it. If Calder called Arik, if Ian had already raised the alarm, if they all joined forces...I didn't know how powerful Nate had become out of his father's stunting shadow, but between him and Arik they had to be able to muster some magical firepower. Ian was a force to be reckoned with, particularly guided by Matt's more restrained and logical judgment.

And Calder—well, I knew what he was capable of.

But they'd forced me to tell him to come alone. They had *defenses*, whatever that meant—wards, maybe magical booby traps. The Armitage territory wards, newly revamped by Nate, could detect who crossed the boundary, not only whether or not someone did. These warlocks would have at least that level of surveillance.

My hope died. I tried to tell myself it was for the better.

Tears streamed down my cheeks, and inside my mind, I screamed at Calder: *Don't come, don't come, it's a trap. Let me die, because they're going to kill me anyway.*

Nothing. I still felt the bond, but it was attenuated and weak, maybe worn out by the way it'd been forced to function as a conduit for more energy than a mating bond should ever have to take.

My stomach roiled, but I didn't throw up again. There wasn't anything left to come up. And Assholedee and Assholedum sure as fuck weren't bothering to feed me. I guessed last meals were more civilized than they could manage.

A lot of time passed. Not days, but more hours than I could begin to keep track of. At some point the need to piss overwhelmed me, and I didn't have the strength to keep it under control.

With a disgusted grumble, one of the warlocks performed some quick magic and cleaned it up.

Well, score one for them having to share an enclosed space with me, anyway.

Other than that, I drifted, in and out of consciousness, with *out* being much preferable considering the agonizing thirst and hunger, and my cramped and aching limbs...and what I had to think about.

I tried to wrap myself in a daydream, imagining being—fuck, not in bed with Calder, safe in his massive arms. That hurt too much. Maybe...hanging out with Ian. No, that hurt too much too. Fixing the fence with Jennifer. Sunshine on my face. Kids' laughter and the yips of little baby werewolves finding their voices ringing in the distance. A mallet in my hands, the thunk of a fencepost being driven into the ground. The breeze brushing over my heated skin.

I drifted again.

The bond snapped me back to something approaching reality. I could feel it again, pulsing, writhing and twisting with the force of the emotion transmitted through it—and strengthened by proximity.

Calder.

He was close by, and I'd have doubled over from the power of his anger if I hadn't been strung up against the wall.

For the first time in the gods only knew how long, I opened my eyes all the way, wincing as my eyelids stuck together and then separated.

Two men bent over something on the counter, the tall scarecrow and a more normal-looking guy, medium height and medium build, with curly graying blond hair. He shifted a little to the side, and I caught a flash of something reflective, a mirror or a piece of polished metal.

They were scrying, almost certainly. And the tension in their stances suggested I knew what they were looking at.

"Good," Curly said. "He found the phone we left outside. Let's hope he can read," he added with a nasty-sounding chuckle.

A phone rang a moment later. Scarecrow picked it up off the counter. "It's him," he confirmed. "We can see you through our surveillance spell," he said into the phone. "So no bullshit."

Calder's low growl came through the phone clearly enough for me to hear, but I couldn't pick up the words.

"Oh, he's alive," Scarecrow said. "Alive and waiting for you. We wouldn't want to separate a mated pair. Go down the stairs and turn left. The door's open. But I would much prefer you didn't cross the threshold."

Calder responded, and this time his tone sent shivers down my spine. Scarecrow went a little pale, and his hand shook around the phone. But he kept it together.

"No, you won't be doing any of those things. The door is protected with an impassable barrier. Or rather, I suppose it could be breached by someone strong enough, but you'll die if you so much as touch it. Have you ever seen someone die of radiation poisoning? Compress that into a few seconds. You'll stay on the other side of it until we tell you what we want you to do. You're the reason we have your worthless mate alive in the first place. If you get yourself killed, we won't have any need for him at all. You'll be killing him too. Remember that."

A burst of static erupted from the phone, and Scarecrow pulled it away from his ear.

"He crushed the phone," Curly commented, raising his eyebrows at the scrying mirror. "I presume he understood you."

"He'd better have," Scarecrow muttered. "I don't want to have gone to all this trouble for nothing."

Curly kept an eye on the scrying surface while Scarecrow moved into the center of the room directly in front of the door.

And then we all waited. I could hear all three of us breathing: my breaths shallow and ragged, Curly's even, and Scarecrow's a little too fast. He was scared, despite the magical barrier, which I could see faintly in the doorway now that I looked for it. A slight shimmer, fuzzy, a little bit like a very thin sheet of that frosted glass people used for bathroom windows.

Well, I didn't blame him for being afraid. I just wished he had more of a reason for it. As far as I could tell, my captors held all the cards. A gun to my head might or might not have stopped Calder, but he was too canny and too experienced to throw his own life away.

Footsteps rang out somewhere in the distance, down the hallway that appeared to lie beyond the door.

The footsteps got louder, heavy and with an odd cadence,

like whoever or whatever was making them wasn't quite human.

And then Calder appeared in front of the doorway.

Chapter 18
The Barrier

Scarecrow stumbled back a step, shock in every line of his body, and Curly let out a strangled sound.

I pressed myself against the wall, heart pounding.

That was Calder, no doubt about it: the glow of his silver eyes and the shape of his nose and cheekbones confirmed it.

But he was a monster. I couldn't imagine being truly afraid of him, not anymore. But monstrous was the only word that fit. He'd half-shifted, but not into any creature I could instantly recognize; a polar bear, maybe. Something huge, something with white fur to match the thick growth on his bare arms and chest...something even larger than Calder was in his human form, given that his head now brushed the ceiling and his shoulders almost spanned the double-width doorway. Six-inch gleaming claws extended from his fingers, and his jaw had stretched, morphed, into something distorted and totally inhuman, large enough to accommodate his dripping fangs.

He looked like a cross between the snow monster from *The Empire Strikes Back* and the Predator.

And I'd never seen anything more beautiful in my life. My heart swelled—with love, it had to be love, nothing else could feel like this—even through the instinctive fear. *Mine*. My mate, in all his fucking nightmarishly terrifying magnificence.

"Give him to me." His voice boomed, snarled, hit me like a wall, with nothing human left in it at all except the words themselves. Scarecrow rocked back another step, and Curly's fingers went white where he gripped the edge of the counter. "My mate. Now. Or you'll both die."

Scarecrow raised his hands, and a bolt of disruption left his palms, like a rippling mirage whipping through the air. It passed through the barrier and struck Calder in the chest.

He stumbled, staggered, shook his head—and drew himself up to his full height again.

"Fuck," Curly whispered. "I told you stunning him wouldn't work."

"It was worth a try," Scarecrow hissed, but he sounded shaken.

Calder bared all of his teeth. "Give him to me."

"No," Scarecrow said, his voice only wavering a little. Christ, he had to be *really* confident about that barrier. Either that, or he'd taken a fistful of Xanax before the phone call. "I'm going to throw this through the doorway." He reached over and picked something up off the examining table: a collar, much like the one Calder had worn in his cell. "You'll shift back, and you'll put it on. Or we will kill this one," he gestured at me, "right here and now."

Calder's hands flexed, the claws glinting. "You're going to kill him once I put the collar on."

Oh, thank gods. Thank all the fucking asshole gods there were that his shift, and his rage, hadn't short-circuited his ability to think clearly. Because they would; of course they would. Did they really believe he'd do what they wanted? What the fuck could their endgame possibly be here? Calder would go, and they'd kill me, and then...then their lives would be like a flipped hourglass.

A small one.

Because Calder would hunt them to the ends of the earth. He wouldn't be able to save me. He wouldn't die for me—he wasn't stupid and I wasn't worth it. But he'd avenge me. That I could count on. Just like he'd promised to do back in our prison, when he'd sworn he'd kill them all for both our sakes if I died giving him what he needed to escape.

"No, of course not," Curly said, his voice high and reedy and strained. "We want you cooperative. We'll keep him alive. You'll be allowed to see him occasionally. If you don't cause trouble."

Calder just stood there for a moment, looming in the doorway, only a foot from the barrier that would kill him if he touched it.

Fuck me. He was thinking about it.

He was *seriously thinking about it*.

About collaring himself, making himself a prisoner again. With any luck he'd contacted Arik and my pack was on the warpath, but if these motherfuckers had Calder under their control? Plus whatever magic they commanded? Plus...I didn't know what else they had up their sleeves. These two seemed to be working alone, and Scarecrow had said they'd lost all their research. So another facility somewhere full of their other experiments, or more allies, seemed not too likely.

But I didn't know that for sure. And that meant they might be able to hide us away somewhere. And if my pack *did* find us, my family...they might die in the attempt to rescue us. Some of them, anyway. Even one would be too many.

Either way, I'd be back in another cell, starved and hurt, alone, knowing Calder was in the same position.

Forever. Seeing him once in a while, maybe through bars. Never able to touch, because they wouldn't risk that.

It wouldn't be living. It'd be a living death.

"Don't!" I cried. My parched throat and constricted lungs made it a hoarse, horrid croak. "Calder, don't, don't do it! Let them kill me, it's better than what they're going to do to us—"

I shrieked, my body convulsing, as Curly spun on me and extended his hand, bolts of crackling energy flying from his fingers and enveloping me. Like Arik's magic worms, only these ones gnawed into every muscle and bone, devouring me in agony from the inside out. My vision went red, and I kept screaming, high and helpless, a keening that didn't even sound like it came from me.

And then, even through the overwhelming pain, came a noise like a freight train colliding with a mountain, a building collapsing, a rending, booming roar that filled the room and battered my ears and whited out every other sensation. The pain stopped, leaving twitching aftershocks, and I blinked back to the world as the roar faded, leaving my ears ringing. Scarecrow and Curly were cringing, curling into themselves with their hands over their ears.

And Calder threw himself at the barrier, landing in the middle of it and—sticking there, caught like a fly in a web. For the first time since they'd captured me, I fought. I tore at my manacles like a beast in a trap, willing to rip off my arms, heedless of the blood running down from my torn and battered wrists, screaming and kicking. Calder was already dead. The moment he touched that barrier, he was a dead man, and my screams echoed off the ceiling…

His face contorted in pain, fangs gnashing, and he shoved with one massive shoulder, his legs straining. "Fuck, he's still alive!" Scarecrow, dancing backward, scrabbling for something, anything—some kind of weapon, but it didn't matter.

Because Calder burst through, the barrier slurping off of him and twanging back into shape behind him. His eyes glowed, but crimson seeped down his face. His eyes were bleeding. His skin reddened and bubbled as I watched, flaking, crisping, his body disintegrating by the instant.

He forced himself forward and seized Scarecrow around the waist, claws piercing his torso, and then turned and flung the warlock back the way he'd come, straight into the barrier. Scarecrow flew through it from the force of Calder's throw and let out an unearthly screech, a wail of pure physical agony, hitting the floor with a wet thump. He thrashed for a second, and blood pooled around him.

And he went still.

Calder turned to Curly, who stood frozen in abject terror, letting out little choking gurgles. Calder was limping, listing to the side, his breathing so raspy and labored it echoed through the room. But he didn't hesitate, taking two steps until he stood over Curly, staring down at him. He took him by the shoulders and dragged him across the room. Curly started to beg, and Calder pushed him into the barrier, pinning him there, suspended inside the deadly magic of it.

He screamed, and he...smoldered and melted, and—I turned my face away, retching. Gods, he deserved it, but I couldn't watch. The smell filled the room, and I choked, hanging in my chains. Calder was dying, he'd killed them, but he was dying—

Calder came back to me, moving more slowly, his face nearly unrecognizable for the horrors of what the magic had done to him. He took one manacle in his hands and ripped it open, the metal squealing and the magic of it sparking. It clattered to the ground. He tore the other off, and my arms fell down, so numb I couldn't hold them up.

And Calder fell to his knees, breathing like a broken bellows, and started to topple over.

Numb or not, I lunged, and I caught him in my arms, choking on sobs, and managed to slow his fall enough that he ended up cradled against my chest, his head tipped back on my arm and my folded knees under him.

"Calder," I whispered. And then stronger, because I couldn't hold it in, "Why did you—fuck you, you fucking bastard, I'll never forgive you! You killed yourself for me, you—" My chest heaved, and I gasped into silence.

He smiled at me, gums painted in bright red, the most gruesome sight of my life and the one I loved the most, because it was Calder, and he was smiling at me. Gazing up at me with those glowing eyes as if he didn't need to see anything else before he died.

"You're alive." The words sounded like they had to scrape their way out of his throat. "Alive. That's—" He stopped, convulsed, coughed up blood. "All that matters."

I stroked his face, my fingertips barely making contact because his skin...oh, fuck, his skin, sloughing away. I bit my lip to keep from howling, tracing the contours of his cheekbone, of his distended jaw.

Only not so distended, now. His shift was fading away: the fangs shortening, his claws retracting, the fur vanishing. He felt lighter in my arms, his body contracting until I could hold him a little more easily.

And the glow faded too. For the first time, I saw his eyes without it. The palest, purest gray, they shone nearly as brightly as his alpha glow, even with the whites of his eyes completely swamped with blood. They were so fucking beautiful.

"Hang on," I said, pointlessly. Every other cliché in the world rushed to my frantic mind. *You can't leave me. I've got you. You'll be fine*. And one other, that I at least knew was true, unlike the others. "I love you. I love you too much to let you go."

It came out broken, nearly incoherent.

But he understood me, and his eyes widened. He shook his head. "No. That's—the bond. Feelings, through it, fuck." He coughed again, longer this time, wracked with it, and more blood dribbled from his mouth. "The bond, Jared. You're feeling what I'm feeling."

"I'm not, I can't be, I'm not in any pain, and you have to be—"

"I'm blocking that as much as I can," he said, with a little smile. "Promised not to hurt you. Remember? Also, physical. Easier to block. But that—you're feeling what I feel. You won't love me after the bond breaks."

"It won't break, it won't break, because if it breaks, that means—don't die for me," I pleaded. "I love you." And I did, so much that it felt like I might rip in half from the bitter joy of it, from the rending grief of impending loss.

And he loved me too, didn't he? That's what he meant. If he thought I was feeling what he was feeling—oh gods, he loved me. It burned, more than any other pain I'd ever felt.

"Worth it," he said, and smiled up at me again. "My mouth's—bloody. But will you kiss—"

"No," I snarled, shaking him. "No! I'm not giving you a, a last kiss. Hold on. You called the pack?" He nodded, and started to talk again. "Shut up! No. Arik will be on his way. He's a healer. A good one, amazing even." I'd finally had the chance to hear what had happened with the pack while I'd been gone, and it sounded like Arik had saved nearly all of their lives at one point or another. "He'll fix you. You just need to *hang on*."

But Calder didn't look like someone who could be fixed. His eyes had dimmed even more, and bloody froth formed at the corners of his mouth with every breath. It might have been funny, the irony of it, if I could've laughed. Those motherfuckers had done this to him. Taken an already extraordinary man and turned him into something truly superhuman—someone who could withstand instant death for long, agonizing minutes, while his body's accelerated healing tried and failed to stem the tide of every cell in his body turning inside out.

"No," he whispered, his lips barely moving. "No time. Just kiss me. Please."

There wasn't time. He was right.

But—my wrists hurt like hell, now that sensation had crept back in. I was healing slowly too, the hunger and thirst and magical fuckery having slowed me down to a near-human level of strength.

And they still bled. Sluggishly, but they bled.

My blood.

If the blood has the right type of magic in it…It's the magic in it that can feed me when I need extra strength. I won't need more. Not under normal circumstances.

Dying had to count as an abnormal circumstance—or at least it ought to, in someone else's life. Fuck mine, anyway.

And we already knew my blood had the right kind of magic in it.

That treacherous hope flared again, my head going light and fuzzy. I could save him. I could save his life, and even if it took mine…I loved him, and I didn't fucking care. In our cell, I'd have died to help him escape because I didn't have much hope left. My life hadn't been worth anything to me or to anyone else.

But now I'd die willingly, if it saved him, because my life was worth everything, and so was he.

I let go of my grip on the other side of his body, shifting my knees to keep him from tumbling to the floor, and held up my arm. "It's not as efficient as the neck, but it'll work," I said.

Calder blinked up at me, slowly, his eyes almost not opening again. "No." His tone held complete finality.

"Yes," I insisted, getting frantic. "Fuck, yes, come on—" I pushed my wrist against his mouth, and he turned his head away, his eyes sliding closed. "Drink it, fuck, Calder! You can heal, you just need more strength—"

His eyes opened again, blazing up at me with the faintest trace of that glowing silver. "Never. Again," he gritted out. "I love you, Jared the werewolf."

His voice trailed into a whisper, and his eyes closed again. He went still. I shook him, hard, hard enough to rattle his teeth.

He didn't move.

I shoved him down onto the floor, pulling my other arm out from under his head.

Something echoed in my ears: my own voice, little whimpers, hitched breaths, the sounds of panic.

No. No no no. I'd lost enough. I'd lost years of my life. I'd nearly died again, and I would die if I lost him…and I could still feel the bond, fading, winking out like the last gasp of a dying firefly.

My wrist had healed a little too much to allow enough blood to flow, so I put it to my mouth and tore into it savagely, mangling it with my too-blunt human teeth, digging deep to open the veins. Blood gushed out, and I pinched his jaw with my other hand to hold it open and shoved my wrist against his lips.

For an endless, agonizing moment, my blood flowed into his mouth and over his lips, half of it running out again.

And then his throat worked, and his mouth clamped over my arm, and he *drank*.

He wasn't conscious—thank gods, or he wouldn't have done it. But his body wanted to live, and I felt the pull of his mouth's suction all along my veins, the blood rushing out of me and into him. The bond pulsed brightly, as crimson and silver as my blood and his eyes. I went dizzy as I lost more blood than I could handle. I hadn't eaten, I hadn't drunk. I'd hung in those chains for at least a day.

But it didn't matter if I passed out, I thought muzzily as I sank down onto Calder's chest. It didn't matter. I lay so that my arm wouldn't move, so that gravity would keep it in place. He might still die.

But if he did, I'd die with him, knowing I loved him. Knowing I'd made my life worth something after all.

And it was more than I'd ever expected to have.

Chapter 19
A Lucky Man

Oh my God, they're both dead! A deep voice. Panicked. Familiar. Floating through my head, and then fading away again.

No, they aren't. I can still see their bond. Lighter. Also panicked. Also familiar.

Shouts, and thumps, and curses. More voices, the same two and two others. Arguing about magic, on and on. Something about a door.

The barrier. There'd been a barrier.

Movement. The voices sounding closer, relieved, but still frantic. Pain and lightness, because I couldn't feel my head. Had I lost it? I'd lost my spleen.

As if someone had read my mind: *You know, the irony is, his spleen would be really fucking useful right about now. It's part of the circulatory—*

Please shut the fuck up. That was the lighter voice again.

Everything went away again.

I jolted in and out of consciousness, hating it more each time. This felt like…I'd escaped. Hadn't I? And it'd been like this. Moments of sensation and pain, interspersed with nothingness.

Calder had taken me somewhere.

Calder!

I tried to force my eyes open, tried to get to him—hands pushed me down, but at least I could tell they were hands, could feel what the fuck was going on around me.

"Jared!" That came in clearly, not all fuzzy and distant like before. "Jared, don't try to fucking move, please, this is hard enough without you getting all crazy!"

Nate. That was Nate's voice.

"Nate," I tried to say, a little slurred mumble.

"He's conscious," Nate said. "He said my name!"

Oh, gods, who gave a fuck if I'd come back to life? Where the fuck was Calder? I tried to make my lips move enough to ask.

"I think he just said he doesn't give a fuck," Nate said. "And then—Calder! He's asking about Calder!" Of course I fucking was, was Nate a fucking idiot? "He's alive," Nate added. "He's still out. But he's alive. Jared? Can you hear me?"

His voice faded out again as all the remaining blood in my body left my brain, shock and relief and joy nearly destroying me.

Calder was alive. I'd saved him.

He'd lived. For once in my life, I hadn't fucked up, and Calder had *lived*.

I could pass out again, and I did.

I woke up for real lying on my side in our bed in the pack house. Opening my eyes felt like more effort than I could handle, but the mattress under me felt familiarly saggy in the middle, and the scents of all my family, and of dust and mildew, and more distantly of the redwoods and the familiar earth of the Armitage lands, all surrounded me.

And Calder.

Opening my eyes might be worth it if I could see him.

Alive, Nate had said he was alive.

At last my eyelids did me a favor and lifted a little.

Calder lay beside me on his back, eyes closed, completely still. And he looked like himself again, his skin pale and smooth, except for a blackened smudge and a trace of blood along his jaw. Someone had cleaned him up and missed a spot.

I shivered, the memory of what he'd looked like as he lay dying in my arms flashing back with horrifying vividness.

But he was alive. I could feel our bond, silvery and warm. I could hear his even breaths and the thump of his heart, and the heat of his body next to mine had the whole bed cozy and comfortable.

I reached up, the movement exhausting, but I had to touch him. I laid my hand on his chest and bit my lip hard to keep in a moan of relief. Calder, alive under my fingers.

"Hey, Jared."

I startled and looked up, tearing my eyes away from Calder. Arik sat by the bed in an armchair, curled up with his legs tucked under him and his head resting on one of the wings of the chair's back. He looked like hell, with huge dark circles under his eyes and golden stubble glinting on his jaw. I realized I'd never seen Arik anything less than perfectly clean-shaven.

"You came for us. I heard you, and Nate, and Ian. Your voices." My own sounded ridiculously rusty and weak. "We're home. Where is everyone?"

"In the kitchen. They were all here too, but having Ian where people are trying to recover is like..." He shook his head, as if an adequate comparison eluded him.

"You don't need to tell me, I get it." I wanted to see him, but I could wait. I felt like I was swimming through Jell-O. Or maybe floating in Jell-O, since my limbs wouldn't have had the strength to swim even if I'd been drowning.

I had been drowning, but Calder had come for me. And then our family had come for both of us, and pulled us out of the water before we could sink out of sight.

Speaking of. "Water?" I husked.

Arik popped out of his chair. "Fuck, sorry. I'm a shitty nurse. I mean, a good healer, maybe the best—" He flashed me a cocky grin that made me smile. Thank gods, he felt up to being an arrogant bastard. That meant everything really would be okay. "But a shitty nurse. I hate taking care of people."

He went into the bathroom and I heard the tap running. A second later he leaned over Calder, helped me prop myself on my elbow, and handed me the glass.

It tasted like fucking ambrosia, even though I dribbled it down my chin because of the weird angle and because I slurped it like a thirsty dog.

I fell back down on the pillow, breathing hard, savoring that coolness spreading up and down my esophagus.

"Better?"

"Yeah, thank you," I managed. Arik might hate taking care of people, but apparently he was willing to make the effort for the ones he cared about. Which seemed to include me. Gods, I was such a lucky man. Despite everything, I couldn't have been luckier. "Calder hasn't woken up yet? Did you heal him?"

"No, he hasn't, and yes, I did." Arik sat back down with a sigh. "As much as I could. But his own body did most of the work. That and your blood. He's still catching up, though. I don't think he'll wake up for a little bit still. Most of his internal organs had failed."

He sounded completely matter of fact, like nothing could possibly gross him out or shock him. I wondered how much it cost him to sound like that, talking about his own brother.

I'd seen Calder dying, seen what that foul magic had done to him. But it still shocked *me*, sending a tremor through me that I hoped Arik didn't see. If he could keep it together, so could I.

"He didn't want to take it." I stroked Calder's chest, running my fingers through his hair and savoring his warmth. "He didn't want to hurt me."

Arik snorted. "Fucking idiot."

I looked up at him, taking in the wrinkled-nosed disgust on his face—and I laughed. It felt so goddamn good. "Yeah. But he passed out, so he didn't have any choice."

"Good," Arik said firmly. "Sometimes he's so fucking stubborn." He looked at me for a long moment, cocking his head, his eyes narrowing. "Are you still planning to break the mate bond? Because he may not realize it, but you're the best thing that ever happened to him. I'm the last person to try to talk someone into a commitment they don't want, okay. I mean, I'm…anyway, that's not me. If you want out of the bond, even if he refuses, I'll break it whether he wants to or not. I do *not* condone unwilling matings," he said fiercely, his eyes gleaming. "But you're good for him. Only you can decide if he's good for you."

I didn't ask. Arik would tell me someday, or he wouldn't. But gods, I was so glad in that moment that he'd found Matt, the kindest and most even-tempered alpha in the world—even if when he did occasionally lose his temper, it was best to run and duck for cover. Arik deserved that. What Calder had told me about Arik's childhood burned in my chest. I wasn't exactly the most kid-friendly dude; I mostly avoided them, since they were sticky and knocked things over and you had to remember not to curse in front of them.

On the other hand, I'd grown up in a pack in which no children were neglected, and any one of the adults would've died before abandoning any of the pack's pups. Even my crappy parents wouldn't have abdicated responsibility for me if they hadn't had the rest of the pack available to pick up their slack. If they'd been alone in the world, they'd have raised me and cared for me to the best of their limited, selfish ability. I'd have been a latchkey kid who ate a lot of frozen chicken nuggets and probably would've gotten the hell out of Dodge the second I turned eighteen, but left to die behind a fucking dumpster? No.

Christ, I was lucky. Despite everything.

"I think you're the best thing that ever happened to him, actually," I said. And I meant it, without a shred of jealousy. A mate was one thing. A child was something else. "Your kids are always the most important thing. At least, that's how it ought to be."

"I'm not his kid," Arik said, but his cheeks went a little pink, and the look he shot at Calder, lying there between us, said it all. Arik adored him—idolized him, even.

"Semantics."

Arik smiled a little. "Yeah, I guess." His gaze flicked back to me. "Either way, he needs you. So if you can stand to keep the bond and see where it goes—you can count on me." That ferocity was back in his tone again. Yeah, bobcats might be a lot smaller than wolves, but I'd still back him in a fight over something he cared about. "I'm an asshole. I'll be an asshole to you all the time either way. But if you care about Calder, and you—if he loves you, then I'll be an asshole you can always count on. Anyway, we're pack now regardless. Just, you know. You have my blessing."

Part of me, the asshole part of my own personality,

wanted to rib him a little about his awkward and slightly incoherent declaration of family loyalty.

And about the fact that I was now his stepdad. Shit, I really was.

But that was the Jared who'd had a spleen, right? And besides…there'd be decades to come for me to tease him and get his back up. I could wait and savor his annoyance later. The word 'stepfather' would cross my lips for the first time when he had a mouthful of coffee. And it'd be glorious.

"Thank you," I said instead. "And—ditto. No conditions attached."

Arik nodded and leaned his head against the chair again, closing his eyes. Apparently he'd tapped out his capacity for heartfelt emotions, and I could live with that just fine.

Decades. I looked back at Calder. I could have many, many decades with my pack. And with my mate by my side.

Except that he'd never indicated he wanted to stay here. Could I leave the Armitage pack with him, leave my family behind? Would he even want me to?

He'd said he loved me. I could hear those words echoing in my head, over and over again. He loved me.

And I loved him. Looking at his harsh, handsome face and the powerful muscles of his shoulders and chest—that strength he'd used to protect me, to care for me—and feeling the swell of relief and possessiveness and joy that he'd survived, I knew I did, down to my bones. We hadn't known each other that long, only a month and a half. But I'd never felt safer, never felt more perfectly myself, than I had with him. Not even before I'd turned to the Dark Side, also known as Jonathan Hawthorne.

And I craved him. Even exhausted and weakened, part of me wanted to climb on top of him and take his cock deep inside me, until that hollow ache I always felt when I didn't have him in me stopped hurting.

Eventually I curled up against his shoulder and slept. Time enough to think about it later. For now, I had Calder, and I was home.

***

That nap caught up to me later in the night, as I lay in bed sleepless and staring at the faint shadows of the tree branches outside cast on the ceiling by the moon. I'd woken up a few hours after my conversation with Arik and crawled out of bed for a shower and all the other bodily necessities. Getting clean felt like heaven, but I hurried—even the ten or fifteen feet separating me from Calder felt like too much.

Matt had replaced Arik at our bedside sometime while I'd slept, but when I came out of the bathroom, Arik had returned, Nate and Ian with him. They all crowded into the room, along with a twelve-pack of beer and a pile of water bottles. And seven pizzas, which Ian proudly presented to me as if he'd hunted them himself, spearing them on the plains and dragging their carcasses home.

"From Marty's," he said smugly. My mouth watered. I fucking loved that place. "I drove extra fast on my way back from Laceyville so they wouldn't get cold."

Nate shuddered and muttered something about dying for a fucking pizza, but I ignored him. My viewpoint on what was and wasn't worth dying for had evolved a bit recently, but seven everything specials from Marty's still topped the list.

I ate on the bed, sitting cross-legged by my mate so that I could be touching him at all times. It was a little weird, eating and talking with him lying inanimate in the middle of it all, especially since Nate had perched at the end of the bed and seemed to be resting his beer on Calder's ankle. But it felt like pack, and the bond thrummed contentedly, reassuring me that Calder was alive and well and healing.

I ate two pizzas all by myself, drank a beer and three bottles of water, and finally collapsed back on the bed, holding my stomach and groaning, while Ian laughed at me—around a mouthful of a slice of his own second pizza, the hypocritical dick.

Once we'd all gorged ourselves, Matt filled me in on what I'd missed, the others chiming in as necessary—or not so necessary. ("I told you that magic barrier wasn't going to respond to your tree-hugging energy thing!" — "Shut the fuck up, Nate!")

But the story wasn't all that complicated, luckily, or I'd have gotten confused by all the interruptions. Ian had called Matt and then Calder once he realized I was gone, and so Calder had already been on his way back—from where, they didn't actually know—when I'd sent my unwilling message through the bond. At that point, he'd been able to pinpoint my location, and he'd called the others. The warlocks had taken me into Nevada, a couple of hours from the border, to an old factory they had set up for times when they needed to kidnap and murder people—or at least that was the only function it seemed to serve.

Matt hadn't been able to question anyone, of course, since both warlocks were about as dead as it was possible to be, and then some, by the time he arrived.

Calder had been closer, and he'd refused to wait. And by the time the cavalry got there, Calder and I were lying on the floor unconscious, with the magic barrier still up and keeping any of them from coming into the room.

They all did their best to skip over the details of that part of the story, and I didn't blame them. I could only imagine what it'd been like, standing in that hallway over the half-melted corpses of the warlocks and watching Calder and me dying, just out of reach and right in front of their eyes, while they frantically worked to undo the warlocks' magic in time.

Nate had eventually gotten the barrier down, and then they'd hustled us out. Arik worked to heal us both, Nate checked the place out to make sure it didn't have any other nasty secrets or anyone in need of rescuing, and then Ian blew it up as they left. ("Where the hell did you even get C4, Ian? And you didn't tell me you had it hidden around, Christ, you're so fucking irresponsible sometimes—" — "I had C4 because I'm just that awesome, dude. Don't ask. You know you'd rather not know.")

It'd taken about four hours to drive home, with Matt going carefully so as not to jostle us too much. And then they'd cleaned us up and put us in bed.

They all filed out an hour after dinner, all of them looking like they hadn't slept in weeks. Arik offered to stay, but I promised him I'd call for him if we needed anything. He hesitated, but Matt wrapped an arm around him and whispered in his ear, and Arik drooped against him like a wilting plant and let himself be led off to bed.

I pissed, and brushed my teeth, and climbed back in bed with Calder, turning off the light because that was what you did in the middle of the night, right?

Only I couldn't sleep.

I'd thought I'd had enough trauma that a little more simply didn't matter, but it turned out that, A, what had happened wasn't *a little more* even by my jaded standards, and B...I needed Calder. Matt and Ian's presence comforted me, and

Arik's healing skills and Nate's magic reassured me.

But I still stared up at the ceiling, Calder's near-death and the echoing agony of the amplified bond replaying over and over again like the world's shittiest clip show.

I needed Calder's arms around me. I needed to hear his voice. Not just because I yearned to know for certain that he'd be all right, but because nothing in the world felt right anymore unless I had him to tell me it would be. He'd seen value in me when no one else had, even myself. He'd saved me twice over. Confided in me...told me he loved me.

A horrible thought struck me, and I stared up at the fluttering branch shadows wide-eyed and frozen.

He'd thought the bond had influenced me into thinking I loved him. That his love had been leaking through and making me feel emotions that weren't mine.

But what if it'd been the other way around? What if he'd been influenced by *my* emotions?

The bond sizzled between us, my fear and worry and pathetic longing lighting it up like a string of firecrackers.

And Calder stirred beside me, breathing in deep and letting out a hitching sigh.

I was up in an instant, reaching across to switch on the bedside lamp and leaning over him, staring down at his face, watching his eyelids flutter.

His eyes opened, and that familiar silver glow had returned, shining up at me.

Chapter 20

Screw the Bond

"Jared," he whispered. And he shut his eyes again, squeezing them tight. Was that…yeah, it was, a tear escaping at the corner of his eye. When he opened them again, both were shiny from more than the glow of his alpha magic. "You're. Fuck. Jared, you're alive."

I gazed into his eyes, caught and held like I had been the very first time I'd looked at him. I'd been afraid of him then.

Fear was the last thing I could ever imagine feeling for him now.

"Because you saved my life. You came for me. You—I'm never going to forgive you for throwing your life away for me." I stroked the side of his face, and he turned his head and pressed a kiss to my palm, still gazing up at me.

"Same to you," he said, his voice still weak but with a growl to it all the same. "You made me break my promise. I almost killed you. Again."

The look in his eyes and the way he kissed my fingertips on the last word kind of negated the growl, and I found myself smiling down at him, helplessly, my eyes wet too.

Allergies. I had allergies to all the dust in this room.

No, no more excuses. I was fucking crying, because I loved him so fucking much and I'd thought I'd never hear his voice again.

I leaned down, a breath away from his mouth. "I think I owe you a kiss."

When our lips met, it wasn't like all the gross descriptions in books for tweens, with the explosions and the flashing lights and the singing birds or the whatnot. Calder's lips were painfully dry, and I was trembling.

But it felt like coming home at last, and when he put his arms around me and pulled me down against his chest, the last of my fear and anxiety evaporated. Calder had me. He'd never let me go, I knew it.

I lifted my head enough to see him, my lips still tingling. I flicked out my tongue to moisten them, and his eyes followed the movement, sharpening in that predatory way I loved so much.

Speaking of. "I love you."

Calder's eyes flicked back to mine, and his brows drew together dangerously. "Don't."

I pulled back a little more, so that he could get the full force of my glare. "Fuck you, Calder! Don't, what? Don't express normal human emotion? You told me you loved me! Are we only allowed to say that shit when one or both of us is experiencing massive fucking organ failure?"

His eyes widened, and his lips twitched—like I'd almost made him laugh.

"You—Jared, you're fucking unbelievable. How can you joke—it's the bond, I told you, you don't feel—"

"I wasn't joking!" I poked him in the chest and turned the glare up a notch, because seriously? "And don't tell me how I feel! I know how I feel. I may be a redneck werewolf who eats too much pizza—"

"*What?*"

"—but that doesn't mean I'm an idiot!"

"Pizza. Fucking—never mind the pizza. Fuck. It's the bond. I couldn't help it, letting what I was feeling through. You don't love me." His voice shook as he said that, and his arms tightened around me until it almost hurt. He was getting his strength back really fucking quickly. "You can't love me!"

"Screw the bond," I shot back, and ducked down to kiss him again—because Calder sounded *anguished*, as if protesting against my loving him was ripping his heart out.

The kiss went on longer than I'd intended, Calder kissing me desperately, his hand wound in my hair to hold me there for him to plunder. I was panting and breathless by the time he let me go.

"Screw the bond," I repeated, slowly and carefully, willing him to understand. "It's not the bond. I loved you just as much when you were unconscious and not sending anything through. I loved you before you tried to die for me like an idiot. I love you now, and I'm not going to stop loving you just because you say I can't!"

I sounded like a petulant child, one step from from stomping my foot, and I turned away, feeling incredibly stupid.

Calder slid his hand from my hair and around to cup the side of my face, gently turning me back to him.

"I've only ever loved one other person in my life," he said softly. "And not like this. I've never loved anyone like this. Like I love you. If you change your mind, it'll kill me. And I'm not even sure I could let you go if you did change your mind. So I need you to be sure. Jared, please be sure."

The look in his eyes was too much for me to take. Calder wasn't a man to beg, but he was begging me: *me*, Jared

Armitage, spleen-less and half-broken, a werewolf who couldn't shift, a man who'd made so many terrible mistakes. I ducked down and buried my face against his neck, squeezing my eyes shut against more stupid tears, wrapping my arms around him and clutching at him like a lifeline.

"I love you," I whispered into his neck. "I'll do anything you tell me, except letting you go."

For a long time, he just held me there, his arms rigid around me and his chest rising and falling quickly under me. "Anything I tell you?"

"Anything." I kissed his neck, and he fucking *shivered*. I held him tighter.

Fuck, I'd used to be the kind of guy who got off on having power. A little bit of it, like being Ian's second-in-command, had gone to my head and made me a total asshole. I'd wished I was an alpha, and I'd tried to compensate for it. And having other people tell me what to do had pissed me off, in large part because deep down I'd kind of enjoyed not having to take too much responsibility, and I'd hated that about myself, and I'd tried to compensate even harder.

I'd had a lot of time for self-reflection over the past two years, and part of becoming a realist, which you really had to in my situation, had been accepting myself for what I was. And part of why I loved Calder so much was that he'd accepted me too, and liked and wanted what he saw in me.

So I wasn't that guy anymore. But…having that kind of power over someone like Calder, someone who always stayed in control—that felt headier than being drunk.

Maybe he called the shots most of the time, and maybe I liked it that way.

But I could make him shiver just by kissing him. Just by handing him the reins and letting him do whatever he wanted with me.

Maybe I could give myself over without any shame and without any regrets, because I owned him as much as he owned me.

Calder relaxed a little at last, letting out a long sigh, stroking his hand down my back and letting it rest just above the swell of my ass. Oh gods, yes, he was going to tell me to do exactly what I wanted to do...

"What if I told you to share the pizza?"

He had to be fucking... "Are you serious right now? Did you just—" I popped up and stared at him in disbelief. "Did you just make a *joke*?"

Calder's lips quirked up, and his eyes shone, an odd vulnerability in them. "I never joke about pizza."

My laugh started as a vibration in my belly and rose up to take me over, until I was laughing and crying and clinging to him, way out of proportion to the cause.

And Calder laughed with me.

***

I'd never seen anyone eat as much as Calder, not even Ian—or me, for that matter. He demolished everything that'd been left over, grabbing a shower while I went down to the kitchen to fetch it for him along with a whole gallon bottle of water.

He polished that off too, sitting on the bed naked, while I curled up next to him. Eating that much and that quickly with one arm wrapped around me had to be a challenge, but he managed. Neither of us wanted to let the other go.

At last he fell back against the pillows, pulling me with him. I eyed his naked body. He'd almost died; in fact, reading between the lines, I was pretty sure a human doctor would've called it, and that only the faintest thread of magic had kept him on this side of the veil.

So he had to be too worn out to fuck me.

Just like I had to be too worn out to get fucked, right?

My cock was half hard.

And his…well, his always looked half hard, it was so goddamn big.

I stroked a hand down over his chest and his muscled stomach, feeling weirdly shy now that all the mundane washing and eating and drinking was out of the way.

He hadn't initiated anything. He just…held me.

And I loved that. I loved him, full stop, so much that it was filling me to the brim, spilling over into my helpless smile and the way I felt like I'd die if I stopped touching him. But he'd always been the one to tell me when he wanted me, and not the other way around, except for that one time I'd pushed him up against a tree and sucked his cock. He'd told me what to do, and sometimes I'd fought it and sometimes I'd given in to it without a fight, but I'd always ended up taking what he gave me. And loving it. Loving him for letting me let go like that.

I'd selfishly let him give me everything, and all I'd given him had been me—I hadn't shown him how I felt.

I rolled over, pressing my lips to the dip between his collarbones, mouthing over his skin.

"Jared?"

One of his hands found my ass, gently massaging, and the other carded through my hair.

"Let me," I murmured into his chest, still unable to look up at him. My courage and my resolution would fail if I let him hypnotize me into lying back and taking. "Let me, love."

I kissed my way down, soft and sweet, submitting to him

in a way I hadn't ever realized I wanted. Giving, instead of taking, or allowing myself to be taken. Cherishing him the way he'd cherished me from the very start, even when everything about him promised violence and brutality. I kissed each of the muscles in his stomach, one at a time, tracing the ridges with my tongue. Stroking his powerful thighs, caressing him until he lay back with a deep moan and let his legs open for me a little bit, enough for me to nestle between, face to face with his cock.

His balls tasted salty and sweet on my tongue, and I lapped at them, laving them, nuzzling into the crease between his thigh and groin. Calder lay still under me. Passive, except for the increasing tension in his body that I could feel under my hands. I'd have done anything he told me to—if he'd commanded me to stop, to lie back and spread my legs, I would have.

But he'd do anything for me, too, it seemed. I didn't even have to ask.

By the time I started licking at his cock, he'd gotten so hard and ready that a few drops of pre-come had slipped out of him, slicking the swollen head. I lapped those up too, and then mouthed down his shaft, getting him wet and teasing every inch of him.

It took a while. He had a lot of inches.

I dared to look up at last. He'd propped himself on his elbows for a better view, and the love and lust and longing in his eyes outshone that alpha silver.

"I love you." I held his gaze, pressing an open-mouthed kiss to the side of his cock. "I love you. And I'll do anything you want. Always."

Slowly, carefully, Calder eased me over onto my back, turning to hover over me, his huge body blocking out everything else in the world. His eyes shone, his expression open for once. Transparent, like he wanted me to see all the way through him the way he'd always seen through me. I settled my head onto a pillow and lay back, spreading out my arms and letting my legs fall open. I belonged to him, just like he belonged to me.

"I only want you," he said, very low, ghosting a hand down over my flushed cheek and my lips, along the curve of my throat, the backs of his fingers brushing my nipples and my belly. "I want you to love me."

"Easy," I whispered. "I won't even have to try."

Calder's smile as he leaned down to kiss me could've lit up a dark night. I wound my arms around him and pulled him in, opening myself to him completely. He only stopped kissing me long enough to grab the lube out of the bedside table drawer, and then his mouth claimed mine again. Calder took his time, playing with my hole, teasing me, kissing me, swallowing my desperate moans and then drawing out more with every motion of his fingers. I lifted my hips to meet him when his cock pressed against me, shaking with the pleasure and the joy of it when he thrust inside.

My head fell back and my body went limp as he impaled me to the hilt. Gods, I'd had him inside me so many times, and every time was a fresh shock: that he could fit in me at all, that it could feel so fucking perfect.

I'd been made for this.

"Yeah, you were," he murmured in my ear, and I realized I'd said it out loud. "So fucking sweet, Jared. So soft and wet for me. How many times do you think I can make you come on my knot before morning?"

"As many times as you want," I gasped, as he drove into me. "As many times as you tell me I can take."

He let out a strangled moan and started to fuck me for real, shoving me up the bed and slamming his cock into me, not hard enough to hurt but hard enough to show me I belonged to him.

I came the first time screaming his name, and the second time sobbing it, wrung out and pliant, draped across his chest and unable to do anything more than cling to him while he thrust his knot inside.

Falling asleep like that felt like heaven. He stroked my hair, whispered all the filthy things he'd do to me the next time he had me, and told me he loved me more than life itself. That I was worth everything, anything, the whole world to him.

I did what he told me: I believed it.

Epilogue

Fucking Saskatchewhat?

Three weeks after our near-death experience, Calder woke me before the sun was even all the way up by biting me on the ass, in the curve right where it met my leg.

I jolted up onto my elbows with a squeak, and Calder shoved me right back down again.

"I'm busy," he growled against the crease of my ass. "Hold still."

Yeah, I'd promised to do whatever he told me, but I still started to argue. So sue me. I liked to argue.

But when he pulled my cheeks apart and thrust his tongue inside me without so much as buying me a drink first, I collapsed back down onto my face and did what he fucking told me after all.

He ate me out until I was writhing against the mattress, desperate to get off, and then slid up the bed and fucked me just like that, holding me down by the neck and making me his bitch, a little rougher than usual with only his spit for lube.

It helped that he'd left me wet and open after fucking me twice the night before—only who was counting.

And I loved being his bitch. When he'd called me that

while I was riding him a few days before, I'd come so hard I'd almost passed out, and then spent the next hour wrapped in his arms while he told me how much he loved me in between kissing and sucking marks into my neck.

Being mated was fucking awesome.

Although Matt and Arik, whose room was the closest occupied one to ours, had started hinting strongly that we ought to move into one of the smaller buildings on the pack lands, one that didn't have any close neighbors.

Well, Matt had hinted. Arik had poured a cup of coffee while glaring at me, and then said as he stomped out of the room, "Move the fuck out of the house, Jared. If I have to hear you begging for my big brother's knot in the middle of the night one more time, I'll fucking bite you. And not in the fun way."

As if he was one to talk. But Arik scared me a little, brother-in-law—or maybe stepson, and I was still saving that one for the perfect moment—or not, so I didn't say a damn word. Maybe I'd begged a little louder the next night, because what was family without a bit of hilarious passive-aggression?

And what Arik didn't know was that I'd already talked to Calder about building our own place near the territory boundary, off in the woods where we'd be alone most of the time. It was kind of a pipe dream, though. We couldn't afford to build a new house, even a small one. The pack could barely afford the electric bill some months.

Calder rolled to the side and tucked me against his chest, idly plucking at my nipples and making me squirm on his knot.

"Once we're not stuck, we're getting in the car," he rumbled in my ear. "Road trip."

"Ungh," I moaned, as he rolled the left nipple between his

thumb and forefinger. "I can't focus. Did you say—fuck, Calder—road trip?"

"Yeah." He let up on me at last and splayed his hand over my sternum. "Where I was going—last time. I had something to do, and I wanted to go alone. Come back and show you I could do something more for you than this." He rolled his hips to demonstrate, and his knot pressed on my prostate and made me moan again.

"That's enough. I might not survive more."

Calder went still, and pressed a soft kiss to my shoulder. "Don't joke about that."

I put my hand over his and laced our fingers together. "Sorry. You know you don't need to do anything more. You're already doubling the amount of hard labor we get done around here on your own."

Since we'd come home for real, Calder had started making more of an effort to integrate with the pack. I hadn't even had to get up the courage to ask him if staying here was really what he wanted; he'd simply gotten up in the morning and gone to Matt to ask him what needed doing, and then done it. No fuss, no muss, and an implicit assumption that since this was my home, it was his too.

When I found him roofing the garage, all sweaty and shirtless and working for the good of my family and pack, I'd been so overwhelmed with love and gratitude and lust that I'd had to make him climb down and come in my mouth. Twice.

He hadn't complained. And I'd made up for the delay by climbing back up there with him and showing him how to properly put down shingles. He learned fast and had the strength of three or four werewolves, but he didn't have any actual construction skills. He'd told me, with breathtakingly sweet earnestness, that he'd get better and be an asset to the pack eventually if I'd teach him how.

Calder didn't reply for a long couple of minutes, and at last, like usual, my curiosity outstripped his talkativeness. "So where are we going? And why? Do I have to play twenty questions?"

He chuckled against my back. Bastard. I was pretty sure he always made me ask because my impatience amused him.

"About seven years ago, not too long before I made another bad decision in a series of bad fucking decisions and got taken captive, one of my employers had a business deal. A shady one. He'd been buying something, and the goods got lost. He thought they ended up at the bottom of a lake when a boat sank. But I took the case, managed to hide it." He paused, long enough to make me start grinding my teeth.

I cracked first. Of course. "Didn't you have a blood oath? I mean, you were supposed to be loyal, right? And what the fuck was in the case?"

I felt him shrug. "The blood oath covered not killing him or his men. I think he assumed I wouldn't fuck him over in other ways, that the oath covered that. But he was wrong. Letter of the law," he said, with undisguised smug satisfaction. "He's dead, by the way, without me having to do anything about it. I looked into it when I left here. Dead and gone."

Another pause. "I swear to all the gods, Calder, if you don't get to the fucking point—"

"Long story short, I have a bunch of uncut diamonds buried in an abandoned uranium mine in Saskatchewan. And I want to go retrieve them."

I blinked at the opposite wall, my mouth falling open. All those words made sense individually, but when you put them together...my brain refused to process that information. "Fucking Saskatche*what*?" was all that came out of me.

Calder's laughter shook me, but he held me still to keep from hurting the rim of my ass when his knot moved. "Saskatchewan," he said, voice tinged with amusement. "I buried the case of diamonds in the mine. No one goes in a played-out uranium mine, for a lot of very valid reasons."

"Uncut diamonds." Another phrase that had a perfectly clear meaning—except in context. "Uranium—dude, you're like that meme. The one with the most interesting man in the world, except that you're just the most insane. A *uranium mine*? Obviously that's a place *you'd* choose to go? Are you fucking kidding me?"

"I'm not kidding you." His knot had finally started to go down, and he very gently pulled out of me and then immediately ruined the effect of his care by slapping me on the ass. "And we're leaving as soon as we're dressed, so up and at 'em, sweetheart."

Sweetheart. While he slapped me on the ass. And told me what to do.

I was smiling as I got in the shower, still smiling when I went downstairs for the coffee and toast he'd made me, and smiling even more when he tossed me the keys to one of the pack's shitty cars and climbed into the passenger seat, the car dipping alarmingly as he did.

He knew how much I'd missed driving, and he didn't even complain when I cranked the radio and sang along off-key. Over breakfast he'd told me that he'd already let Matt know we were taking off for a few days and cleared borrowing the car.

Which meant I didn't have a damn care in the world.

Other than the fact that my mate apparently had a case full of uncut diamonds sitting in a uranium mine in an un-spellable Canadian province.

And, as the drive went on, the discomfort of being in a car for eighteen hours at a stretch after my ass had been knotted open that morning.

Still. Even that felt good, since it reminded me I was with my mate.

I'd turned into such a slut.

We made it to the far frozen north in a little under three days of driving, by dint of switching off often and not stopping for more than a couple of hours, sleeping in the car in turns. Calder drove as we crossed the border, taking us along a shitty narrow side road that he said used to be a smuggling route.

And then I took over, driving for endless, uncountable hours and miles across the flattest plains to ever flat until my eyes burned. I loved my mate, but hearing him snoring in the passenger seat after the first couple of hundred miles of it made me want to kick him in the balls.

He woke up to take over again for our journey through northern Saskatchewan, and I fell asleep as the terrain went from grassy to rocky and wooded.

We found the mine on the third day.

It had been burrowed and blown into the side of a large hill overlooking a lake, one of hundreds of identical lakes that spread out for hundreds of miles. I had no idea how Calder had remembered where to look, given the approximately seven billion identical forest-covered rock formations we'd driven past, and the dozens and dozens of clear, rushing rivers. Granted, they were all fucking beautiful. But they looked exactly the same.

He parked on a small access road and we hiked in, slapping at palm-sized mosquitoes and huge biting flies, and wading through thick heaps of fallen branches and brush beneath endless trees or climbing over exposed chunks of rock.

Eventually we reached a tall chain-link fence with a bunch of rusty, weathered signs bearing reassuring things like radiation symbols and dire warnings of danger.

The radiation warnings didn't concern me much. Shifter healing could deal with a few rads no problem, and it wasn't like we were walking into an active reactor or anything. On the other hand, it looked like something out of the part of a horror movie right before the first people on screen got eaten by the mine monster.

It reassured me a bit that the mine monster, if it existed, was more likely to take one look at Calder and run away howling than attack us.

Calder wrapped his hands through the fence's links and pulled, and it ripped apart like tissue paper, leaving a tall, jagged rent.

We ducked through, and a couple of minutes later we reached the entrance to the mine, a dark, timbered structure with a padlocked gate.

"Huh," Calder said. "I guess they replaced the gate since the last time I was here. I had to pull the last padlock off to get in. I hid the case well," he added, in response to my look of dismay. "Anyway, you should stay out here. It's not great in there."

No shit, Sherlock. "Not great is something like, I got the wrong meal when I went through the drive-through," I groused. "This is an eleven on the scale of not great."

Calder laughed, his eyes crinkling. Gods, I loved his laugh, even though it probably sounded like a predator issuing a challenge to most people who didn't know him. I loved that he laughed with me, for me, even more than the sound of his laughter itself.

"More like a twelve," he acknowledged. "The spiders

alone are epic."

Yeah. "I'll keep watch, since two of us just means more weight to collapse something. And your night vision's better than mine. But I'll be listening right by the entrance. And be careful, okay?"

He nodded, kissed me, ripped off the padlock, and disappeared into the bowels of the giant-spider-infested, uranium-poisoned earth.

They were probably mutant spiders.

Yeesh.

I paced near the entrance to the mine, amusing and horrifying myself in equal measure by imagining what would happen if Calder got bitten by a radioactive spider. He'd probably turn into the Hulk, only ten times more terrifying.

Finally, as I started to get antsy, I heard footsteps returning, and Calder reappeared a moment later, shoving the gate open a few more inches with a screech of rusty hinges. He had a metal suitcase in his hand, the kind people chained to themselves in stupid movies.

My heart beat a little faster. Money had never been a big motivator for me, partly because I'd never had any to be motivated by and partly because my chances of getting any were so fucking slim, why worry about it? But this...this wasn't money, like you won a hundred bucks on a scratch-off ticket.

This was money with a capital M, the kind people killed for.

Calder grinned at me. "Right where I left it. Apparently spiders aren't that interested in gemstones."

He shoved the gate closed again behind him, maybe to keep the hordes of mutant spiders from escaping and ravaging central Canada, and set the case down a few feet from the entrance, kneeling down beside it. I joined him, crowding in close as he pried up the lid.

I held my breath. The case creaked open.

And I blinked down at a heap of not-nearly-as-shiny-as-I-expected stones, each one a lot bigger than what you thought of as a diamond. Diamonds fit in rings, or on necklaces.

These wouldn't. Unless maybe you were a Kardashian, or something, and I was pretty sure even Kim would think these stones were tackily large. There weren't that many of them, but it didn't seem like there needed to be.

"I'm not sure what we can sell them for," Calder said, answering the question at the forefront of my mind. "I don't want to use any of my old contacts, for obvious reasons. But my boss at the time was buying them for a million. And he was getting a deal on them, since they'd been smuggled and were too hot for the original owners to sell openly right away."

"A million…dollars?" I croaked. "American dollars?"

"This is Canada, baby. A million cups of Tim Horton's coffee."

I gaped at him, my eyes wide, until he burst into laughter and pulled me roughly into his arms, squeezing me tight.

"Yes, a million dollars U.S.," he said. "We won't be able to sell them for that much, since we don't know the right people. But even if we only get half of what they're really worth…"

He didn't need to finish that sentence. Half a million dollars—and I was willing to bet we could get more than that, with some of the contacts the pack had, leaving Calder's completely out of it—would be enough to change everything. A few of the younger pack members had gone to Matt and the council recently with an honestly pretty kick-ass business plan for a microbrewery. But we didn't have a fucking dime to put into it, and they didn't have the credit for loans. One girl, a human member of the pack, was graduating from high school in a couple of weeks and wanted to get a double degree in agriculture and business and then come back and start an organic dairy farm. We couldn't even afford to send her as far as the Lancaster community college.

But this…and then it was like a record scratch, because I'd been thinking of all the things the pack could do with all that money, when—it wasn't theirs. Or mine, even. Sure, Calder would use some of it to build that little house for us, but…

I pulled back and looked him in the eye. I had to get the tone just right. Any hint of pressure, or expectation, would make me an entitled fucking scumbag. Packs worked like that, but Calder wasn't a pack animal. And he didn't owe us a fucking thing.

"What are you planning to do first?" I grinned at him as naturally as I could. "Buy a car you actually fit into?"

He grinned back at me and leaned in to drop a quick kiss on my lips. "No. First priority? Soundproofing Matthew and Arik's bedroom so my brat of a brother stops making inappropriate pointed remarks." He grimaced and added, "And it's not like they're so fucking quiet themselves." I choked on a burst of hysterical laughter. Oh gods, was he saying— "And then send Meghan to college," he added more seriously. "Obviously. I actually like cows more than I like most people, they're peaceful. And she promised me she'd have a line of homemade ice cream. I'm sold."

If anyone had ever asked me where on earth I expected to finish falling completely, hopelessly, head over heels in love with another person—not to mention who that person would be—a six-foot-seven polar bear shifter with permanently glowing eyes who fucked me three times a day, while kneeling on the weedy contaminated dirt outside an abandoned Canadian uranium mine, would have been…maybe infinity down that list.

I'd become a realist. And I'd thought that meant accepting all the awful things the world could do to me.

But it turned out reality could be infinitely better than anything my imagination could've produced. And all I had to do was accept it.

Calder smiled at me, and I wound my arms around his neck and pulled him down into the filthiest, most suggestive kiss I could manage, not withdrawing until he'd bruised my lips and stolen all the air from my lungs.

And he wasn't breathing evenly either, eyeing me like I tasted as good as that future homemade ice cream.

"I only want you, too, Calder," I said. "The diamonds are fucking great, don't get me wrong, but—"

He tackled me to the ground, laughing and kissing me breathless again.

I forgot all about the diamonds.

Calder was worth more to me than anything with a price, and—I knew I was worth more to him, and always would be.

The End

Acknowledgments

Super-duper thanks to Alessandra Hazard for alpha-reading the hell out of the first few chapters of this book (and the whole thing, for that matter). She made it so much better with her advice!

Many thanks to Amy Pittel and Jem Zee for beta reading!

My husband gets a shout-out for thinking of the title of this book. Mr. Grayson, did you ever know that you're my hero…?

Last but not least, I'm very grateful to Erica for setting me straight about northern Saskatchewan and Tim Horton's. She's my favorite Canadian!

And as always, thank you to my readers for your kind encouragement along the way.

Get in Touch

I love hearing from readers! Find me at eliotgrayson.com, where you can get more info about my books and also sign up for my newsletter or contact me directly. You can also find out about my other books on Amazon, or join my Facebook readers' group, Eliot Grayson's Escape from Reality, to get more frequent updates. Thanks for reading!

Also by Eliot Grayson

Mismatched Mates:
The Alpha's Warlock
Captive Mate
A Very Armitage Christmas
First Blood
The Alpha Experiment
Lost and Bound

Goddess-Blessed:
The Replacement Husband
The Reluctant Husband
Yuletide Treasure
The Yuletide Runaway

Portsmouth:
Like a Gentleman
Once a Gentleman

The One Decent Thing

Need a Hand?

Deven and the Dragon

Brought to Light

Undercover

Made in the USA
Monee, IL
31 January 2025